D1648629

THE STONE PONIES

Books by Tom Willard

The Dolomite Memorandum
Strike Fighters
Bold Forager
Sudden Fury
Red Dancer
Desert Star
Blood River
Golden Triangle
War Chariot
Death Squad
Afrikorps
Iron Horse
White Rhino
Sea Stallion
Lion Mountain
Cobra Curse

THE BLACK SABRE CHRONICLES
Buffalo Soldiers
The Sable Doughboys
Wings of Honor
The Stone Ponies

THE STONE PONIES

Book Four of the Black Sabre Chronicles

Tom Willard

A TOM DOHERTY ASSOCIATES BOOK
New York

THE STONE PONIES

Map and ornament by Ellisa H. Mitchell

A Forge Book
Published by Tom Doherty Associates, LLC
175 Fifth Avenue
New York, NY 10010

www.tor.com

Forge® is a registered trademark of Tom Doherty Associates, LLC.

Library of Congress Cataloging-in-Publication Data

Willard, Tom.
    The stone ponies / Tom Willard—1st ed.
        p. cm.—(The Black sabre chronicles ; bk. 4)
    "A Tom Doherty Associates book."
    ISBN 0-312-85763-2 (acid-free paper)
    1. Vietnamese Conflict, 1961–1975—Participation, Afro-American—
Fiction. 2. United States. Army. Airborne Division, 101st—Fiction.
3. United States. Army—Afro-American troops—Fiction. 4. Afro-
American soldiers—Fiction. 5. Afro-American families—Fiction.
6. Fathers and sons—Fiction. I. Title.

PS3573.I4445 S76 2000
813'.54—dc21   00-028805

First Edition: August 2000

Printed in the United States of America

0 9 8 7 6 5 4 3 2 1

To:

Sergeant First Class John Franklin Hughes (Ret.)
Colonel David H. Hackworth (Ret.)
Command Sergeant Major Leo B. Smith (Ret.)
Warrant Officer Four Charlie Mussellwhite (Ret.)
Lieutenant Colonel Dennis Foley (Ret.)
Sergeant First Class Chuck Knowlan (Ret.)
Specialist Four Earl Wilson (Memphis, Tennessee)
Specialist Four Gaines Wilson (Fort Lauderdale, Florida)
Sergeant Jeffrey Letson Kockritz (KIA)
Master Sergeant Phillip Chassion (KIA)
Brigadier General John D. Howard (Ret.)
Sergeant Sheffield (KIA)
Specialist Four Eddie Carreon (San Antonio, Texas)
Specialist Four Willie Murrel (Gary, Indiana)
Specialist Five Jessie Copeland (Oklahoma City)
Specialist Five Juan Ybanaez (KIA)
Brigadier General George Shevlin (Ret.)
Colonel Ted Crozier (Ret.)
Command Sergeant Major Russ MacDonald (Ret.)
First Lieutenant James Alton Gardner (KIA), Posthumous
    Recipient, Medal of Honor

And all the many others . . .

I lie in my tent
Thanking God for free rent
While outside the rain pours
And inside my buddy snores
Muddy floors and a wet cot
But still thanking God a lot.
Got hot chow every day
Rain or shine, come what may,
Got a dog 'bout two weeks old
Eats C-rations hot or cold.
Special Forces all around
Keeping safe this hallowed ground.
1st Cav in the air
Landing, fighting here and there.
Ain't got much but could be worse
Just ask the men in the 101st.

—"Ode to the Infantryman in RVN,"
   by an anonymous Signal Corpsman in Nha Trang,
   Republic of Vietnam
   (from the *Vietnam Reporter,* October 1965)

You see, a private had no right to know anything, and that is why generals did all the fighting, and that is today why generals and colonels and captains are great men. They fought the battles of our country. The privates did not. The generals risked their reputation, the private soldier his life. No one ever saw a private in battle. His history would never be written. It was the general that everybody saw charge such and such, with drawn sabre, his eyes flashing fire, his nostrils dilated, and his clarion voice ringing above the din of battle. . . .
—Private Sam Watkins, Maury Grays,
  First Tennessee Regiment,
  veteran of Shiloh, Perryville, Chattanooga, Chickamauga,
  Murfreesboro, Missionary Ridge, and Atlanta

This piece was provided to the author by a great friend and soldier, Colonel John D. Rosenberger, 11th Armored Cavalry Regiment (OPFOR), 58th Colonel of the Regiment, Commanding.

Ever go to the park? See the statue of a great general sitting on his horse, sabre extended, riding to glory?

The general got all the glory, but it was the "grunt" . . . that "stone pony" he's riding on . . . that carried him to glory.

—Anonymous

North Vietnam

Hanoi

Luang Prabang

Laos

Gulf of Tonkin

Hainan

Dong Hoi

17th Parallel

DMZ

Ho Chi Minh Trail

Phu Bai

Danang

Chu Lai

Thailand

Cambodia

Pleiku

Qui Nhon

South

Tuy Hoa

Vietnam

Nha Trang

Cam Ranh Bay

Phan Rang

Phnom Penh

Bien Hoa

Saigon

Vung Tau

South China Sea

Gulf of Siam

SOUTHEAST ASIA

0   50   100 miles

Foreword

*   *   *

In the history of the United States, there has never been a more important time of personal decision for the African-American soldier fighting for his country than the war in Vietnam. In 1965, many aspects of the United States were segregated, schools as well as bathrooms, restaurants, and motels. People of color couldn't share the same drinking fountain with white people. But they could share their blood on the same battlefield.

Employment was not based on equality, rather on the color of a man's skin. The American economy was flourishing while a great void existed between the white and black races.

But changes came about, though slowly and often subtly. The Korean War was the first major foreign conflict utilizing integrated military forces. In Vietnam, for the first time, Negro officers led white soldiers into battle.

Yet racial disparity continued in the United States, where a white soldier and black soldier from Mississippi could fight and die alongside each other on foreign soil, sip from the same canteens, but couldn't drink from the same water fountain in Hattiesburg. The white and black soldiers could hold each other in the frightful moments of war, while in the streets of America whites and blacks fought each other over equality.

From Vietnam arose two distinctive factions: the men and women wearing the uniform and those opposed to the war. At war's end, both sides claimed victory. Both sides moved forward with their lives.

But the Vietnam soldier continued to harbor a resentment, to both the government and the people who turned their backs on them. The Vietnam soldier didn't want a parade or a welcome home party. A simple "Thank you" would have sufficed.

America sent its children to war and turned its back on them on both the battlefield and the home front. Unlike the Desert Stormers—offspring of the Vietnam soldier—who received well-deserved support and praise, the Vietnam veteran was left with the task of sorting out his place in history on an individual or collective basis.

This is a story of the *grunt*. That down-in-the-dirt, too-often-unappreciated reminder of war that society seems to want to avoid, except on Veterans Day.

The soldier who would follow a great leader through the gates of hell, put out the Devil's flames, and fight his way back up to good ground even if his hair was on fire.

Prologue

Franklin LeBaron Sharps's journey to war would begin the same way as his father's and grandfather's: standing on the railroad platform at Willcox, Arizona. Franklin's great-great-grandfather, the sergeant major, who served with the 10th Cavalry, joined the army at eighteen on the frozen plains of Kansas in 1868. He had heard the old stories, knew of the glory days of his great-grandfather riding to victory with the Buffalo Soldiers; his grandfather charging across no-man's-land in the Meuse-Argonne with the Sable Doughboys; his father screaming through the skies in a fighter plane, sleek and shining. He knew about their valor, lived with their legend.

Now it was his turn.

He had learned to overcome fear; one must confront fear. To understand fear, one must survive fear. To know fear, one must only be in a fearful place.

He was twenty, a high school dropout and, to some extent, an embarrassment to his father, Brigadier General Samuel Sharps, one of the original "Tuskegee Airmen" fighter pilots.

Franklin was a paratrooper, tall and lean like his father, and lighter-skinned, which he attributed to his mother's partial Cherokee blood.

He had been given his two weeks' leave, like the other 5,500 troopers in the First Brigade, 101st Airborne Division. Now it was time to get back to Fort Campbell, Kentucky, and prepare for another journey.

"You'll be fine. Just fine," his mother said. Shania ran her hand across his forehead and kissed him lightly on the cheek. "Just don't go and try to be a hero."

He smiled that boyish smile she adored. "I won't. One's enough in the family."

Her face saddened. "You know your father would be here if he could."

He nodded. "Maybe we'll run into each other in Vietnam."

"Don't fill your heart with anger, baby. It'll only make things worse for you."

"How can you say that about him? After what he did to you. To our family!"

She had not forgotten the betrayal. "That's between your father and me. You and Kevin are both grown men, starting your own lives. Don't let his mistake destroy a lifetime of love and respect."

"Respect? He was carrying on with another woman! His secretary, for Chrissakes! He betrayed us all. And him, always talking about honor. I despise him."

She began to cry and reached into her purse and handed him a miniature replica of a cavalry sabre. "All Sharps men go to war carrying a sabre. Your daddy has your grandfather's. This one is for you."

He recognized it. It was the same sabre that had been returned with his brother Adrian's personal effects six months ago. After he was killed in Vietnam. A West Point graduate, Adrian had been killed by the Vietcong at an overrun Special Forces camp in the Central Highlands.

He slipped the sabre into his pocket. He gave no thought to

the possibility it might bring him bad luck. He felt the kinship bleed through the blade and into his soul.

He would look at it later, on the train, and remember those moments that bring so much pain to the healing heart. He would remember.

And God help the sonsabitches who killed his brother. He was going to balance the books!

Two weeks later, Franklin studied the miniature sabre as he lay on his bunk, gear packed, trying to remember *not to remember*. He had been told not to think about yesterday—it's forgotten— or today, for it's uncertain; or tomorrow, for it doesn't exist.

From outside, near the barracks, at the beer garden Bastogne Club, the music and words of "You've Lost That Lovin' Feelin'" and the pristine voices of the Righteous Brothers cut through the still of the night with agonizing reminders of where he was and where he was going.

Intermingled was the nervous laughter of men and women spending their last night with soldiers stationed at the fort.

But for most of the young paratroopers, like the words of the song, there was a strong sense of being alone. Especially in the medical platoon of the First Brigade's Headquarters Company, First Battalion, 327th Airborne Infantry, where no one could sleep. And everyone listened.

They all knew two things: The song would end, and tomorrow they were going to war.

"You asleep, man?" PFC Tommie Wilkes, one of his fellow medics, asked softly. Like Franklin, he lay dressed in fatigues, his Corcoran jump boots unlaced. All the troopers were sleeping in similar fashion, waiting for the sudden thunder of First Sergeant Leo B. Smith's voice.

Franklin had heard Smith's voice on many occasions. The most memorable was on the day he went searching for his job as medic for the recon platoon. Breaking the chain of command, he went directly to Master Sergeant Phil Chassion, a Korean veteran, and applied for the position . . . which was not allocated in an Airborne infantry unit.

"Recon don't have medics," Chassion snapped.

"It could, Sergeant," Franklin said.

Chassion eyed him warily, then asked in his gritty, low voice, "Why do you want to be in recon?"

Franklin didn't flinch; he had prepared his answer. "Medics carry forty-five pistols, Sergeant. If I'm going to war, I want to carry an M-sixteen rifle. As your medic I can carry an M-sixteen rifle. I'm infantry-trained and fired expert on the range. It'll give you another source of firepower."

Chassion jumped directly into Franklin's face. "Have you discussed this with your platoon leader and platoon sergeant?"

Franklin shook his head. "No, Sergeant."

That was the beginning of a long line of ass-chewings that would include his platoon leader and platoon sergeant, first sergeant, and, finally, company commander, Captain George Shevlin.

By the end of that day Franklin would have little ass left; however, he was given the position, along with an M-16 rifle. He was also allowed to keep his .45 pistol. And for the first time in its illustrious history, the 101st Airborne Division assigned a permanent medic to a recon platoon.

Franklin sat up and looked along the long bay. Every bunk gave off some sign of wakefulness. "Naw. Who can sleep?" he said to Wilkes. The glow of a match touching a cigarette across the bay caught his attention. "Damn. I wish we was on the move."

"What's the matter, Sharps? Can't wait to kill somebody?" a voice asked from the bunk where the cigarette glowed.

Franklin had started to reply when the barracks filled with

light; then a voice boomed, and there was the thundering of a garbage can ricocheting off the floor.

"On your feet!" the voice of First Sergeant Smith roared. A short, muscular man, a combat veteran of the 187th Regimental Combat Team of Korea fame, Smith marched through the bay jabbing his fingers at each soldier, ordering them to their feet. Behind him walked several other noncommissioned officers, all wearing grizzled faces with eyes peering hard and relentless. "What are you!" Smith's voice again bellowed.

The troopers, now standing ramrod straight at attention in front of their bunks, responded in a chorus, "Air-borne!"

"How far!" Smith barked.

"All the way! First Ser-geant!"

Sergeant First Class Bill Trout, new in the unit from the unit from the 173rd Airborne Brigade, walked behind Smith, staring for a single sharp moment at his troopers. He said nothing; his presence spoke for itself. He had broken his collarbone a week before and, now wearing a cast, he refused to be medically relieved from the shipment to Nam. A tough, no-nonsense soldier from Hershey, Pennsylvania, he had personally built the medic platoon, throwing out the shirkers and slackers with the ease of a butcher trimming fat from a slab of beef.

"The chow hall is open for thirty minutes," Smith blared. "Get yourselves fed, gear up, and report in formation in front of headquarters. Don't leave any of your gear behind. If you do . . . you'll go to war without it. Is that clear?"

"Yes, First Sergeant!" the troopers shouted.

Smith looked at Trout, nodded, then marched sharply away. Franklin watched as the platoon sergeant scanned the bay, his face tightened by the pain of his injury. "Any questions?" he asked.

There were none.

"Move out!"

The bay shook from the heavy paratrooper boots slamming

against the floor until there was silence and the barracks was empty except for Trout, who checked the stacked duffel bags, helmets, weapons, medical aid kits, and assault packs of each man.

The OPORD—Operational Order—the method by which the brigade would be moved to Vietnam, was the written masterpiece of Major David H. Hackworth, Captain Hank Lunde, and Sergeant Major Grady Jones, and was nearly a foot thick when finished. The plan called for a combined use of commercial air travel for the troops and railway transportation for the massive amount of equipment required for an Airborne brigade. All were designed to reach the shipping point at the same time, which they did. In Oakland, California, the USS *General Eltinge* lay gray in sunlight and darkness. Franklin stared in awe at the huge transport ship and, like the other paratroopers, was still in shock from the rapid deployment from Fort Campbell, which had taken less than a day. The troopers boarded in long lines, carrying their duffel bags, with packs on, weapons shouldered. Used to jumping from planes in flight, they would now ride the waves of the Pacific, standing at the rails, sleeping in bunks of canvas, all likely longing for hard, even cold ground, rather than enclosed spaces.

The brigade arrived in Cam Ranh Bay, Republic of South Vietnam, on a hot July day in 1965. There to greet them was General William Childs Westmoreland, who had once been division commander of the "Screaming Eagles." As a special tribute to "westy," officers and NCOs who had served with Westmoreland in the 187th Regimental Combat Team in Korea, his first general command, formed a special detail to greet their former commander of the "Rakkassans," all wearing their combat patches of the "Angels from Hell."

Hackworth, a decorated battle veteran of World War II and

Korea, watched the brigade assemble and listened to the words of Westmoreland, who, along with Ambassador Maxwell Taylor, also a former division commander of the 101st—his son an officer in the brigade—gave stirring speeches of the necessity of American forces to serve in Vietnam.

Hackworth, referred to as "Hack," always the realist, listened to the speeches and, when finished, muttered softly, "Ready or not . . . here we are!"

PFC Franklin Sharps, sweating profusely in the hot sun and out of range of Hack, muttered, "Here we are. . . . I hope we're ready!"

PART 1

★

TIM'S TRAVELING TROUBLE

1

* * *

The thump and beat of the helicopter rotors made the air inside the Huey vibrate, giving Franklin the sensation that the chopper was alive and he was feeling its pulse. He sat on his helmet, as he and the others had learned to do in order to protect their private parts from enemy ground fire.

Gone were the heavy Corcoran jump boots, all of which had rotted from the troopers' feet within weeks of arriving at Cam Ranh Bay. Moisture and humidity had eaten the leather soles away, forcing the Americans to use tape, even communications wire, to bind the boots together until they were finally replaced by the new Vietnam jungle boots. Gone were the heavy fatigues, designed for cold weather, replaced by the looser-fitting and more practical poplin jungle fatigues.

And, as would be expected, gone was their innocence of war, and the short-lived bravado that began fading the first night in the bush. In less than six weeks, the brigade had been battled, blooded, and baptized by fire from an enemy they barely saw and could rarely catch in an open fight.

The brigade had became known as "Tim's Traveling Trouble" in honor of brigade commander Colonel James S. Timothy.

A West Point officer and decorated veteran of World War II and Korea, Timothy was widely known as a "no bullshit commander," whose philosophy regarding the enemy was simple: Find them. Fix them. Then kill them.

Certainly bullshitless.

His troopers rolled out in the morning, on choppers gilded with guns spitting the hellfire of death.

His troopers took hills known to only the enemy.

His troopers pressed on.

Casualties had started early upon their arrival, ranging from gunshot to fragmentation wounds, malaria, intestinal disorders, and punctures from the punji stakes, dipped in human excrement, concealed in pits that lay on silent trails or a step over a log in the path.

Charlie knew the American better than the American knew himself.

Most American soldiers had run track.

Run the hurdles.

Charlie knew that . . . Americans go over . . . they don't go around.

Even the MACV—Military Advisory Command Vietnam— "rules of engagement," requiring American troops to carry unloaded weapons until fired upon, were rescinded. Due, no doubt, to the fact that Charlie would jump out, spray soldiers with automatic fire, then disappear. By the time survivors were loaded up, there were only the dead and wounded.

The brigade had traveled from Cam Ranh to the mountains of the Central Highlands, where their current mission was to clear Route 19 for the arrival of the First Air Cavalry Division. Patrol operations were under the most brutal of physical conditions, exacting from the troopers every ounce of their courage and stamina. Rugged terrain, monsoon rain, mosquitoes, leeches, even wild tigers in the jungle added to the danger. But the elusive Charlie was their greatest frustration, living in holes and popping up at night to harass units and patrols. The fight was becoming one that required the Americans to get down into the dirt and dig Charlie out of his underground sanctuaries.

The sudden yaw of the chopper snapped Franklin back to reality. The weather was lousy and they were flying through mountains above the rugged central highland plains west of An Khe.

He glanced at the door gunner, who leaned against his M-60 machine gun, his eyes scanning the terrain below. It was black as night and raining like hell, and all the recon team members were soaked to the bone as the rain whipped through the open doors, stinging their faces, numbing their bodies.

All wore a common expression on their camouflaged faces: They'd rather be somewhere else!

"Get ready!" shouted the door gunner.

Franklin and the others slipped condoms over the muzzles of their M-16s to prevent mud and water from getting into the barrels, adjusted their harnesses, locked and loaded their rifles, and swung their legs outside, planting their feet on the skids. A recon "insert" was quick and risky, forcing the men to drop from as high as ten feet from the moving helicopter. The trick was to hit the ground running and not break any bones or become mired to the knees in mud. Both would make the trooper a sitting target for the enemy.

Franklin braced his feet, felt the chopper's nose rise, then heard the gunner shout, "Go!"

They slammed onto the wet, slimy, and deadly sharp elephant grass, dropped to a prone position, and lay still until the chopper roared away.

Then they rose and, bent low, started toward a village that was the first stop on their ten-day long-range patrol.

2

The recon team slipped through the dense foliage like ghosts moving through walls, touching nothing as they worked their way carefully toward a large opening where a small village was seen. The monsoon rain fell in windswept slants, nearly obscuring the tiny ville, nothing more than mud huts with thatch roofs, dividing the village into two sections, with a community gathering place between the two.

That was what recently promoted Spec Four Franklin Sharps was studying through his binoculars. What he saw wasn't pretty, twisting his face into a mask of fury. Although still officially a medic, he had become a valuable member of Recon Platoon, which was now a fast-moving, hard-hitting, "take back the night" commando force. He not only carried his rucksack and aid kit; he also carried greater responsibility.

Private John Dawes eased to his side and whispered, "What's the plan?"

Franklin whispered, "You take Kirkwood and Burkett and cover the back door. I'll take Marion and Elliott and we'll go in and scope out the ville."

Dawes nodded and turned to Private Burkett, whose white

face was a myriad of camouflage paint. He motioned with one finger toward thick jungle near the south end of the village. Then they disappeared without making a sound.

Three more scouts appeared wearing tiger-stripe fatigues, carrying rucksacks laden with explosives, ammunition, and other equipment vital to a long-range recon patrol team.

The night suddenly turned gray as a loud crash of thunder preceded a finger of lightning, highlighting the three scouts as they moved from the jungle. When Franklin reached the first hut he looked right, then left, removed his bayonet, and showed it to the other two. He carefully locked the bayonet on the muzzle stud, then switched off the safety on his M-16 rifle.

Franklin slid along the edge of the hut, his heart pounding. He peered into the hut and found it empty. A small cook fire was smoldering, with only a slight wisp of smoke, telling him the owners had been gone for some time.

As he started toward the second hut there was a loud "squeal!" as a frightened pig shot past him. His heart was now racing, so he knelt and tried to calm his nerves by breathing in long, deep breaths. When he had settled down, he continued his sweep.

He quickly checked the second hut and found it empty. As was the third. One by one each hut was checked.

The three joined up on the far side of the first section and started forward. Franklin held up his fist and pointed. Marion and Elliott squinted and through the rain saw the hooch. He motioned them forward, raising his weapon, at the ready to fire.

Ten yards away, beneath the poncho hooch, four Vietcong soldiers slept in hammocks, their Kalashnikov AK-47s lying across their chests. On the ground lay several empty bottles of Bamiba beer.

Franklin took aim, as did Marion and Elliott, then shouted, "Let's rock-and-roll!"

A startled Vietcong awoke just as Franklin opened fire with his M-16 fusillade. The jungle then came alive with the thunderous roar of the weapons as the hammocks swung wildly, bullets tearing bits of tissue and body.

Within seconds the four VC were dead, their blood running onto the wet ground, forming rivulets of red that ran onto the jungle boots of the LRRP (Long-Range Reconnaissance Patrol) soldiers. Smoke drifted lazily upward, then flattened as the humidity and rain seemed to want to deny it to the sky.

Marion stepped forward and kicked one of the dead soldiers in his hammock. "Sleep on that, sucker!"

Franklin pulled his knife from his harness and cut the rope attached to one end of the hammock of a dead Vietcong. The VC's body spilled onto the ground, his face in a pool of his blood. "That's for my dead brother Adrian, you son of a bitch!"

He stood there breathing heavy, smelling the gunpowder, the death, and loving every moment, as he had each time before when he avenged the death of his brother. Then he knelt heavily and said to Marion, "Check them out for papers. Money. Anything. You've got two minutes; then we move. We'll hook up with the others at the back door."

Franklin looked around, knowing there was still one piece of work left. He walked off, reloading a fresh magazine, as Marion and Elliott began searching the bodies. "Wire the bastards!" he said.

Marion checked the first body, found nothing, then took a hand grenade, pulled the pin, and placed it in the VC's armpit, rolling him carefully onto that side. If he was turned over by other Vietcong, a loud surprise would be waiting!

When Franklin reached the open area he felt sick at the sight before him. Dawes, Burkett, and Kirkwood stood looking at two Vietnamese children. "Are they still alive?" he asked Dawes.

Dawes tossed a cigarette onto the ground. "Barely."

Franklin looked at the two children suffering before him.

"Charlie sure gets pissed when the locals step out of line."

The two small children appeared to be standing but weren't, their small feet dangling inches from the ground. Their tiny bodies were held by bamboo poles planted in the ground and shoved up their rectums. The little girl squirmed pitifully, then closed her eyes. Blood and excrement slowly oozed down the pole.

"How you want to do this?" asked Franklin.

"Can you do anything for them?" asked Dawes.

"Yeah, but you ain't going to like it. Only trouble, there ain't enough morphine to do the job right." He hawked and spit with disgust. "Otherwise, they're going to suffer. Can't get a chopper in with this weather. Besides, it wouldn't matter. Neither one's got a snowball's chance in hell. They're just living on minutes."

Franklin looked at their faces, then lifted the girl from the pole as Dawes lifted the boy from his stake. They laid the children on the ground, side by side. Franklin knelt and ran his hand along her face, pushing back her matted hair. He was surprised to see a brief moment of gratitude, as though she knew what he would do to relieve her torturous misery.

Franklin stood, as did Dawes, and lowered his M-16 to her head. Dawes did the same to the boy.

Both pulled their triggers at the same moment the earth shook with thunder and lightning forked through the sky.

3

Franklin thought constantly of those wily little bastards called "Charlie." After six days there were plenty of signs of the VC, but no Charlie to be found. Roads had been rendered impassable by deep trenches cut diagonally, preventing farmers from transporting their crops to market. Whole villages had been forced to become staging areas and sanctuaries, even training and recreational sites. Charlie was smart. From the moment Americans arrived "in-country," he hid in the mountains and lowlands, watching, always watching, learning everything he could about American tactics and deployment. He even learned their eating habits and turned their garbage into a weapon.

Empty C-ration cans were turned into booby traps. Grenades found on the battlefield were planted near American areas to be discovered, the fuses shortened to nearly nothing, becoming instant death for soldiers who pulled the pin and released the safety spoon. Claymore mines were reversed, aiming their deadly ball-bearing swath of explosive at the soldier firing the device. And there were other psychological mind benders used by Sir Charles: Coca-Cola sold with ground glass in the bottles, baby carriages rigged with blocks of C-Four explosives, left to detonate near restaurants and bars in major cities. Even mouse-traps became instruments of death: bullets were imbedded in doors, over which a mousetrap was placed, the spring loaded arm cocked above a nail pressed lightly against the percussion cap. When the door was opened—"boom"—another body bag bound for the "world."

Tough. Smart. Rice balls and bamboo rats their diet. When they did fight they fought on their terms, hugging the Americans' belt, fighting close in, denying effective use of tactical air and artillery support, grating on the emotional strength of the American soldier.

The Americans had learned that Charlie had more tricks than a monkey on a hundred yards of grapevine!

The team had patrolled all day, cutting through the thick entanglement beneath the canopy of trees flourishing on the highland terrain. Finally, they reached a road, which was nothing more than a narrow path winding through the brutal bush. Each man's eyes carefully studied the road from the thick foliage off the gravelly trail. Smiles filled their camo-covered faces as they looked at the edge of the trail, then above.

Poles had been driven into the ground on each side; at the top, another pole ran across the trail, joined to another. Latticed across the framework were thick branches, forming a crude tunnel, providing cover from air observation. This was a feed-off of the trail and less sophisticated than that which snaked toward the north, becoming more sophisticated with each mile.

Construction on the Ho Chi Minh Trail began in 1959, near the 17th parallel of North Vietnam. A guerrilla society, the North Vietnamese required a covert means of delivering supplies and personnel to the south while avoiding detection and attack. The trail ran more than fifteen hundred miles, winding from North Vietnam, through Laos and Cambodia, and into South Vietnam, a wondrous engineering feat. Hundreds of

thousands of workers toiled and lived along the trail, construct-
ing the supply route with every means imaginable from humans
to trucks, carts, elephants. Where rivers or gorges appeared,
makeshift bridges were constructed; bombings by the South
Vietnamese or American forces were only minor inconven-
iences, as work crews would hurry to the damaged area and
quickly make repairs.

The Ho Chi Minh Trail was more than a supply route; it was
a society within itself, complete with small cities, rest and recreational areas, hospitals staffed with doctors and nurses.
Newspapers were printed along the route, sending word north
and south of the status of the war. The trail was defended with
antiaircraft gun emplacements, artillery, and tanks secreted into
the caves and deep trenches covered with camouflage. The Vietnamese grew crops at various locations, manufactured ammunition and combat clothing, built schools and day-care centers
for the children of the worker/soldiers, all underground in lab-
yrinths of sophisticated tunnel systems or beneath thick jungle
canopy impenetrable to the human eye from airborne platforms.

The trail was also a military training facility, although on the
move, taking young Vietnamese men and women with no military experience and honing them into soldiers as they made the
six-month journey from the north to the south. By the time a
soldier had reached the sector of the south where his unit would
be deployed, they had been trained in the rudiments of guerrilla
warfare, which often included ground-to-air antiaircraft fire and
artillery bombardment along the way. Overcoming the hardships of nature, including malaria, dysentery, poisonous snake-
bites, even attacks by tigers, the NVA were hard as nails and
eager to fight once they reached the Vietcong unit of assignment.

The Americans knew this, especially the Special Forces teams
living in outposts along the trail. The problem was the Vietnamese and American governments, who refused to believe such
a sophisticated supply line actually existed. That was the job of

the recon elements: to probe the trail, find its weak spots, harass the enemy, disrupt supply and communication lines. To get in close to Charlie, find where he slept, and turn the night or day into a fiery hell.

In August 1965, the mission of the First Brigade was to clear the An Khe area for the arrival of the 20,000-man First Air Cavalry Division's arrival and hit Charlie along the trail, cutting it wherever possible.

MACV in Saigon had ordered that every ounce of rice, bullets, and soldiers coming down the trail would be paid for by the North Vietnamese and Vietcong with their blood.

"I think we've found something," Marion whispered to the team. He motioned Franklin onto the trail.

Franklin crawled onto the trail and lay beneath the canopy. His eyes slowly scanned the dirt, which was still wet from the heavy rain. A grin suddenly filled his face. He reached and ran his fingers onto what appeared to be a small, narrow tire tread embedded in the dirt. It was no secret Charlie wore what were called "Ho Chi Minh sandals," crudely made footwear from discarded automobile tires. Carefully Franklin eased back into the protective concealment of the bush and crawled beside Marion.

"We got beaucoup troop movement on this baby," he whispered. "Plus deep grooves. Looks like bicycles. I think we've found a supply route."

Marion took out his map and, after confirming their position, reported to headquarters on the PRC-25 radio. The squelch was turned all the way down, eliminating the scratchy static from the radio. His words were low, no more than a whisper. "Tiger Base, this is Tiger One. Over."

There was a pause; then a voice replied, "State position and sit rep. Over."

Marion gave their position, then a situation report. "Have

found heavy-duty signs of enemy troop and supply travel on canopied trail. Over."

There was a long pause; then the voice of platoon leader Lieutenant James Gardner was heard from the recon platoon base at battalion headquarters. "Roger, on the find. Continue recon from your position. Maintain radio contact. Do not—repeat—do not make contact with Charlie. Sit rep every fifteen minutes. Do you copy?"

"Roger. Copy five-by-five. Out."

Marion said, "Let's grab some chow while we can. It might get active here tonight. Check your socks, strap your shit down tight, and dust off your weapons."

Like the others, Franklin reached into his pack and pulled out several cans of C-rations, all bound together by tape or commo wire. This was done in order to keep the cans from clanging together, a dead giveaway in the bush, where sound traveled like lightning and could be a dead giveaway of their position.

He opened a can of turkey loaf with his P-38 can opener and dipped his mess spoon into the chow. He ate slowly, listening while chewing, his ears pricked for the sound of unexpected company.

Marion eased beside him, his face a mass of scratches from the prickly "wait-a-minute" vines they had fought through since leaving the village for the dense bush. He pointed down the right of the trail. "I'm going to put Burkett twenty meters to the right on this side of the trail. You go twenty meters to the left on the other side of the trail. That'll give us both enfiladed and cross fire if the balloon goes up. Set up claymores with angles on the center of the trail in front of my position."

Franklin shook his head, his face equally as scratched. "Your ass will be in the hurt locker if we have to use the claymores."

Marion grinned. "I'll keep my head down. If we have to fight it out, move straight back from your position and to this point, five clicks to the south. That's extract Bandit. We'll hook up at dawn and call in a chopper." He tapped a spot on his map that was circled in red, a relatively low area five kilometers from their location where an extract helicopter could land to remove the team. Or what was left of them.

Franklin didn't like the situation, knowing there was more combined firepower in numbers if the team stayed together. But if the shit did hit the fan, there might be a chance for some of them to escape if they weren't in one concentrated group.

"OK. See you in the morning." They shook hands and Marion crawled toward the others to lay out the plan. Franklin reached into his pack and pulled out two squares of tire tread the size of the soles of his boots. With string he tied the squares on, giving him a portable set of Ho Chi Minh sandals. He checked the trail in both directions, then hurried across the trail in a diagonal path. When Charlie's point man came along the trail, even using flashlights at night, he would see only tire tread prints, not the distinctive sole print of American jungle boots.

Reaching the spot Marion had designated, Franklin took a claymore from his pack and braced the deadly device against a tree to give added blast force, connected the detonator wires, then moved to a position that would give him protection from the blast of the mine and good observation of the trail. He laid out his equipment for ready use: two grenades with the pins straightened for quick use, his M-79 grenade launcher beside his pack, loaded and ready to rock-and-roll, and his "quickie" magazine unit, three magazines taped top-and-bottom to give him fast reloading capability without reaching for another magazine. He turned on his radio, which was set to the same frequency as headquarters and the other men, making sure the squelch was off, and covered everything, including himself, with loose foliage.

The cover gave him a sense of security, like when he was a child, lying beneath a blanket during a thunderstorm, hiding from the darkness within a suit of armor made of cloth that brought warmth and security. Hiding from the darkness inside another darkness.

Around him he could hear the trees breathe with each slight breeze at the tops, the only point where the trees could be touched. Beneath, the air was stifling, the heat sucking the bark and pulp dry.

He felt a bug crawl onto his face but didn't slap at the insect. Movement was critical now. He had learned to lie motionless and endure the agonies of the jungle and rice paddies.

Leeches. Mosquitoes. Snakes. Each had their particular form of deadliness in the war, brought about by movement. Pull at a leech while lying in a rice paddy and the water rippled or gave off a slight splashing that could alert a nearby Charlie. Slap at a mosquito and the sound could travel through the night as though he had fired his weapon. Snakes were different. A snake has its own personal death delivery system—with a snake he had learned to lie motionless, let the reptile slither over his body and disappear toward another place. He felt secure beneath the cover, he did what all soldiers in a combat area hated the most: He waited.

4

* * *

Beneath the triple canopy of tall trees, smaller trees, and high brush, the cascading foliage made starlight impenetrable. So dark, Franklin thought he could see the veins in his eyes as he stared into the nothingness.

Most important in an ambush was sound. The enemy would not arrive with an orchestra playing; nor with talk, laughter, or the clanging of equipment. Charles would slip along the trail with the silence of a single drop of rain sliding down a leaf and dropping quietly onto the heavy ground cover. His rubber sandals would not kick up the dirt as he walked, nor his feet drag listlessly; each step would be an exercise in stealth and subtlety, as he was carefully trained to become one with the ground over which he traveled. There would be no glow of a lit cigarette, nor metal-to-metal contact between weapon and harness.

When Sir Charles entered the arena, it would be with no more warning than a bolt of lightning. Only there would be no brilliant flash of light, nor clap of thunder.

But even Charlie couldn't see in the dark. He might be good in the shadows, but he was neither bat nor owl, although as quick and wily.

An hour after darkness fell, Franklin saw what he had hoped and prayed for: A small, reddish light danced along the trail, coming in his direction. He knew the VC point man would carry a flashlight with a red filter and over that a piece of cloth to further cut down the glowing signature.

The point man was moving slow, the light low to the ground, as though he were searching for something lost. Franklin knew a second VC was close behind, within touching distance, only his back to the point man, his flashlight serving as a beacon for those who followed, like a lighthouse on a darkened shore.

Franklin heard the soft patter of the point man's feet as he passed, followed by the second, and carefully reached to his radio. He keyed the transmitter button—"breaking squelch"—for a long three-second count, a signal back to headquarters that Charlie had arrived. Slowly, the caravan began to appear, and only sound, though barely audible, now served as the recon squad's eyes. And it became something of a quessing game, trying to calculate how many soldiers and bicycles or carts were passing. He listened so hard his brain ached as he tried to judge the count. For every ten men, break squelch once on the transmitter. For every bicycle or cart, two clicks. Electronic Braille.

Not a perfect science, but the best they had under the circumstances.

From time to time there would be a soft cough or a scuffle of sandals on the dirt, but rarely. He lay there in his sweat, his finger on the button, his ears tuned to the mystery of what traveled through the night only a few feet away.

He felt a presence, froze. He nearly panicked as he realized one of the VC had stepped off the trail. A foot stepped onto his hand. He lay motionless. Then, he felt the warm stream of piss, smelled the ammonia.

The VC stood above him, one foot on his hand; Franklin fought to lay motionless as the piss splashed off the side of his face, flooded his ear, his mouth. Then, he felt the vibration as the VC shook himself and stepped from Franklin's hand and slipped quietly back onto the trail.

Franklin lay there, his heart pounding, his stomach rising into his throat. He felt the wetness in his crotch and realized that aside from the darkness, the war, and the danger that lurked, he and the VC shared another common denominator: Both had taken a piss together.

5

Hours after the caravan had passed, Franklin remained in place, whispering to Marion over the PRC-25. It was agreed that all would remain in their position in case of further activity. Near dawn, thin shafts of light filtered through the canopy, slowly illuminating the trail, then the dense wooded floor. When he heard Marion's voice over the radio calling him and Burkett to his position, he crossed the trail diagonally, still wearing the treads strapped to his boots.

The team sat in an area of thick brush, only discussing what had happened. Franklin gave his report, leaving out the pissing incident: Even in war, some things remained personal.

Marion spoke the obvious. "This is definitely an active trail and it has to lead to somewhere. We've been ordered to follow it and see where those supplies and troops were headed. We report back, then head for the extract point and call for the chopper."

Before anyone could respond, the team heard a strange creaking sound, followed by a hellish bellowing. The team snapped to the edge of the trail, their weapons at the ready. When the subject of the commotion came into sight, the troopers stared incredulously. Franklin, like the others, could only watch and wonder. An old man was driving a cart filled with cut branches. It rolled on a pair of rickety wooden wheels, pulled by a single water buffalo.

Franklin looked at Marion. "You thinking what I'm thinking?"

Marion nodded and the team stepped simultaneously onto the trail, where the terrified old man drew the buffalo to a stop.

"Hey, Papa-san. What you got in the cart?" Marion said.

The man, short and squat, his arms thin, face emaciated from age and hardship, shook his head and bowed politely.

Burkett walked around to the rear of the cart and began sifting through the branches. Franklin ran his hand along the buffalo's brisket. His hand came away wet and slimy with white, frothy sweat.

"This animal's been pushed mighty hard."

The old man was now sweating himself, jabbering away in a language the Americans had not yet mastered. But they all understood fear. And the old man radiated it—his eyes went quickly to Burkett, just as the trooper said, "Look what I found."

Franklin took the old man by the wrist and led him to the rear. Burkett removed some branches. They all whistled in chorus. All eyes moved to the trembling old man.

Beneath the branches lay an unexploded American artillery round. The troopers knew that Charlie was a master at turning unexploded ordnance into deadly mines and booby traps, even detonating entire rounds in populated areas.

Marion radioed headquarters. "The lieutenant thinks the old man can help lead us to Charlie's base camp."

"We can't understand a word he says," Franklin said, his eyes staring coldly and hatefully at the Vietnamese. His brother had been killed when his jeep hit a land mine fabricated from an American artillery round. "Besides, if he does talk it'll be nothing but lies. Probably lead us into an ambush."

Marion had a demonic grin on his face. "That's not what the lieutenant has in mind."

"What then?"

"The lieutenant wants us to make some noise. Charlie will come and investigate."

"Then we follow them back to their base camp," Franklin said.

"Roger that, Brother Franklin. Makes our job quick and easy. Then we catch the bird out of this shithole and report back to headquarters."

"What about Charlie? Won't he know we're in the area?" Dawes wondered.

Franklin grinned. "What will they find? Shard. A hole in the road. And nothing but blood, meat, and bone. Probably figured he hit a bump and the round detonated."

"What about this bastard?" Burkett angrily snapped.

"He stays with the artillery round. He'll be remembered as a hero of the Revolution."

The troopers laughed; the old man shook like a leaf in a gale.

"Tie his ass onto the cart," Marion ordered.

While the old man was gagged and tied, Burkett took a block of C-Four explosives, shaped it to the nose of the artillery round, and inserted a blasting cap attached with three feet of detonation cord.

The fuse was lit and the six troopers raced to the underbrush, where they found cover behind trees and in ditches carved into the landscape by the heavy rains.

The explosion tore a gap in the road and overhead canopy, shaking hundreds of branches from the surrounding trees, showering the troopers with branches and leaves.

Again it was time to play the waiting game.

An hour later the troopers, now lying in a concealed "star" defensive perimeter two hundred yards from the road, saw a

Vietcong soldier appear suddenly near the demolition site. He looked around, then motioned to his left, and three more VC came into sight.

"Just a scout patrol," Franklin whispered to Marion as he watched the enemy through his binoculars. "I only see four."

Marion was doing the same. "Roger, on the four Charlies. Now, let's see what they do."

They watched in silence as the VC picked their way onto the trail and walked about, inspecting the remaining debris of cart, animal, and human. Two of the Cong stood guard while the other two took entrenching tools and began filling in the hole in the road.

"It's working," Franklin whispered. "They bought it."

When the hole was filled and smoothed over, the two enemy soldiers cleared the debris from the road and slipped back into the trees, in clear enough view of the troopers for them to see which direction to follow.

All the VC withdrew, except one, who sat watching the area, a silent rear guard. After ten minutes he followed in his comrades' path.

"Let's go," Marion whispered. "Keep five and stay low and quiet."

The "keep five" order was obeyed, each man maintaining five yards' distance from the other to avoid a burst of automatic weapon fire hitting them all at once. The troopers moved with the same pace as the single VC, who never looked back and never knew he was followed. The troopers, however, maintained constant situational awareness, being careful not to be detected by either the rear guard or the forward element.

The rear VC met up with the other three, who moved out again, allowing him a breather. Franklin eyed the soldier through his binoculars, wishing he could fire, knowing how much he wanted to kill the little bastard. But not now. Now was the time to play Charlie's game, hug close to his belt, find his camp, then bring in the artillery and tactical air support. Then would come the extract and the flight to their base camp.

The leapfrog advance and pursuit continued for about an hour, with the VC still unaware they were being trailed. Finally, the flat terrain began to descend into a small valley.

And there the four Vietcong disappeared!

"Shit!" Marion cursed. All were studying the valley through binoculars, their vision made unclear by their rapid pulses' causing their field glasses to move erratically in their hands.

"I got nothing," Burkett whispered.

"Nothing here," Franklin whispered.

The others checked in with the same report.

"Watch for any sign of movement," Franklin whispered. Then he saw something, slight movement. "There're the little bastards. Ten o'clock. At the base of the slope."

All binoculars swung slightly to the left, where the four appeared in an open clearing. They dashed across the clearing, and their formation was a sign to the veteran recon troopers.

"They're bunched up; they're getting close to the front door," Franklin said.

"Or the back door," Marion suggested.

The recon team watched as the VC scampered toward an outcropping of boulders covered by brush. Then the brush moved, revealing an opening between the boulders no larger than a man's body, and bushes closed over the opening.

They stared at the silent valley below, knowing that the enemy lay hidden beneath the ground in a labyrinth of tunnels concealing them from air reconnaissance.

"Not this time, Sir Charles," Franklin said aloud. "We know where you live now."

Marion pressed the transmitter button on the radio, sent in his report, checked his map, and relayed the coordinates to headquarters. He looked at the others. "Tomorrow morning, Battalion's going to launch a combined air and artillery strike. We're to remain at this position and direct the fire." He pointed to the map. "ABU Company is going to be helicoptered into this point." His finger tapped the north end of the valley. "Cobra Company will be deployed to the east, west, and south. ABU Company will push from their landing zone, Cobra Company sets up an ambush. All we got to do right now is keep giving them a sit rep every fifteen minutes and keep low."

The troopers knew the extract would not happen; it didn't matter. They were finally going to get Charlie in a box and wear his ass out.

An hour later their worst nightmare began to unfold as they held their position above the small valley that was Charlie's base camp.

It began to rain and the afternoon sky turned black and ominous.

"Damn," Franklin cursed. "The weather's going against us."

Marion studied the sky. For five hours the rain poured, the wind whipped and roared through the valley, lightning cracked, and the thunder rolled like a mad drumroll. He contacted headquarters with the weather report. Radio contact ended with the same order: "Sit tight. Sit rep every fifteen minutes."

Night came and the recon troopers knew there would be no battle. Mother Nature had given the Vietcong another day to avoid the fight the First Brigade had dreamed of having. That was confirmed around 2100 when hundreds of flashes of lightning provided enough illumination for the troopers to see the Vietcong begin to slip from their underground labyrinth and deploy in every direction on the compass, carrying on their backs what appeared to be their entire base camp.

"They're skying out!" Marion snapped throatily into the radio, his anger uncontrollable. "They're skying out! Goddammit! The little bastards know something's going on!"

Watching through his binoculars, Franklin could see the Vietcong during the intermittent flashes. The valley was peppered with the elusive enemy popping from the ground from "spider holes," appearing for a moment, then gone the next, like fireflies on a hot summer night.

"They know," Franklin said angrily.

"The bastards always know," Burkett said.

One of the frustrations the brigade had suffered in getting Charlie to come out and fight was his uncanny ability to know where and when American forces would strike their camps. Having spies and agents near large American units, especially helicopter squadrons, often determined when an operation was about to be mounted. The recon troopers watched helplessly.

"How many you make?" Marion asked Franklin.

"Can't tell, but there's beaucoup," Franklin replied. "But right now we got other problems. Some of them are going to be coming our way."

"Find a tree and climb as high as you can," Marion said. "We don't want the shit coming down on our head. Spread out and stay off anything that looks like a trail."

The men climbed quickly into the trees and hugged the thick trunks, hoping the height and the darkness would give them ample cover. Franklin stood on a thick branch, his weapon at the ready, and knew that, unlike the night before, Charlie's approach would not be so subtle.

The Vietcong's approach was signaled by the clatter of weapons banging off harnesses, grunting, heavy breathing, and the snapping of branches. The recon men hugged the wet trunks and branches as the wind whipped at their bodies, while clutching the swaying trees, making it nearly impossible to keep a tight grip on the wet bark.

Suddenly the enemy seemed to be everywhere, streaking through the bush like deer scattering in the forest. Lightning flashed and Franklin saw a group of three VC running directly toward his tree, but they didn't stop or look up. They ran headlong past his position and disappeared as quickly as they had arrived. Another group passed seconds later, and Franklin nearly laughed: They were carrying bicycles.

Although the exfiltration by the Vietcong past the Americans took only minutes, the time seemed interminable. Finally the forest returned to its pristine quiet, except for the rumble of thunder. An hour later, the troopers heard Marion's soft voice ordering them to regroup. Franklin climbed down, his muscles cramped from squatting on the branch, and joined the others.

Marion had that unique look of being calm and said, "We ride out the night in a tight defensive perimeter. Every other man awake for two hours."

That was the procedure: Keep the surveillance; get some sleep while the others covered your ass.

"Set out claymores?" Franklin asked.

Marion shook his head, his eyes steady. "No claymores. If there's stragglers, let them through. We don't want to make contact."

Contact. What they all longed for but not could have, at least not in strong force. That was the greatest source of frustration about being in recon. Contact was forbidden.

The troopers formed a six-man star, their weapons at the ready, every other man awake.

Franklin took the first watch, with Dawes and Burkett. They lay beneath the darkened triple canopy, seething that they had not had a chance to draw first blood.

6

The recon team moved from their position at first light, quickly covering the distance to the rim overlooking the valley, and reported to headquarters. Rain continued to fall, but not in the torrent of a few hours earlier. The small valley appeared quiet and empty. Marion listened to the platoon leader's orders and briefed the others on their next move.

"We're going to recon the area, but first there's going to be an artillery strike at zero-seven-hundred. If everything is cool, we move to the extract point." He grinned. "At least we get to make a little noise."

The men took cover in an outcropping of rocks overlooking the valley and, though maintaining vigilant watch for the enemy, found time to relax for the first time in days. Franklin removed his harness and sipped from his canteen as the first signal of incoming artillery whistled through the air.

A terrific explosion erupted two hundred meters south of the opening in which they had seen the VC disappear, then another, only closer, as the rolling barrage crept toward the base camp. Marion gave elevation adjustments until the rounds were hitting square in the center of the camp. "Fire for effect," Marion called on the radio.

Giant plumes of black-gray smoke rose as rounds began to saturate the area. Marion continued to guide the attack, moving carefully to the flanks, back to the center, then forward, slowly sweeping the enemy area until there was nothing but twisted trees, shattered rock, and potholes rapidly filling with the rain.

"Wow!" Burkett laughed. "Fourth of July!"

"Out of sight!" Dawes chimed in.

Franklin watched the massive destructive force of the 155 howitzers pound the valley into fodder, wishing there were Vietcong on the receiving end of the artillery. He watched through his binoculars and saw a round strike, caving in what appeared to be a tunnel system, which now, with the upper level blown away, looked like a long open trench, a deep, ugly scar where once there had been lush green natural beauty.

But Charlie was nowhere to be seen.

The troopers watched, eating C-rations like children licking cotton candy at a fireworks display, only not cheering aloud as they had as youngsters. It was a strange sight for all; none had ever had a front-row seat to such devastation. They had only heard it from a distance and were awed at the horrific destructive power of modern warfare. Theirs had been a silent world for the most part. Calling in mortar strikes and throwing grenades paled in light of what they now watched as the air shrieked with the telltale whistles; the ground shook, and huge masses of rock and dirt spewed from the earth as though it was being spit to the surface by some mammoth unseen subterranean force.

"It's beautiful," Franklin said softly. "Man, I don't want none of that shit to ever come down on me."

Suddenly quiet settled over the valley. Smoke clung to the ground, drifting along the shattered earth in eerie fingers of gray, ghostly and spooky, creeping into the trenches as though seeking the souls of the dead. All wondered if the enemy were dead.

The troopers could only watch, and all felt a chill, knowing that soon they would be in those trenches and wondering what they would find.

For a split second, Franklin found admiration for Charlie, who was willing to endure such massive destruction and deprivation to fight for his cause.

Then Marion ordered, "Let's move out. Two-by-two spread. Franklin and Dawes on the point. Elliot on me at the center. Burkett and Kirkwood bring up the rear. Each team keep ten from the other. Move out."

The recon teams employed a standard operational procedure when advancing across unknown ground: In pairs, one watched the ground for trip wires and punji pits while the other watched the trees for snipers. Charlie loved the game of mind-fuck; he had a Ph.D. in psy-war ops. But the Americans were fast-learning students, unlike when they first arrived and did "their Sunday afternoon walk in the park with their heads up their asses."

Progeny of the saviors of the world in World War II, reminded by uncles who had been at "Frozen Chosin" and parachuted onto "Munsenei" in Korea, the American soldiers in Vietnam felt an invincibility that required nothing more to survive combat than a good weapon, dry socks, and a piece of local pussy for an occasional reward for studious work.

In reality, class was just beginning.

Sir Charles was a great teacher, with a body bag and flag-draped coffin as a diploma for each of the Americans who failed to negotiate his course.

Signs abounded of the Vietcong's hasty withdrawal: sandal tracks, broken or twisted branches, pieces of black pajama clinging to the saw teeth of the wait-a-minute bushes, and a few bandoliers. Franklin even found an AK-47, dropped by a frightened VC he figured must have been a recruit. No veteran Cong would lose his Kalashnikov. He'd die first. Franklin examined the weapon, which was filthy, but he knew it would fire, even if rusted. Unlike the M-16, the AK could take any kind of abuse. Americans were not allowed to carry recovered AKs, for if they were fired in combat, their distinctive "*clatter*" might give their own people the mistaken notion they were Cong and draw friendly fire. It had happened many times, with deadly results.

Where the wall of the ridge met the flatter terrain of the valley the earth looked as though huge fingers had clawed through the ground, leaving indelible etchings they recognized as collapsed tunnels. "Man," Franklin said to Dawes, "Mr. Charlie must be part gopher." The extent of the tunnel system was mind-boggling. No more than two feet wide and three deep, the maze wove from outer entry points to a central location that was much larger in dimension. Splintered support beams jutted from the floor; some lay twisted inside the opening.

Franklin's eyes narrowed, and the stench stung his nose. Though it was covered with dirt and debris, he realized what he had found.

This is not my fault, Franklin reminded himself as he stood staring into a deep crater. *I didn't start this war. But you killed my brother and I owe you no sympathy!*

"Must have been the infirmary," Dawes said. He pointed his rifle at the twisted remains of enemy bodies lying mangled and dismembered on the floor of the crater. "I count seven. Most of them bandaged."

"Yeah. Charlie skyed so quick, he had to leave behind the wounded." Franklin dropped into the infirmary and knelt beside a body. "She looks no older than ten years." A young girl, her head bandaged, lay twisted, the dressing black with dried blood. Clutched in her small hand was a wooden doll.

Odd, he thought. Children the world over have their specific needs. Little girls have their dolls. Like when he was a boy, only his toy was a cap gun. Charlie probably grew up playing with a cap gun. And like him, now the guns they played with were real.

And deadly.

"Look here." Dawes pointed to another body. "An old mama-san. Must have been a nurse or something. I suppose she stayed behind to comfort the wounded." The upper torso of an old woman, her long gray hair in a ponytail, lay in the center. "Wonder where the other half is?" Her intestines hung from her sunken belly, turning black as the air sucked at the tissue and the blood drained onto the ground. Flies would dwell on her soon, breeding maggots that would wind into the cavity, devour all that was flesh. Leaving only the bones. Symbolic of war. When it's over, there's nothing left but the bones. Everything else belongs to whoever stakes the first claim.

Franklin shook his head and turned, raised his fist, and pumped his arm, signaling the others to follow.

The team regrouped and were delighted to hear Marion say, "We'll be extracted from this point. The chopper's inbound." That was good news. Tired from the long patrol, the men looked forward to a hot shower and a long sleep, even if it would be on hard ground.

Franklin looked again into the crater and for a moment felt pity for the child and old woman. Then he spit and said acidly, "Don't mean nothing!"

That had become the "phrase" of the American soldier. To mean something, there has to be value. In Vietnam, life had become an equation that meant nothing.

Then, the greatest sound they had heard in nearly two weeks: the rotor slap from an incoming helicopter.

The chopper flew the team away, all knowing the Vietcong would return.

So would the Americans.

PART 2

HUGGING THE BELT

7

Brigadier General Samuel Sharps was tall and sapling lean, his physique strong and durable, like that of a long-distance runner. He wore his hair shaved two inches above the ears and close-cropped on top and allowed himself a narrow mustache, highlighting full lips. He wore a light blue jumpsuit as he sat at the large ormulu desk commanding his office at MACV headquarters in Saigon, where he served as liaison officer between the U.S. Air Force and South Vietnamese Air Force.

He glanced to the mahogany wall, slowly swiveling his leather chair as he studied a panorama of family photographs, awards, and decorations earned during a military career that spanned nearly three decades. When one particular frame caught his attention, he felt a sense of pride, followed by sadness, as he always felt when remembering the most painful day of his life.

The photograph was of his son Adrian, taken the day of his graduation from West Point. The next frame held the photograph of Adrian's wife, Darlene, proudly holding their daughter, Argonne, a daughter he never lived to see. She had been born while he was in Vietnam. Beside the picture was another, a photograph of son Franklin, taken the day he graduated from airborne school at Fort Benning. General Sharps's emotions were in conflict between the two young men. Adrian was the disciplined, methodical son, always ambitious and dependable; Franklin had always been a mustang, wild and undisciplined.

A sudden knock on Samuel's office door broke him from his reverie.

His secretary, Jessica Kovar, entered, carrying a cardboard box. "I have these for you, General, just as you ordered."

He forgot about all else and looked into the box, containing five smaller cartons, each in its original wrapping. "Outstanding!" he said to Kovar. "You have the addresses?"

"Of course." She reached into the box, removed one of the cartons, and laid it on the desk. "But this one is for you. I'll get the others in the overnight mail bag immediately."

He removed the cellophane wrapping. The tape recorder was just what he needed, the others what his family needed. Separated by so many miles—and differences—he yearned to begin bringing his family back together again. The sting of shame struck him, reminding him of past mistakes, particularly his betrayal of the ones he loved the most in the world.

After leaving his office at MACV headquarters, Samuel strolled along the wide boulevard. The air was muggy, thick with the moisture, nearly to the point of rain, that dogged the Vietnamese people hurrying about their business, past outdoor vendors selling the Vietnamese version of hamburgers and fries: slices of beef in French bread with thick fried potatoes in their crinkly peels. He enjoyed being among the people, even though his height made him stand out like an oak tree in a cornfield. Perhaps due to his race, the Vietnamese treated him friendlier than they did white Americans, whom they called "long noses," a throwback name to French colonialism.

As he reached the building where he and other high-ranking

officers were billeted, there was a thunderous explosion. Fire belched from the building; then a second explosion followed, sending chunks of plaster and mortar in every direction.

Samuel felt a smothering blast of heat, then an impact and blinding, searing pain and blackness.

8

The mission of the First Brigade, as defined by Colonel James Timothy, was to serve as "a reserve reaction force capable of airmobile or parachute assault anywhere in the theater." The troopers of the First Brigade learned that quickly. Crack assault troops, such as Airborne or Marines, were being used for operations that were designed for infantry units. Instead, these elite assets were deployed as "search-and-destroy" units.

Only the recon element was acting in its traditional role: searching for the enemy and providing constant intelligence. That meant long-range patrols and isolation, which sat well with the 1/327 Recon Platoon.

By the end of August, the clearing of the An Khe Pass had become one of drudgery and disappointment. *Where was Charlie?* was the question on everybody's mind. He was out there. That was certain, but where?

There were some certainties. The young paratroopers were receiving fine-tuning points of soldiering from seasoned combat veterans of Korea, many of whom had also fought in World War II and pulled a tour in Vietnam before assignment to the Screaming Eagles, the boldest, most courageous fighting unit in

American military history. One of the finest—who took keen interest in the training of the young soldiers—was Major David Hackworth. He knew there was more to educating soldiers than a rough commanding voice and telling war stories.

" 'What's a soldier?' " Hack—as he was called—would ask. Rarely did he get a good answer. Hackworth would explain: "A soldier is a trooper who can fire a three-round burst at a charging enemy and hit three targets." Hack hated weapons fired on full automatic. "If you fire full automatic you'll generally miss everything. It's a waste of ammunition, and more important . . . it tells the enemy you're scared and inexperienced."

Combat was the true classroom for Vietnam. Hackworth always reminded his troopers, "You'll be fighting an enemy who feels his country has been invaded by you. On his terrain, which he knows better than you. And the population is more on his side than yours. Don't think of this enemy as bowlegged slopeheads who can't soldier. They've known war all their lives. They defeated the Japanese and the French. They were born in this country. Not New York City, or Dallas, or Los Angeles, where there are no trees or rice paddies or mountains. This is their ground. They'll choose the time and place to fight."

The brigade had learned fast that in a firefight a soldier never saw the totality of what was happening. There was too much foliage, places for the enemy to hide, too much smoke, and too much noise gnawing at the senses. Noise. God, was there noise. Gunfire. Grenade and artillery explosions. Mortar rounds crashing to the earth, ripping apart trees and chewing up the ground in large chunks. Helicopters screaming low over the ground. Bombs and napalm exploding, searing the blue from the sky, turning it charcoal. Radios crackling. And the most unforgettable, the screams of the wounded and dying.

The only silence came from the dead.

"Hugging the belt" was a terrible tactic. It meant getting close, trying to tear at the will of Charlie, to drive him back and into the open, then brutalize him as he scurried for his village sanctuaries or underground bunkers.

It had become Charlie's greatest strategy. Hackworth convinced the brass it was time the Americans "took back the night."

The tactic was employed at night with good effect. Instead of Charlie harassing the brigade, the troopers sent out ambush patrols, sat in the night along trails worn smooth, like ruts from wagon wheels. An M-60 machine gun commanded the trail; claymore mines were posted to provide a sudden deadly swatch of hellish steel.

The brigade was learning how to take the fight to Charlie, and it was paying off, but with a price higher than expected.

There were other new tactics evolving, and not all of them to the liking of the troopers. Especially to Franklin Sharps, whose next patrol included a Vietnamese soldier leading a German shepherd that looked as scrawny as his master. The Americans called him a Kit Carson scout—one of hundreds of former Vietcong who had come over to the Americans. And not necessarily for patriotic reasons as much as the fact that they were tired of being hounded in the bush, bombed by airplanes, or shelled by mortar and artillery. Most Americans thought it was the better food and the odds-on bet that they would live longer fighting against their former comrades than fighting the Americans.

But these men knew the habits of the Vietcong, and the dog was trained in tracking the Vietnamese by the distinctive odor of *Nuk Bam*, a foul-smelling cooking oil derived from fish drying in the sun, seeping into the oil during decomposition. Most Americans thought the oil smelled like liquid manure and tasted worse. The only drawback for the Kit Carsons was that they were allowed to eat only American chow; otherwise their smell might throw off the dog's ability to pick up Charlie's scent.

Franklin looked at the man, pockmarked face, high cheekbones, and flat, dead eyes. He thought more highly of the Vietcong than the Kit Carsons, who most Americans viewed as traitors. And, he thought, *he might be the motherfucker that killed my brother!*

Major Hackworth gave the briefing as platoon leader Lieutenant James Gardner looked on. The major pointed to a map, an area marked in black. "Intelligence reports from popular forces indicate the Vietcong are using this area as a staging point. They are stockpiling weapons, ammunition, rice, medical supplies . . . all the good shit Charlie needs for an offensive. We need you to get in there and sniff out the bastards. There'll be recon units from Second Brigade operating ten clicks from you." He tapped the map and warned, "Don't fire on each other, goddammit."

A week before, a soldier had fired an M-79 grenade launcher onto his comrades' position and wounded eleven troopers.

"Charlie's in there. Be assured of that. I want good eyes on all of you. Get sloppy . . . and you'll sleep in a body bag." He paused, grinned, and gave his classic final words of farewell: "And remember . . . always keep five!"

Hackworth glanced at Staff Sergeant John "Dynamite" Hughes and added, "Sergeant Hughes, you know the drill. Keep your squad tight." Hughes was a professional soldier; small, but strong as an ox, he could carry more weaponry and ammunition than any other man in the unit. He had acquired his nickname Dynamite from that very characteristic. It was a common joke that should he ever take a direct hit he would detonate like an atomic bomb.

"Yes, sir." Hughes looked at the men and gave his standard piece of advice: "We do our job. No heroes . . . and everybody comes home!"

The briefing over, the soldiers had started to leave when Captain George Shevlin, the headquarters company commander, motioned for Franklin Sharps. Shevlin, a stocky, robust man, who was considered one of the finest officers in the brigade, took a sheet of paper from his blouse pocket. He handed it to Franklin. "This communiqué came in from Saigon." He paused, then added, "I didn't know your father was a general."

"It's not something I discuss, sir. It's not the sort of thing that makes a guy popular among the troops."

Shevlin understood. He added, "Read the message. If there's anything I can do, I'll help."

Franklin read the message. His father had been wounded in a bomb explosion in Saigon.

"Do you want to go to Saigon?" Shevlin said.

"No, sir. I'm going out on a mission. Anything else, sir?"

"No. Good luck on the mission."

Franklin and the others climbed into waiting jeeps for the short ride to the chopper pad. The team began loading under the glaring eye of the door gunner, who stared curiously at the dog, then shook his head and said nothing. The dog was hoisted inside by the Kit Carson and the aircraft lifted off and raced toward the landing zone west of Pleiku.

9

* * *

The beauty of the landscape was mesmerizing: a quilt work of rice paddies, framed by green forests, that sat surrounded by towering mountains that formed the Central Highlands. Like a black widow, thought Franklin, so beautiful, and filled with the deadly poison of a hidden enemy. Sprinkling the rice paddies were Vietnamese, bent over, pulling at rice shoots, a water buffalo in each square section to carry the harvest. But the Americans knew that lurking beneath many of those baskets were AK-47s, RPG-7 rocket launchers, and hand grenades. Charlie was prepared to go down only after putting up one hell of a fight.

The sudden *stammer* of the door gunner's M-60 cut the air, getting everyone's attention except the dog's.

"Got you, motherfucker!" The gunner was blazing away at the paddies, where Franklin saw the peasants breaking frantically for cover. Another burst left the air tasting of gunpowder, and he saw a water buffalo twisting and jerking in the paddy.

"Yeah! Have that for supper, you little bastards!" The gunner was in a near state of grace as he continued his staccato of death aimed at the peasants.

Another burst rippled, and the gunner looked at Hughes, saying, "Have to clear my gun."

Hughes just looked at him with contempt. In the two months the brigade had been in the bush, they had seen it all. Nothing surprised any of the troopers anymore. Except for maybe the presence of the dog.

The chopper raced along the paddies, then banked toward a tree line in the distance. Passing over the leading edge of the tall trees, the Huey slowed up and began settling in an open area covered with elephant grass. Hughes's eyes narrowed; then he called to the pilot, "Get out of here! Charlie has this spot bracketed!"

The pilot throttled up, eased the nose forward. Hughes pointed at the opening. "Look at the elephant grass. It's been cut short. Each blade is like a sharp stake, and there's no cover from Charlie." He looked at the door gunner. "Cut loose on the tree line."

The gunner grinned and began firing; red tracers marked the deadly fusillade's path.

But Charlie wasn't to be denied his moment. The trees suddenly came alive with gunfire and the Americans instinctively ducked, as though that might save them. The door gunner screamed and fell over the skid into empty air, his fall cut short by the safety harness secured to the floor. Franklin and Hughes reached, grabbed the strap, and began pulling the heavy body into the fuselage. He had been hit in the throat; blood poured from his neck. His eyes were rolled back, face ashen, and Franklin knew he was dead.

Hughes hurried to the pilot. "Put us down at the far end of the tree line!" He was pointing at an area that was nearly a mile from where Charlie had opened fire.

The pilot nodded and looked at the gunner. "What's his status?"

Hughes shook his head. "He's bought the farm."

Hughes and the others perched on the skids, ready for a "hot insert." "Keep low and move out quick," Hughes ordered. "Charlie's in there." He looked at the Kit Carson and yelled, "Carry your dog. We ain't waiting!"

The Kit understood. The dog would be in water over his head, forced to swim, becoming a juicy target.

The Huey dropped low over the water but near the tree line when the troopers unassed the chopper and hit the water on the dead run, charging toward the security of the trees. Franklin looked back and saw the Kit Carson, dog in arms, both of their eyes filled with fear.

They crashed through the edge of the trees and spread out, forming a horseshoe defensive perimeter. No one spoke; all eyes were searching, ears tuned for the slightest sound. But they saw nothing and the only sounds were the labored breathing of the Kit and dog and the fading rotor slap of the Huey.

Hughes gave a hand signal, and the seven Americans and Kit began moving out in pairs, one watching the trees for snipers, the other watching the ground for booby traps. They moved quick, careful, and silent, threading through the thick trees like shadows, saying nothing, unseen—they hoped—knowing that Charlie was in the area.

An hour later they stopped for a break. While Hughes checked his map, Franklin slipped around to each of the men. He always carried two extra canteens with a heavy salt concentration in each. Loss of body salt in the extreme heat took nearly as high a toll as malaria and booby traps.

When the Kit Carson grunted, pointing at the canteen, Franklin gave him a look the Kit immediately understood. Hughes, watching the exchange, knelt by Franklin. "The dog could use some of your saltwater mixture."

"I ain't no goddamned veterinarian, Sarge. Let the dink look after his dog."

Hughes's lips tightened. "You unload your hatred on the

Cong, young man. On a patrol you're the medic for everyone along . . . including the Kit Carson and his dog. Do I make myself clear?"

Franklin tossed his canteen to the Kit and sat against a tree watching the Vietnamese pour the water into the dog's mouth, then wet a bandanna and wash the dog's face. For a moment, Franklin almost felt sorry for the two creatures. All they had in the world was each other, and to Franklin's way of seeing things, that meant neither had much.

"Let's move out," Hughes ordered.

Tired and sweat-soaked, the troopers got to their feet, hoisted their heavy packs onto their backs, and started forward. The Kit led out with the dog walking to the front. The others on the team followed, with Hughes at the center. Franklin took up his usual position at the rear.

PFC Jesus Marquez was a tall, muscular Hispanic from Fort Worth, Texas, and had the dubious role of carrying the M-60 machine gun, the largest weapon in the American infantry arsenal. Size was important where this weapon was concerned. Humping hills and paddies with the '60 was a backbreaking job, even for the strong. Strands of ammunition were wound around his upper torso, adding to the burden and giving him the appearance of wearing brass armor, gleaming in the sunlight.

PFC Miles Walker carried the PRC-25 radio behind Hughes. From Macon, Georgia, Walker was tall, rawboned, and tough. He loved the bush and moved through the thick foliage with the ease of water moving over hard ground.

Spec Four Boyd Graves was a black kid from Chicago with large hands and feet, giving his short frame an awkward appearance.

PFC George Has No Horses was a full-blooded Sioux from Wounded Knee, South Dakota. Square-faced and wiry, his eyes dark, brooding, a grandson of Sitting Bull, nephew of One Bull, George was born to the lance and smell of battle.

Spec Four Jessie Stark was black and the "cherry," the new member in the platoon.

With the exception of Hughes and Franklin, they were all still teenagers, kids playing for keeps in a deadly adult world.

After nearly an hour, Hughes stopped the patrol to check his map, then reported their position over the radio. They moved out, following a trail that would take them to a village tucked deep in the bush, which the Vietcong preferred, as compared to the rice paddies with their openness. Thick, razor-sharp vines tangled their bodies, stinging the skin and impeding their advance. Mosquitoes buzzed, adding to the aggravation. The misery.

From the rear, Franklin watched the Kit and dog, both appearing to flow through the tangle of foliage. The Kit's eyes were trained on the ground when his hand shot upward. He squatted and took out his machete. Hughes eased up to his side, where the Vietnamese had run the blade beneath a clump of branches. Carefully the clump was removed, revealing a hole in the earth.

"Punji pit," Hughes whispered to Marquez, who passed the word along to the others. Sharp stakes hardened with fire at the tips and dipped in human excrement lay planted in the hole, a painful welcome mat to the Vietnamese village.

"Move off the trail," Hughes whispered. "Move abreast and keep ten."

The going became more than a physical challenge; it was equally demanding on the mind. The bush was thicker, visibility nearly zero, where seeing a few feet ahead was nearly impossible. Monkeys scurried about in the treetops, chattering and swinging from the branches, adding to the intensity. And the nervousness. Sweat poured from the men's faces, each knowing that any moment contact could be made with a concealed enemy.

There would be little cover. The Vietcong would be in bunkers covered with logs, and there would be the mines: Bouncing

Betties that exploded at the ground, rose five feet, then detonated a second explosion; and the Chinese "button mines,"
plastic devils the size of a silver dollar but capable of blowing
off a foot or leg.

Booby traps were Charlie's forte. The psychological effect
was as important as the physical destruction. Fear and appre-
hension gnawing at the mind caused mistakes, which took a toll
on others if a trip wire was triggered.

Franklin was on the left wing of the advance when the explosion ripped through the thick brush. The heavy thunder of
the M-60 roared through the dense vines; a scream echoed from
his right, and he recognized the voice of Has No Horses. Automatic weapons fire filled the air; there was the deep "crump"
of a grenade exploding from Franklin's right front, followed by
the cry he knew he would hear: "Med-ic!"

He charged head-down, his weapon poised to the front, ignoring the thorns and pain; the sweat burned his eyes, and he
could barely see. Hackworth had been right: "You don't see
war. . . . You hear it!"

He followed the sound, the distinct chatter of AK-47s firing
from the front. The sound of bullets passing over his head
cracked sharply in the stifling air, then more shouts and another
report from an exploding grenade.

Franklin reached Has No Horses, who lay cradled in
Hughes's arms. Hughes was talking slow and calm into the radio headset, ordering an artillery fire mission. He looked up at
Franklin and nodded at the wounded Has No Horses. There
was a look in his eyes that chilled Franklin to the bone.

While Walker kept his weapon leveled toward the sound of
the firefight, Hughes kept talking on the radio and Franklin
knelt beside his wounded comrade. Both legs were gone at the
knees. Blood gushed from the stumps, soaking the loam ground
a dark brown where he lay. His legs were nowhere in sight.

Franklin removed his pack and took a Syrette of morphine,
pushed the plunger in, releasing the medication, then injected

Has No Horses in the neck. He slowly squeezed the Syrette until it was empty, then took two tourniquets from his aid pack. Has No Horses stared emptily at Franklin.

Around him, the clatter of M-16s and exploding grenades stunned the ground, the air, and the senses within its touch.

Stark suddenly appeared; his eyes wide as he looked at Has No Horses, turned away for a moment, seized his composure, then said, "There's a Charlie bunker twenty meters to the front."

"Just one?" Hughes snapped.

"That's all that's opened up for now. Could be more. What do we do, Sarge?"

Hughes took the handset and spoke quickly. "We're too close for arty. Negative on the fire mission." He tossed the handset to Walker and told Stark, "We move straight on the bunker. You from the right flank with Graves. I'll take Walker and Marquez and go up the middle and keep them busy." He looked at Franklin and said, "You and the Kit hit them from the left flank."

Franklin nodded and looked at Has No Horses. "I can't do any more for him. We need to get a chopper in here."

Hughes looked up. "No way in hell a chopper can land in here. Right now we got to take out that bunker." Hughes looked at the wounded man. "When you hear Marquez open up with the sixty, start moving in."

Franklin understood. He finished wrapping the second dressing on Has No Horses's bloody stumps, then stood and motioned for the Kit to follow him. The Vietnamese tied his dog to a tree and followed.

The men broke away and moved quickly toward their positions. Franklin let the Kit take the lead, following in his footprints and maintaining a separation in case of more mines. They moved swift and steady, bent low, their weapons at the ready, until the Kit stopped and pointed to his right.

Franklin's eyes strained to see what the man was pointing at.

Then he saw a slight movement at ground level no more than ten meters away. The barrel of a rifle. He watched the Kit take a grenade, pull the pin, and point toward the bunker. Franklin did the same and waited.

Suddenly the loud stutter of the M-60 erupted; bullets struck in the ground in front of the bunker, kicking up dust and keeping the enemy occupied. When the Kit's arm swung back, Franklin did the same, and both men threw their grenades and dived for cover.

At the moment the grenades exploded, Franklin caught movement from his left. No more than a flash of black.

He saw a Vietcong racing through the trees, snapped to his feet, and charged after the soldier. He fired a short burst, then another, and suddenly reached an opening that revealed a slight ravine. Franklin could see the VC wasn't armed with an AK-47. He fired another burst that hit the VC in the legs, dropping him instantly.

Behind him was more gunfire from the M-60 and the M-16s, telling Franklin the others must have taken out the bunker. But now he had a wounded enemy soldier, and even wounded, he was still deadly. Franklin walked slowly toward the man, then stopped suddenly. It was a boy of no more than twelve. He was on his stomach, trying to crawl away.

Franklin wasn't sure what had caught his attention, whether it was the movement of the boy's hand or the slight metallic ring, but his instincts told him to dive for cover. He had started to dive, his finger on the trigger, firing toward the boy, when he saw the grenade fall from the VC's hand and roll only inches from his body.

The explosion tore the boy to shreds, showering Franklin with dirt, debris, and bits of metal that stung at his arm. The concussion thundered in his ears, setting off a ringing in his brain unlike any he had ever known. He felt himself still rolling, as most of the shrapnel mushroomed over his body and ripped at the trees. Had he been closer the concussion would have killed him; any farther away and the deadly metal fragments would have torn his body to pieces.

Then it grew quiet and he saw the Kit suddenly appear at his side. He looked into the man's eyes; they appeared saddened, not heartless and cold. Franklin tried to rise up, but the Kit gently forced him to lay back down, then removed his canteen and poured water over Franklin's face. Franklin rolled up his sleeve and checked his wounds. He was fortunate. The wounds were small punctures he could easily clean and dress with Band-Aids.

Both turned suddenly at the sound of movement and pointed their rifles. The dog appeared and ran straight for his master. Franklin figured the dog had pulled himself loose during the ruckus and followed the Kit's scent. The dog licked at the Vietnamese's face, and while only moments before there had been the fury of war all around, now there was no other sound except for the heavy breathing of the two soldiers and the dog.

10

* * *

When Franklin and the Kit reached the rest of the team at the bunker, Sergeant Hughes was examining what remained. The grenades had torn holes in the ground, and two mangled bodies lay off to the side. There was only one weapon, a Chinese machine gun that had suffered as poorly in the grenade explosions as the Vietcong.

"This must have been a listening post. By now the ville will be empty." Hughes looked at Franklin and asked, "Did you make contact?"

"Scratch one VC. But not much of one. He was just a kid with a grenade."

"Yeah, and the will to use it. Deadly combination." He pointed at Franklin's bloody sleeve. "You square?"

"Just a scratch. No problem."

Hughes took off his helmet and poured water over his head, then pointed at Has No Horses. "Better get him ready for a medevac." He looked up at the tall trees. "If we can get him out of here."

Franklin went to George Has No Horses, who lay nearly lifeless. He was unconscious, and that was a blessing, thought

Franklin. He injected Has No Horses with another Syrette of morphine and started an intravenous drip of saline solution. There was nothing more he could do, and he felt helpless. He knew that Has No Horses had been a rodeo rider before volunteering for the army. His eyes went to the blood-soaked bandages covering the stumps and he said softly, "Guess you won't be needing any horses, George."

From behind him Hughes's voice could be heard giving a situation report and calling for a helicopter evacuation.

One of the main purposes of the helicopter was for medical evacuation of the wounded and a quick trip to a waiting team of surgeons at a field hospital. The dust-off, as it was termed, was a psychological ace in the hole for the American soldiers in Vietnam. Long trips over difficult roads in frontline ambulances were passé; the chopper was the modern angel of mercy. However, terrain played a major role in making the extraction of the wounded often as deadly as the enemy. Charlie knew it was far better to wound an opponent than to kill him because the wounded required extraction, which demanded manpower, putting other personnel and assets at risk.

Charlie knew that where an American soldier lay wounded a big, conspicuous helicopter would arrive.

Hughes knew that if he didn't get a medevac for the Indian damned quick, the man would die. It was decided to deploy the team and set up a defense perimeter to protect the chopper, which would hover over the site and lower a harness through the trees. Franklin and Hughes would connect the wounded recce soldier, and then a winch would raise him to the Huey.

Franklin knew of this extract procedure only in theory. He had never done it before. Though risky, it was the only available option to save the man's life.

Franklin and Hughes stayed with Has No Horses and waited for the Huey while the others set up the perimeter. Franklin had given Has No Horses several more injections of morphine sulfate, rendering him totally unconscious. The tourniquets were stanching the flow of blood, and by the time the chopper arrived he was resting easy. Hughes tossed a purple smoke grenade, marking their position, and stood staring through the trees until he saw the helo suddenly appear at the tops of the towering forest.

Hughes had kept the PRC-25 and radioed the pilot to lower the harness. The lifesaving apparatus came down, and despite becoming entangled in a tree, it was freed when the pilot lifted the chopper slightly, then lowered the nose, allowing the tether to drop to the waiting Hughes.

Franklin and Hughes moved quickly, harnessed the wounded soldier, then signaled the crew chief, who sat in the open door, to begin winching the wounded man up.

The wounded paratrooper, Has No Horses, rose straight up, slowly, oblivious to what was happening. Franklin had taped the intravenous saline bottle to the harness. The continual flow would sustain the wounded soldier until he was received by the waiting surgical team.

Franklin and Hughes stood watching as the wounded man neared the tops of the trees. Then, without warning, they saw Has No Horses fall from the harness and plummet toward earth.

"Run, goddammit!" Hughes shouted.

Franklin stood frozen, heard Hughes shout again.

A huge cloud of dust rose from where the trooper impacted on the hard ground.

Franklin walked to the body, knowing there was no hope.

PFC George Has No Horses had landed flush on the stumps and died instantly, his mind unaware, narcotized by the morphine. He stared emptily into the trees above through dead eyes, as one might look on a sunshine-filled beach, buried to his waist in sand.

Hughes walked over, put his hand on the neck and felt for a pulse, stepped away, and said to Franklin, "Tag him . . . and bag him."

Minutes later a body bag was lowered, and Franklin "tagged and bagged" his comrade. Hughes tied the bag to the harness, securing it with rope he carried for just this purpose.

Franklin watched in silence as Has No Horses's body rose again toward the opening in the top of the trees. Seconds afterward, the chopper peeled off and disappeared.

Hughes's voice thundered, "All right, let's saddle up. We've got a ville to recon."

11

* * *

The team reached the edge of the hamlet and found the ville empty. This was typical of the highland villages most sparsely populated, except for the Montegnards—the "mountain people"—who lived farther to the west. The mere existence of the village was evidence enough for most military leaders to suspect it was Vietcong. The National Liberation Front—the Vietcong—built small villages in isolated areas for one specific purpose: to serve as supply dumps for the guerrilla units operating in the region. The VC used these supply depots, well concealed and appearing harmless, to store supplies brought south from North Vietnam. The tiny hamlets would suddenly appear to serve as a momentary base of operations, then would be abandoned, the guerrillas moving to another area.

Hughes scanned through his binoculars and saw no movement. "I was right about the bunker. Not a soul."

"What now, Sarge?" Marquez said.

"Let's go in from three points. Nice and easy. We've already lost one of our men. I don't want to lose any more."

They moved toward the hamlet from the tree line in the same

groups as the assault on the bunker. There was not a sound coming from the ville, which was no more than a half-dozen mud huts.

The team moved from hut to hut, staying outside, until they were convinced there was no one to be found. Then they gathered up and took the next step. Each man took a grenade and tossed it through the crude glassless windows. The demolition took only seconds, with each explosion destroying the hut and any booby trap that might be planted inside. The Screaming Eagles had learned the hard lessons of the past few months: Take no chances.

Hughes ordered the Kit to turn loose the dog. "Let's see if that son of a bitch has a Tennessee coon hound's hunting nose," he muttered.

The paratroopers stood watching as the shepherd sniffed and pranced about the debris, appearing more playful than serious. He rooted beneath the thick blocks of mud that formed the huts, pawed at splintered wood, avoided spots where fires still burned.

"Nothing," Hughes mumbled. He was about to call off the dog when the shepherd stopped, stood motionless, then lay on the earth, on his side, his ear against the ground as though he were going to sleep.

When the dog barked, the troopers jerked alert, and the Kit smiled, walked over to Hughes, and pointed to the smooth ground. "VC," he said excitedly, pointing at the ground. "VC here."

Franklin stepped forward and looked at the dog. "I think the dog is dumber than the Kit."

Hughes shook his head. "Give me your ET."

Franklin took the entrenching tool from his rucksack and handed it to Hughes, who began digging into the ground until he had dug no more than a foot and an opening appeared through the ground. It was common among Vietnamese villagers to build shelters beneath their huts to provide a quick and accessible shelter from bombs and artillery or to use as storage areas for supplies.

"Underground shelter," Hughes said. He spaded around the edge until the hole was the size of a sewer cover, then lay down and peered inside. The sunlight filtered into the hole; beyond the light provided by the sun he saw nothing. "Probably a bomb shelter." He looked at Franklin. "Drop a Willie Peter in there, kid."

Franklin took a white phosphorus grenade from his harness and released the spoon. At the moment he tossed the grenade, he saw movement in the hole and the shepherd leaped forward, soared through the air, and disappeared into the ground.

The Kit shouted and started forward. Hughes grabbed him by his harness and threw him back. Franklin was mesmerized by what he saw in the floor of the shelter: two brown eyes stared helplessly at him from within.

"Move, dammit!" Hughes shouted.

Franklin stood frozen, his eyes joined to the child's in the shelter.

"Get down!" Hughes grabbed Franklin's harness and with all his strength jerked the young trooper away from the hole. The earth shook as the grenade exploded, collapsing the shelter, creating an even larger crater. White phosphorus smoke spewed from the crater, acrid and billowing, forming a volcanic cloud that rose, flattened, and descended to where it spread ghostlike across the ground.

The silence that followed was broken only by the whimpering of the Kit, who sat staring helplessly at the empty crater.

Hughes screamed in Franklin's face, "What the fuck's wrong with you, boy!"

Franklin said nothing. He walked to the edge of the crater and looked down. "The shelter wasn't empty."

Hughes looked and saw several arms and legs sticking up from the dirt. One leg appeared older than the others. There were five limbs altogether. The squad leader dropped into the hole and pulled at the legs, tossing them out of the crater until he came to one with a sandal still on the foot. He examined the foot closely, noting the decrepit toenails and the withered skin. "Looks like we got us a papa-san and a couple of kids." He reached down and picked up a bloody, furry mass, tossed it out, and said angrily, "And one fucking German shepherd."

"Hell of a body count," Marquez said as he poured water onto a towel and wrapped it around his neck.

Franklin felt sick and wanted to throw up, wanted to kill Vietcong, not old men and children, wanted to go back to that moment and grab the grenade, put the pin back in, and walk away.

But he couldn't. It was too late. Death offers no rehearsal. Casualties of war, they had been told, would be a common experience. See it. Smell it . . . then move out. That's what the brass passed down from on high.

The grunts in the bush had another way of putting it: "*Fuck it . . . don't mean nothing.*"

12

Hughes and the others knew the mission had been a bust when they took initial fire from Charlie at the tree line earlier that day. He had decided to push forward, hoping their presence would not compromise the mission, but he knew that would not be the case. The fact the ville was empty only reinforced that notion. Charlie had gone to ground and would not surface so long as he thought there were Americans seeking out his positions, especially if he suspected it was a recon team probing the area.

Hughes contacted the command post and arranged for an "extract" the following morning. He would have called for a daylight pickup but, knowing Charlie would be watching, he chose the early morning darkness when Charles could only hear the rotor thump and not actually see the team being airlifted from the arena. "Let Charles wonder if we're still here," Hughes said, "Maybe he won't sleep too tight tonight."

The team spent the night sleeping in trees high above a trail that meandered through the dense forest. Each man had tied himself to the trunk, straddling a heavy branch, perched on his rucksack for crotch protection. Then they played the "Close Watch" game.

The worst thing a recon specialist can do is lose focus, to forget where he's at and what's going on in the immediate area. Unlike the regular infantry soldier, one hundred yards means nothing to a recce grunt. That may as well be the edge of the earth. To the scout, the game is played out in a matter of feet and inches. Smell is important. A foreigner's smell can be as distinctive as rotting carrion, a trigger mechanism that can set off the alarms. But stealth is the most important, to move unseen in front of the enemies' eyes, and not make a sound.

Sound travels in the darkness like a crash of thunder from the sky, and can have a devastating result. A soldier on ambush patrol takes his turn to sleep, starts snoring, and before long incoming rounds start pulverizing the area. That is when the recon team's job is abruptly finished: when their presence is known to the enemy.

In Nam, word of a recon team's presence carried more swiftly than dry land lightning, or sound in the night. Which was why they knew their job was finished. The team was too small to be a fighting force should contact be made with a Vietcong unit of any size.

Hughes knew that Hackworth had devised a plan to combine the recon and antitank platoons to form a battalion-size "Tiger Force," as he called it, a fast-hitting, power-packed fighting unit that would pounce on Charlie with lightning speed and murderous firepower. Thus far it was theory, but in the works. He hoped it would come about soon, for he and the others were tired of being outnumbered.

Two hours before daybreak the team slithered down from their concealed heights and formed up. With Marquez on point, they slipped quietly through the forest toward the extract point. It took nearly an hour to reach the area, termed "Vegas," where tall elephant grass washed lazily back and forth in a slight breeze. The razor-sharp grass-edges offered a formidable and painful welcome.

Franklin's first experience in the grass was a nightmare he'd never forget. The wind whipped with near gale force, and the grass became what he could only describe as a meat grinder. By the time the team had moved through the field, not an inch of skin was left unblooded on the face and hands of the team.

The men sat waiting, nervous, knowing they had no protection from incoming bullets should Charlie know their presence, and rip off "spray and pray" automatic weapons fire. It was the same technique used by Americans: spray the area with automatic fire and pray that you hit a target.

Hughes sat stolid, his ears tuned for the sound he would recognize. Franklin glanced at him, and asked, trying not to laugh, "How's Butch?"

Hughes grinned and took a rubber doll from his harness. Butch was his good luck charm. Long black hair; no clothes, and uglier than Barbie on her deathbed.

"Butch's doing just fine," Hughes said, then stiffened and looked to the south.

The sound was distant at first, a low, pronounced thump that seemed to rumble overhead, then the distinct slap of the rotors as the Huey flew east of their position, giving the enemy the impression the chopper was bound elsewhere. In the cockpit, the pilot would reach a coordinate, drop low to treetop or paddy level, then run flat out to the rendezvous point.

But in the grass there was no real joy as the Huey flared above the team, turning the sea of elephant grass into a whipping storm of knives.

The men scrambled aboard through both open doors, lay flat, and turned their weapons outward. The nose of the helicopter lowered, the Huey pilot throttled up, then the craft raced across the grass in the first traces of dawn.

During the ride Franklin thought of Has No Horses and the dead children, and wished again he could change the outcome. He glanced at the Kit, and even felt sorry for the poor bastard. The man had lost his best friend; the team had lost a good friend.

13

Samuel Sharps awoke to the feel of a razor against his face. When his hand touched the thick gauze over his eyes, a woman's voice said, "Please lie still, General. I'm not the greatest in the world when it comes to shaving a man's face."

He found something humorous in this and chuckled. The smell of antiseptic filled the room. "How long have I been here?"

"Three days," the woman said.

His mind flashed back to his last conscious moment. He remembered the explosion but nothing else except the pain. "What's your rank, miss?"

"Captain Jane Caulder, sir. I'm the shift supervisor." She placed the razor in a basin of water and began toweling the residual shaving cream off his face. "There. All done."

He felt his face. "You missed your calling. You should have been a barber. I couldn't have done a better job myself."

He could feel her breath as she leaned close to him. "I think I'll keep the one I have."

He heard the sound of a door open; voices rushed into the room, most of them screams and shouts familiar to a hospital in wartime. "Good morning, General Sharps. I'm Major Dan Eades, chief of ophthalmology."

"Good morning, Major. Pardon me if I don't get up." He went straight to the heart of the matter. "Am I blind?"

There was a pause. "No, sir. But you've suffered damage to your right eye," Eades said.

"What is the extent of the damage?"

"I won't know until the bandages come off and give you an examination."

"When will that be?"

"Now that you're conscious, I'll conduct an exam."

That suited him fine. He wasn't a man who liked surprises or having to wait if there was bad news. He felt a wet cloth wipe at his face, then the slight sting of aftershave on his face. There was the shuffle of feet, the sound of movement nearby, and the physician's voice. "Captain, close the blinds."

The bandage was carefully unwound. Thick pads covered his eyes; when removed, he continued to see only blackness. "I can't see anything," he said.

Suddenly—a burst of light exploded in his brain and he lurched forward. He felt hands pushing him back onto the bed and heard the doctor's voice speaking in a calm, measured tone. "Lie back, sir. This will be uncomfortable for a few moments. But . . . it's good news, General. Your reaction to the light is a positive sign."

Slowly, his eyes adjusted to the light; he could see the light move from one eye to the other. He heard Eades tell the nurse, "Open the blinds. Very slowly."

Gradually, the room filled with light; he began to make out shapes, then objects as the interior clarified. But the light flooding the room was diminished by the relief filling his soul.

He had suffered injuries in life, wounds in France during World War II, airplane crashes, even jet ejections. He had walked away from them all. None were so frightening as this experience.

14

* * *

General Sharps was released from the hospital one week after being wounded in the hotel explosion. He went directly to his office at MAC-V Headquarters, where his aide, Major Leif Svenson, was waiting to brief him.

Svenson, a burly Swede from Kenmore, North Dakota, was an F-4 fighter pilot who had been shot down six months before. Injured when he ejected, and spending nearly a week evading the enemy, despite a broken leg, he wanted to complete his tour in Vietnam rather than be shipped stateside for a desk job. Sharps, who had known him as a young lieutenant in his F-88 fighter squadron in Korea, gave him a job as his aide.

The two talked for nearly an hour on the deployment of several air force reserve units that would be arriving in-country in a matter of days from the United States. The war was cranking up; hundreds of thousands more U.S. ground troops were scheduled to arrive from CONUS (Continental United States), bringing the total number to over 300,000 by the end of August.

Sharps glanced at the photographs on the wall. "What do you hear on the Screaming Eagles?"

Svenson was surprised at the question. In his own roundabout way the General was inquiring about his son, which he had never done before. He knew the relationship between the two was strained, but naturally never pursued the matter. "They're still up in the Central Highlands, digging out the Vietcong, clearing the An Khe Pass for the First Air Cav. It's damn rough going up there, General."

Sharps leaned on his desk and rested his chin on hand. His dark eyes seemed to drift back in time. "The monsoon must be beating the hell out of our boys up there."

"It's relentless, sir. The troops on the coast—especially the Marines—are up to their asses in the rice paddies. Air-to-ground support has been mostly ineffective, what with the lousy weather and the VC striking from close range, then disappearing like ghosts."

Ghosts, thought the General. Another nickname for the elusive Cong. He glanced over to the corner of his office and saw a pile of clothes that lay neatly folded on a chair. "Is that all that's left of my personal property from the hotel?"

Svenson nodded. "You're lucky to have that much left over. The place damned near burned completely to the ground." He paused, then added, "From where you were found, another thirty seconds and you would have . . ." His voice trailed off.

Sharps rose and went to the window. He stared through the glass for several minutes, saying nothing, watching the throng of mopeds and bicycles stream along the streets like salmon swimming upriver. What he knew—what everyone knew—was that most of them were either Vietcong or sympathizers. He also knew that America had put itself in a situation similar to the French in the 1950s: a one-way street that never ended.

"Do you think we can win this war, Leif?"

Svenson stood and stepped beside the general. He looked out the window at the stream of Vietnamese flowing along the boulevard. "This is their country, sir. They've known nothing but war and invasion for centuries. They see us as no different from the French, the Japanese, or the Chinese. They see us as invaders. We are the Spartans at the gates of Troy, and we don't have a wooden horse."

"Hell," Sharps said, "we don't even have a beautiful Helen to hold hostage. Instead, *we're* being held hostage. What are they thinking in Washington?"

"I understand General Johnson's Linebacker plan has been put on the back burner."

Operating from 8th Air Force Headquarters in Guam, Lieutenant General Johnson had conceived a plan called Linebacker, in which his B-52 Strata-Fortresses would bomb nearly one hundred key industrial and military complexes in North Vietnam, eliminating manufacturing and shipment of valuable war materials, while concurrently destroying national morale and resolve.

Sharps nodded. "Yes, it has. President Johnson doesn't want the United States to appear as some Goliath stepping down hard on the tiny David."

"This David doesn't carry a slingshot, sir. He's well equipped, knows the terrain, and is certain he is right."

The general went back to his desk and began poring over the pile of correspondence that had collected since being wounded. As always, there were the daily letters from Shania. He opened them first, reading each word as though it were the first he had heard from her. She wrote of Kevin, who was in college, and her recent letters from Franklin, and asked again, "Have you two gotten together yet since he arrived in Vietnam? I truly wish you would, Samuel. I think it would do both of you a lot of good. You're fighting a war together on the other side of the world. He needs his father. You need your son. Can't you find a way?"

He had been invited to Cam Ranh Bay by General Westmoreland to welcome the 101st Airborne when it arrived in-country, but he had passed on the offer. Knowing the bad blood that still existed between him and his son, he didn't want Franklin to start his tour in the war with an angry beginning. It would be difficult enough in time; no need to make the first day tense because of family problems.

Christ! How could I have been so stupid! To throw away a family for a romantic fling with a woman half my age!

He spent the next hour listening to Svenson brief him on the status of the Ho Chi Minh Trail and the ongoing air operations designed to create as much havoc as possible for supplying the Vietcong in the south.

"It's like walking up a muddy slope, General. For every two steps forward, we fall back one. We blow a bridge, the VC rebuilds overnight. We cut one branch of the trail, they use an alternate, or carve out another."

"What's the bottom line on this situation, Leif?"

Svenson shrugged. "We've tried taking away the jungle by defoliation, but that's simply not working. At least, not the way we hoped."

"What do you suggest?"

Svenson went to a map of Indo-China and pointed at the red lines depicting the Ho Chi Minh Trail. "A two-pronged attack, using B-52 bombers for saturation bombing, and lighter aircraft to mine the trail inside South Vietnam, Laos, and Cambodia."

"Mines?" Samuel asked dourly.

"Yes, sir. Antipersonnel mines. We'll put the same fear of God into the little bastards as they have in our people."

"You want to mine nearly fifteen hundred miles of jungle trail?"

Svenson was now getting excited. "Yes, sir, plus we can airborne insert sensor devices to pick up movement of personnel and equipment."

"Sensors?" Samuel was wondering how warfare had gone from man and machine fighting one another to high technology.

"Yes, sir. The boys in the labs back home are coming up with a lot of new scientific gadgets for us to use in this war. With sensors we don't have to send our people into that hellish place. We can target them through the sensors and send in the bombers to waste them. Our people can sit on the outside and watch the fireworks. Safe and sound. It can be Charlie's worse nightmare."

"Or ours. You know as well as I do that Charlie turns everything against us that isn't nailed down. He'll find the sensors, set them up near our people, and we'll be bombing American personnel or Vietnamese villages. The mines will be added to their already existing inventory of American antipersonnel ordnance they're using to kill and maim our troops. No, Major, forget the sensors and mines. The only way to cut off the trail is to go inside and dig the little bastards out of their holes and tunnels. To do that we'll have to use more ground troops. God help them when they venture into Charlie's living room."

"Is it better to let them venture into ours," Svenson wondered. "At least by fighting them on the trail we can control the action. Keep them busy. Pinned down. That's why the Air Cav is being deployed to An Khe."

All the while he spoke, Sharps had his eyes fixed on the neighboring countries of Laos and Cambodia. If the Ho Chi Minh Trail was shut down, the Vietcong would more than likely use the two neighboring countries as supply depots from which to continue the flow of supplies into South Vietnam. It would be more difficult, but then, the Vietcong understood hardship. That had been proven since World War II.

The question was: Could the American forces endure the same hardships? He doubted that. There was a major difference: the Americans were considered invaders by the Vietnamese. A war of attrition is won by the side willing to give up more than the other side is willing to give up. He knew there would eventually be a watermark the American people would not allow the government to surpass.

But what was that watermark? How many killed before this war was either fought and won the right way, or abandoned completely? History had taught the United States nothing. The Japanese. French. Now America.

Ten thousand Americans killed in action? Twenty thousand? Thirty? Certainly, no more than that. All Charlie had to do was hold on. He didn't have to defeat the American soldiers. America would do that for him.

15

Franklin Sharps knew Sergeant Bill Trout as about the toughest son of a bitch in the battalion, with the exception of Chassion, Smith, Musselwhite, and a few dozen other top noncoms. As a new sergeant first class and medic platoon sergeant, Trout was continuing in Vietnam the reputation he had begun building at Fort Campbell before deployment: "Do your job, don't whine, and if you've got a personal problem, see the chaplain. If you don't like me, tough fucking shit! Write your congressman. When he contacts me, I'll tell him to talk to my congressman. We're going to war, gentlemen, not to some sorority house party. You're going to see your friends die. You're going to see all sorts of people die. In fact, *you* might die."

When Franklin reported to the battalion aid station to resupply from the last mission, he found Trout sitting in front of the command tent sipping a beer, his M-16 nestled against his chair. His blue eyes narrowed on Franklin as he approached.

"Wilkes was hit yesterday," he said. "Pretty serious shit. He was medevaced to the Third Army Field Hospital in Qui Nhon."

Tommie Wilkes. Franklin's crazy buddy from Airborne

school and medic school at Fort Sam Houston and close-in bunkie in the barracks at Fort Campbell. A heartbreaker with the ladies and a hard charger on the battlefield. He'd already been awarded the Bronze Star with Valor and the Purple Heart, the first medic to get hit since arriving in Nam. More important, he was a friend.

The word was that Trout was finding a new reality within himself, one that men often found on the battlefield. Three days before, he had killed a Vietcong sniper with a single shot from over one hundred yards. Franklin figured he was chilling out, letting it all sink in. Real deep. That was never Franklin's problem. He didn't kill for God and country. He killed for revenge. That kept life simple.

Trout pointed toward the brigade commander's tent. "How many whores are standing in front of Colonel Timothy's headquarters?"

Franklin looked. "There aren't any whores in front of Colonel Timothy's tent, Sergeant."

Trout took a swig of beer, shook his head. "Your eyes must be going bad. I'm going to send you to Qui Nhon. I want you to get your eyes examined at the field hospital." He handed Franklin a prepared authorization signed by the battalion surgeon ordering Franklin to report for an eye examination.

He had started to walk away when Trout's voice stopped him. "Tell Wilkes I've written a letter to his family. I've told them what happened. How he was wounded. How he saved the lives of three American soldiers. Tell him the plat daddy is very proud." He added, "Don't worry about Chassion. I'll square it up with him."

16

The view from the Huey was breathtaking as Franklin studied the scenery stretching from the highlands to the South China Sea. The tall mountains gave way to lush paddies, dotted with Vietnamese tending to the rice crop. Franklin could see Route 19, which was still marked with burned-out French vehicles of Mobile Group 100, the French Foreign Legionnaire task force annihilated eleven years before by the Vietminh. It was common knowledge the Vietcong had purposely left— even brought in—other derelicts to be a constant reminder to the Americans of what awaited foreign invaders on the stretch of deadly highway.

Sitting across from him was a black trooper from C Company, wearing a grin as large as his helmet. He was going back to the world, his short tour from Campbell to An Khe finished. No more mosquitoes, leeches, land mines, or snipers; hot food and a soft bunk were waiting at the bottom, then the ride back to the world.

Franklin nearly envied the man, who said nothing, but stared at the passing terrain below, his grin growing ever wider as the mountains disappeared and the thin blue of the South China Sea could be seen in the distance.

"I'm out of this motherfucker!" he suddenly yelled, eyes dancing like two lanterns swinging in the wind. "Yeah! Airborne! Going home to my baby."

Franklin leaned over and extended his hand. The trooper, a buck sergeant, gripped him firmly and long, not seeming to want to let go. "You take care of yourself, young blood," the sergeant said, even looking slightly embarrassed. "Don't go getting your ass shot off."

Franklin shook his head. "I'm going home in one piece. Just like you."

The trooper shifted over beside Franklin, took out his wallet, and began showing photographs of his wife and three children. "They're back home in Alabama. My wife says, 'No more army. No more Nam.' I'm going to college on the GI Bill and be somebody." He looked severely at Franklin. "What about you, young blood? You going to college when you get out?"

Over the thump of the rotor slap Franklin shouted, "I don't know. Just trying to get out of here alive. That's all I got on my mind. I'll worry about that river when I get to it, Sarge."

The sergeant slapped him on the back. "The only chance the black man has in this world is to get an education. Without that, we just going to be carrying the Man's load all our lives. Do your tour, put in your time, then get the hell smartened and educated up. That's the package. We done fought for this country all over the world since freedom; now we got to make the big fight back home if we're going to get a piece of the pie."

He had heard it before. The refrain was typical of the philosophy expounded by many black soldiers: Do the time, get the hell out, then get the sheepskin. Work with your mind, not your back. Build from within, not from without.

"We've got to operate like the Cong," the sergeant went on. "We can't tear down the system from the outside. That won't work. We've got to do it from within. Just like Charlie. Get sneaky, and get smart. One day the white man will wake up, and without warning there we're going to be. Standing tall. Proud. Educated. Ready to take our place. We can only do that with education. That's the ticket that'll get us from the back of the bus to the front. You'll see, young blood. You listen to me. We're not going to be denied our rights any longer."

The war had begun to bring out such attitudes in the black population. What was being called the Civil Rights Movement was growing in the United States, especially in the South, where Jim Crow law still ruled in many states and the races were "separate but equal." Added to that was the expanding antiwar movement, and Franklin could only imagine what the United States would be like if the two ever merged. America could become more violent than Vietnam.

The chopper landed at the airstrip, and the two Screaming Eagles shook hands on the tarmac. The sergeant grinned, then gave Franklin a hurried hug and said, "Take care, young blood. Come home alive. We're going to need young brothers to help in the cause."

Franklin watched him walk toward the operations center, where he'd catch another flight to Ton Son Nhut, then the "freedom bird" back to the "big plantation."

But for Franklin there was the current situation. He was in Vietnam; he wouldn't take that ride for long months to come. He had no idea what he would do when he returned. He had not given it the slightest thought. Right now he was in a war, and he had to say good-bye to a friend.

17

* * *

The first thing that struck Franklin's senses when he entered the Third Army Field Hospital was the stench of decaying flesh and antiseptic; the second were the flies, clouds of them in the air, black patches of them on the blood-soaked bandages of wounded soldiers. Moans and screams echoed; metal clanged; flies buzzed.

The beds were lined on each side of the tent; a slight breeze drifted in where the flaps had been raised, but the heat was stifling. He didn't know what he would find, but he didn't expect the heat. It was more torturous than being in the bush. The medical personnel walked around with dour, blanched faces, more mechanical than human. And he could understand why. There were wounds of every type: gunshots, fragmentation grenades, amputations from mines and booby traps, bandaged eyes that would never see again, broken backs and legs, arms and skulls from explosions or dismounting helicopters improperly. But the worst were the burn victims, their bodies covered in heavy white bandages, oozing gel designed to soothe the pain and prevent the skin from scabbing against the dressing.

There were Marines, army, air force, and navy personnel in

the ward. Officers and enlisted men shared the same space, where rank no longer meant anything, where the common denominator was suffering.

Franklin eased along the aisle, his eyes searching for his friend.

He stood frozen at the sight of his friend. Tommie Wilkes's left arm was heavily bandaged and suspended from an IV pole. Intravenous tubes ran into his feet and one large one into his right bicep, where a "cut-down" had been performed to allow direct insertion of the tube into the artery. A heavy bandage covered his left shoulder and chest area, which Franklin knew was the exit wound of the bullet that had hit Wilkes in the back. Gone was his typical smile; his face muscles were set hard and tight. Gone was the laughter in his eyes; he rarely blinked, but he stared at the ceiling as though expecting God to come through the top and retrieve him from his torture. Gone was his left hand; the blood-soaked bandage covering his stump hung suspended, as though he were raising his hand to ask the teacher a question.

Franklin eased down on the bunk and waved away the flies that stirred from the bandage covering Wilkes's shoulder. The gauze was bluish, seepage from the massive doses of antibiotics he had been given to combat infection. Hard as it was to believe, gangrene was still a potent enemy of the wounded, especially those who had to crawl through the filth and slime of rice paddies after being wounded. Packing wounds with mud often saved the lives of wounded soldiers, but the bacteria introduced set in motion a new set of problems.

Franklin ran his fingers over Wilkes's close-cropped hair, which brought the young trooper out of the trance. A smile threaded across his face, then his lips quivered, and tears suddenly filled his eyes. "Hey, killer. How's my main man?" Wilkes asked.

"Good to go. You?" He knew the answer but wanted to get Wilkes talking.

Wilkes shrugged, then looked at the stump. "Don't mean nothing, man," he replied.

Franklin knew Wilkes was trying to be tough, acting out the bravado of the paratrooper code. But he knew the young man was in a lot of pain, both physically and mentally. And why shouldn't he be? Franklin said to himself. Wilkes was eighteen; he'd been shot to pieces and had lost a part of his body. That's enough to break the strongest. But Wilkes wasn't going to break. Franklin felt and believed that in his heart. Wilkes just needed a little "remindering," as Franklin's great-grandmother used to say.

He tapped Wilkes lightly with his fist on the side of his jaw. "Are we tough?" he asked.

Wilkes's eyes glistened; the smile started to return. "Yeah. We're tough."

Franklin tapped again. "Are we bad?"

Wilkes nodded. "Bad to the bone."

"Are we going home?"

"Home, to drive-in burgers and the pretty girls in short-shorts."

"We going home heroes?"

"Heroes and heartbreakers."

"That's my main man. You're tough. You're bad. You're a hero and a heartbreaker."

Wilkes was now smiling. "Thanks, man. I needed that." He tried to raise up but fell limp onto the pillow.

"Lay still, bro. Don't jerk those tubes out."

Wilkes sighed heavily. "I hate this backside-laying bullshit, Franklin. I wish I could get on my feet and walk around. Anything but lay here and feel these fucking flies chewing on me. I swear, I've fed half the flies in the province since they rolled me out of surgery."

Franklin glanced around and saw the dark clouds rise, then descend again onto the wounded soldiers. "This sucks. Can't the medics do something about this shit?"

Wilkes snickered. "The only time they fan them off is when the brass tour the place. I hate the flies worse than the Cong."

"You need a smoke. That'll keep them off you for a while."

Wilkes's eyes lit up. "You got one?"

Franklin took out a pack of C-ration cigarettes. He lit the Marlboro and held it to Wilkes's lips. The trooper took a long, slow drag, held it in for what seemed an eternity, then slowly exhaled a cloud of smoke. He giggled as he watched a storm of flies get airborne and fly away to torment someone else.

A few more drags and Wilkes was cruising in the good lane, sounding chipper and talking like they were back in the barracks at Campbell. When they were interrupted by a nurse, who injected him with Demerol, the chatter stopped only long enough for the shot; then it picked back up. They talked about their buddies in the bush, what was up ahead for the brigade, and Wilkes told him what had happened on the day he was wounded.

"Snipers everywhere, man. It was unfucking real. Must have been twenty or thirty of them. All of them in the trees. We called in artillery, but that didn't have an effect, so the plat daddy sent everybody forward in two-man teams. One held up stationary while the other advanced drawing fire. The action and delay trip, you know?"

Franklin knew. The action man drew the fire; the delay man sighted on the enemy muzzle flash. A deadly method of taking snipes, but the only effective means in thick terrain.

"One of our guys got hit. I went out to get him. I was just about to him when I took the one here. . . ." Franklin looked down at his thigh. A heavy bandage covered the area between his left knee and hip. "I managed to hobble to the wounded dude and was trying to drag him off when *blam*!" He looked up at his stump. "The fucking bullet hit the outside of the wrist, came out the other side, took it off cleaner than a sharp ax to a chicken's head. That's when I knew I was in trouble. I threw the dude over my shoulder and started running back to our position. Then I took the one in the back. It came out my shoulder and tore me open pretty good." He paused and looked again at the arm suspended from the pole. "I didn't feel any more pain in the hand. The bullet that hit me in the back and came out the shoulder clipped the nerves to the arm. Looks like the whole fucking arm's going to be paralyzed forever."

Franklin reached and held the cigarette again to Wilkes's mouth. The narcotic was starting to take effect. The pupils of his eyes were dilated; his words were becoming slurred as the narcosis began taking hold of his system.

"You did good, buddy," Franklin said, again giving him a hit from the Marlboro. "Trout told me to tell you he's proud of you. He's going to write your folks and tell them what happened."

"Tell him I appreciate that. But I'll probably talk to them before the letter gets home."

"They sending you stateside?"

"Yeah. Walter Reed. I evac tomorrow morning. We get to call home from Clark Air Base in the Philippines."

"Walter Reed's the best. My old man was there during the second big war. They'll take good care of you."

Wilkes scowled as he said, "Right. Then what? A fucking cripple getting in everybody's way?"

"You ain't a cripple, Tommie. You're young and you'll adjust. My grandfather lost his arm in France during World War One. He's dead now, but he rode horses, drove cars, even played golf. He didn't miss out on anything. You just need to rest and heal up. Then you'll come back strong. You're alive, man. That's more than some have, and there's a lot more going back draped in Old Glory. You made it, man. You're a little chewed up . . . but you made it."

This seemed to put some fire back in Wilkes. But there were still other losses to consider. "Guess I'll have to forget about playing pro baseball." He laughed. "Unless they need a water boy."

Franklin knew that Wilkes had been professional baseball material. He had played for the Fort Campbell team, even while in basic training, and had been scouted by the St. Louis Cardinals before the brigade left Fort Campbell.

"Fuck a bunch of baseball. Get well. Go to college. Get married. Have a shitload of kids and enjoy your life, man. You're only eighteen and you've been through more than those Jody fucks back in the world will ever know. You got that going for you: You survived Nam. They're still waiting to get here. You made it, my man. You made it."

Wilkes looked sadly at Franklin. "What about you? You going to make it? Or let that damn hatred get you greased?"

Franklin shook his head. "The hatred's gone, man. Or near about. I just want to stay alive."

"That's a one-eighty reversal. What brought that on? You go and get yourself full of religion?"

"Not religion." Franklin told Wilkes about the grenade and the dead children. "I never meant to kill kids, man. I just wanted Charlie. I got what I come for. I've avenged my brother. I can go home today and never look back on this shit."

The Demerol was bringing Wilkes down hard. He began dozing, and Franklin knew it was time to leave. "I better go, babe. Trout said I could stay overnight. Think I'll hit the enlisted barracks, grab some sleep, and see the city tonight."

Wilkes could only nod. Franklin went to the nurses' station and got a pen and paper. He wrote down his address in Arizona, then nudged Wilkes awake.

"Here's my address and phone number in the world. If you can, call my mother and tell her I'm doing good. She's a great lady. When I get back, I'll come visit you in Georgia."

Wilkes was fading fast, but despite the intravenous tube he raised his right hand. Franklin held it gently, almost lovingly. This was his friend. A white boy from Georgia he had grown to love like a brother.

Franklin leaned over and hugged him. "Stay in touch, my brother."

18

Qui Nhon was a teeming city on the coast, flanked by the South China Sea to the east, the Central Highlands to the west. It was a mecca for every form of entrepreneur in Vietnam, whether the goods were entertainment, libation, narcotics, gambling, or flesh. Pimps patrolled on their mopeds searching for GIs in town for a day or two, eager to help relieve them of their pent-up frustrations and their money. They were called cowboys, or "piss-ants," who should have been patrolling the rice paddies and highlands with M-16s instead of running an ongoing pussy patrol through the streets.

French colonial villas stood as a reminder of the previous war, their stone walls trimmed with barbed wire or broken glass embedded in cement. Old women sold flowers and fruit on the corner; most of them were the Vietcong intelligence-gathering network. Young girls strolled the streets in long silk dresses, looking voluptuous and innocent, carrying multicolored parasols while all the while observing movement of trucks and troops; children hustled ice-cold soda pop to the grunts used to drinking from rice paddies and muddy rivers or warm water from the unit Lister bag.

Franklin bought a bottle of Coke from a kid and snapped off the top. Before drinking, he put a handkerchief over the mouth of the bottle just in case the kid had put ground glass in the bottle. As he started to drink he thought he saw a momentary look of disappointment on the boy's face, which made him feel good. He started walking, followed closely by the boy, who was waiting for him to discard the bottle. When he finished, he sat the bottle on the sidewalk and continued on his way, drawn by the sound of rock-and-roll.

The Philadelphia Bar—all the bars had U.S.-flavored names— was typical, smelling of cheap booze and stale sex from the whorehouse at the rear. He found a seat near the front, located near a small stage, where three Vietnamese musicians brutalized Buddy Holly's "Maybe, Baby" with two guitars and a snare drum. The noise was deafening, the mangled lyrics lost in the loud talk and laughter of the troops at the bar.

All the military branches were represented, except the Vietnamese armed forces. They knew better than to come on American ground in the city. There was little respect between the fighting men of the two countries, mainly because the Americans didn't regard the Vietnamese as fighters. They considered them cowards, no better than pimps and laundry boys. Which, for some odd reason Franklin didn't understand, made him think of the Kit Carson scout.

At least the sonofabitch showed up for one roll call, he thought. Which was more than he could say for the "cowboys."

They were a sight to behold, wearing their tight Levi's, their little asses twitching nervously around hardened men carrying loaded pistols beneath their jungle fatigue jackets. Most, anyway. M-16s weren't allowed in the cities, but no GI in his right mind walked the streets anywhere in Vietnam without carrying some heat.

Franklin turned to the bar, spotted several delicious-looking young ladies, then motioned one to join him. She was young, no more than seventeen, he figured, wearing bright red lipstick and a bikini.

Her name was Monique. Odd, he thought, a Vietnamese girl with a French name. She said she was part French. He liked that. Maybe she wasn't all round eyes, but she had some in her, which meant she might be trusted not to shove a crochet needle through his ear and into his brain if they played boom-boom in the back room.

He ordered a drink for the two of them, and they talked; later, they danced on the small floor. The drinks kept coming until he was feeling light-headed and sat back in his chair. He started to order another drink, but she shook her head.

"This place too loud. We go for walk outside." He watched her go to the bar and speak with the bartender, a short, squat man with a wide forehead and broad mouth. Franklin thought he looked like the Buddha statues he had seen in pagodas around the country.

He had seen it coming, and now it was time to talk serious. "How much, for boom-boom?"

Her eyebrows rose seductively; then she whispered in his ear.

"I can handle that." He reached into his pocket and pulled out a roll of piastre, scrip money issued to the GIs. It was forbidden to use American currency in Vietnam. He peeled off the agreed amount, and after she gave the bartender his cut they left.

The night air was muggy and thick with that special heaviness he had known only in-country. Not even in the South, in America, had the air felt so oppressive. Unlike the mountains, where the air was thinner, the coastal regions were known for their humidity.

They walked unsteadily along the street, avoiding children darting about, some offering to shine his boots, others offering their sisters or mothers. Monique shooed them away in Vietnamese, all the while clutching his hand, steering him to wherever she intended to go.

After nearly half an hour they had left the busy city center and were in a small neighborhood of homes. This surprised him, since most of the Vietnamese whores operated from the back rooms of bars or cheap hotels.

"My father was *Légionnaire Etrangère*," she said. He was born in Brussels. I never knew the man since he was killed at Dien Bien Phu. My mother adored him and never remarried. She was Annamese." Franklin understood. Annam was a former French administrative region of central Vietnam, a culture within a culture that included their own language. There was a mystical look of pride in her eyes, as though she were unveiling some great secret in her life.

They reached a wrought-iron gate that opened into a small yard overgrown with weeds and framed by a pond that was drained and darkened by decay. The cement path to the house was cracked and pocked with what appeared to be bullet holes or shrapnel. They were both feeling the effects of the alcohol and moved unsteadily to the heavy front door, where she fumbled with her keys. Finally, she opened a series of three dead-bolt locks and led him inside the house. What struck his senses first was the smell of it, a mixture of dankness, rotting wood, and decrepitude.

The front room was bare except for a chair where she kept a kerosene lantern. When the flame illuminated the room it was clear the house had once been elegant, the walls bearing a vague mural, cracked and peeling and no longer artistically discernible; all the windows were secured by iron bars. Monique locked the bolts and they started up a winding staircase Franklin thought would surely collapse from their weight. But the hard teak structure held solid as they reached the upper level, where the light danced along a neatly painted hallway. Pictures covered both sides of the walls, his eyes noting each one, a small historical tour of the woman's lost past.

"This was my father, Major Henri Ricard." She held the lantern to a photograph of a dark-haired man dressed in a French

Legion uniform. The light drifted to another picture nearby, depicting a woman with long dark hair and deep brown eyes. "My mother's name was Mai Li. She was sixteen when she married my father."

"She was beautiful. How did she die?" Franklin asked.

She shook her head. "She did not die. She was murdered after the Vietminh conquered the French. I was spared because I was a child. I was put in a convent in Da Lat."

Franklin felt the sting of the irony. She had been raised in a convent to become a whore in order to survive. She was as much a second-class citizen in her country as black Americans were in the United States.

He followed her to the end of the hall, where she opened another locked door and entered her light-flooded bedroom. There was the sweet smell of ambrosia and a sudden flutter in the air. He saw a bird flap its wings in a cage beside a window.

It was as though he had stepped from one world into another. From the agony of a persecuting present to the elegance of a forgotten past. She went to her bed, pulled back the mosquito netting draped from the ceiling and lay down, and motioned him to lie beside her.

Franklin sat on the side of the bed and removed his boots, took his .45 pistol and shoved it under the pillow. He undressed, watching her do the same.

They made love, slept, made love again, slept some more, under watchful canary eyes and within hearing distance of sporadic gunfire echoing from beyond the walls.

He felt safe, even if the Vietcong were roaming the streets in search of drunken Americans.

He fell into a deep sleep—and the nightmare began.

He saw himself lying motionless with an agonizing paralysis gripping his mind and body. At first he found the place unfamiliar but gradually began to recognize the surroundings. There was a thick, rich smell of blood in the air. In the distance, a bright light shined through the thin fog that shrouded the ground where he lay, a graveyard, rising like a promontory in the rice paddy.

He was surrounded by men who had been breathing only hours before, but now were stacked like cordwood to give him protection from the evil advancing in the night. He froze, neither thinking nor moving, and watched as a light grew closer, swaying, as though it were dancing or being carried.

From the mist a man appeared, his features growing clearer with each advancing step. The man was short, clad in black pajamas, and stared emptily from dark eyes sunken in a shadowed, pockmarked face expressionless beneath a weathered pith helmet. In one hand the man carried a flashlight, the type used by American troops; in the other, an AK-47 Kalashnikov assault rifle.

Franklin tried to move, to rise—anything but lie there—but he remained frozen to the soggy ground of the graveyard. He wanted to scream, curse, but nothing came out, not even a whimper. He saw the VC's delight in his dilemma, grinning, revealing rotten teeth from behind lips that were no more than a knife wound.

Franklin knew him; knew the leer, the smell, the stench of rotting flesh that clung to the emaciated, malaria-ridden bodies of the men he had hunted and was hunted by.

The soldier stopped near the stack and looked over the bodies of the dead, resting his AK on his hip, weaving like a cobra as the breath strained from his lungs. To Franklin, this particular face was not familiar, although he may have killed this man. But Franklin knew the soldier; he recognized the wiry man who ate rats and rice balls, who spent his days in underground tunnels, then surfaced in the night to hunt Americans.

When the soldier pressed the muzzle of the AK against his face Franklin fought to rise, but to no avail. Then, he saw why:

One of his dead comrades' hands had gripped his arm, the man smiling insanely at him, holding him down.

Then the VC began to laugh, his voice joined by the laughter of his dead comrades, their voices rising in a deep, guttural cachinnation that seemed to rise from the bowels of hell. Louder the symphony grew, until Franklin felt lifted by it, swirling upward, as though caught in a tempest.

He tore himself from the terror of the dream and found himself standing in the middle of the bedroom, his pistol clutched in his hand. Monique stared at him from behind the mosquito netting, her eyes wide with fear. The canary was fluttering wildly in the cage, feathers flying.

She eased through the canopy and walked carefully to him, her hand outstretched. He sensed she had been in this situation before, perhaps with other Americans, perhaps with the Vietcong. Qui Nhon was an R and R center for both armies.

Her hand touched the barrel of the pistol, pushed it to his side, and she stepped close and put her arm around him. He felt himself trembling, felt her trembling.

"You are safe here," she whispered.

He picked her up and carried her back to the bed, where they made love again, this time not gently as before.

19

It was noon when Franklin and Monique left the house and strolled back to the streets lined with small cafés and bars. Traffic was heavy, the sidewalks packed with soldiers hung over from the previous night of carousing. They had a light breakfast of scones and hot tea. He allowed a boy to shine his boots, never taking his eyes off the kid. It was a favorite trick of the kids, taught by the Vietcong, to whip out a straight razor, slash the tendons behind the knee or the Achilles tendon, and run away and become lost in the sea of people, leaving the soldier crippled for life.

Charlie was a treacherous bastard, even in childhood.

When they reached the bar, they stood a long moment, saying nothing. He held both her hands, kissed her lightly on the cheek, and reached into his pocket. He took a wad of piastres and added to her payment from the day before. She didn't refuse him. She needed the money more than he did.

Rarely did a combat soldier return from a short R and R with any money. There was no need for currency in the bush. Only bullets, and they came free from Uncle Sam.

He turned and walked away, glancing back once, to see her step into the bar.

He knew they would never meet again.

20

An hour later he caught a ride on a helo from the brigade's 101st Aviation Battalion that included several "cherries," fresh from Airborne school. Their jungle boots and fatigues were new and clean, camouflage helmet covers sparkling, LC-1 harnesses fresh off the presses.

Fresh meat for Charlie, Franklin thought.

"You with the Screaming Eagles?" a cherry asked, a lanky kid.

He nodded; his thin smile made the inquisitor nervous. "I came over with the brigade from Fort Campbell. What about you guys? You come from Campbell?"

They shook their heads. "Nah," one said, his M-16 shiny and without a scratch. "We all graduated from jump school together." He looked at the others and grinned like a puppy eating shit. "They sent us over to help you guys." He wore his "blood wings"—parachutist wings issued upon graduating from Airborne school—on the retaining band over the cover of his helmet. A five-jump commando.

The third trooper sat also grinning, playing with his bayonet, which he was trying to attach to the stud on the barrel.

Franklin nearly laughed out loud. He looked at the door gunner, who had a big wad of tobacco in his mouth and leaned over and spit toward the opposite door, spraying the cherries' helmets and pretty fatigues.

The three jumped to their feet; the gunner whipped out a .45 pistol and aimed it at the one with the bayonet on his M-16 rifle. He had to shout over the roar of the rotors and the windblast coming through the open doors, but the kid heard him clearly. "Mine's loaded. How about yours?"

The trooper shook his head.

"Then sit your narrow John Wayne ass the fuck down before I throw you out of this fucking bird." He looked at the others and said, "That goes for the rest of you cherries, too!"

Franklin grinned at the gunner, took his pistol out, jacked a round into the chamber, and laid it beside him. The three quickly seated themselves.

Below, the rice paddies were meeting the base of the mountains. Franklin pointed at the French vehicles lining the roads and said to the cherries, "Those were the French Foreign Legion's vehicles. The Cong slaughtered them. I was told you could mark their point of retreat from where the bodies started stacking up near the top. They couldn't go up the highway . . . only down, and the Cong had ambushes waiting for them at every turn in the road." He pointed a finger at the one with the bayonet and said, "You remember that, Cherry. If you do, you just might last out the first day."

The lanky kid looked surprised. "We were told we wouldn't be near combat our first day in the bush."

Franklin shook his head, pointed to the jungle below. "We had a guy come into the unit. He arrived at zero-seven-hundred, was issued his gear at zero-seven-thirty, climbed in a jeep at zero-eight-thirty, which hit a land mine at zero-eight-forty-five, killing him and two others." He paused for effect. "Nobody knew his name. Not the platoon sergeant, not the company commander. They got his name off his dog tags, which they had to dig out of the roof of his mouth. The concussion blew those babies right through his throat and up. They were embedded so deep, the plat daddy had to use a pair of pliers to pull them free." He pointed at his boots. Each of his dog tags was threaded through the bottom lace of each boot. "You wear them like this. Even if you step on a mine, we'll find at least one boot."

The door gunner slapped the lanky kid on the shoulder, spit another stream of tobacco juice, and shouted, "Welcome to the prom . . . ladies!"

When he arrived at his hooch he found Marion sitting alone, reading a letter from his wife. In his lap was a tiny puppy. He was playfully stroking the dog while reading, wearing that special smile a man has when he's hearing good news. He looked up as Franklin dropped onto his rack.

"Hey, brother. You're back soon enough."

"Yeah. Got my business taken care of in fine style."

Marion chuckled. "Was she pretty?"

Franklin smiled just slightly. He rolled over and went to sleep, his thoughts on Monique.

21

A few days after Franklin returned from R and R the word
came down that the ground element of the First Air Cavalry Division was moving onto the "Golf Course," the huge
helicopter complex at An Khe. The name of the massive area
that would base the more than four hundred choppers was easy
enough to understand. From the air, the distinctive circular heli-
pads uniformly splotching the earth gave the terrain a country
club look. It was only natural that the Screaming Eagle troopers
began calling An Khe the "Country Club." But on this course,
the airmobile couldn't get out of the rough with a five-wood.
And there was plenty of rough in which they could lose their
balls.

It had been the task of the First Brigade to clear Highway 19
from the coastal city of Qui Nhon through the rugged An Khe
Pass, if for no other reason than to ensure that the young cav
soldiers wouldn't get their asses shot off before they made it to
the top. What pissed off the Screaming Eagles the most? The
Eagles had to continue clearing the surrounding pass and Central Highlands since the cav had been promised thirty days to

get into position and adjust to the area before beginning operations.

The Eagles had begun operations only days after arriving incountry and were now busting their backs for a full division, three times the brigade's size.

The job had been dangerous and difficult, from the squad level to battalion, with all support elements kicking in and doing a masterful job in a short time. The road was open; engineers had made improvements under the watchful guard of the Airborne infantry placed at key outposts along the route, while the rest of the brigade harassed and chased Charlie, keeping him away from the highway he so loved to violate.

Even the whorehouses flourished around An Khe, indicative of what was laughingly known as "tight security." It had become common knowledge that anyone needing to know anything about anything need only ask the whores. They knew the game schedule before the high command. The mama-sans who ran the joints—which cropped up overnight, with names like Club Arizona, Club Southeast Asia, and Ho's Whores and were typical flesh parlors—were not exotic madams, neither in conduct nor in appearance. Most were repulsive, but they had a product they could sell. After all, one sergeant said, "Even a moron can sell ice in hell."

The whores were young, beautiful in that special Oriental way, many virginal when they hit the bamboo mat the first time with an eager trooper. By sunrise they would be a little older, a few dollars richer, and overloaded with information they would pass along to Mama-san, who in turn passed it along to the Vietcong.

The only respite in Nam was getting laid, and even that required some tactical determination. Sergeant Chassion always reminded the recon troops that "if Uncle Sam wanted you to have pussy, he'd have issued one to your buddy!"

Pussy was amazing in Nam. It bought a few minutes' pleasure

for a trooper who might lose his dick on the next helo assault; it created a flashback for another to the backseat of his Chevy with his girlfriend that last night before reporting back to Campbell. It might generate a few bucks in a trooper's pocket for directing his buddies to a particular *hooch lai* laden with *bambi ba,* cheap scotch, or expensive San Miguel beer. To the married soldiers who indulged, it was a reminder of his wife's refrain: "Don't bring nothing back I can't cook or play with!"

Pussy also got a lot of men killed in Nam. In the long, tedious nights of guard duty at the barbed wire, branches in the distance took on the voluptuous shapes of girls from the past, mesmerizing with their steady advance, eyes soft and glowing from the moonlight. Then the face turned ugly, the outstretched hand held a grenade, and the dick went soft just before everything else in his world turned hard.

"Pussy kills!" one crusty old sergeant warned.

"Yeah," countered a young trooper, "but what a way to go!"

The whores followed the troopers like the laundresses followed the soldiers on the Western frontier in the late 1800s. Hell, they'd even wash your socks and drawers for a few extra piastres. What did the trooper care? He liked being pampered, it was the second best thing to being home with mom. Like soldiers down through the ages, he thought only about three things, besides staying alive: his feet, his stomach, and his dick. And not necessarily in that order.

Everything else was relative to the moment.

But the most incredible thing that had occurred, in Franklin's way of seeing the "Big Picture," as it was called, was the matter of race.

Back in the world, whites and blacks had maintained a distance, friendly for the most part in the barracks, always separate off-post, maintaining that line of demarcation that said: "You can't cross over. Your shade ain't right for the place."

Not in Nam. Race seemed to have stayed aboard the USS *General Eltinge* where the 101st was concerned. A white man stayed alive because the blacks were cooking Charlie with their weapons and looking after the real estate, and vice versa. They drank out of the same canteens, ate from the same tin cups, mixed tears over wounded or dead buddies, and got their asses shot off hauling one another from sure death to safety.

War, thought Franklin, was a dichotomy, a situation of mutual exclusiveness. White hates black; black hates white. Until the shooting starts. Then everybody's the same color: scared birdshit green!

Franklin never saw this to be more true than the day the grunts of the cav started coming up the An Khe Pass. He watched a long, seemingly never-ending string of what appeared to be cattle trucks, loaded with the young "sky soldiers," move steadily upward toward the plateau. It was near sunset and the procession had continued for hours, the sound of double-clutching and grinding gears, and nervous young soldiers trying to look cocky and arrogant, some shouting obscenities at the troopers. The procession would end as dark neared; danger lurked from the blackness like rattlesnakes in the desert: hidden and ready to strike.

Franklin had been assigned to Dawes's team to guard an important bridge over a deep gorge. Charlie had blown the crossing a dozen times in the past, but not since the Screaming Eagles took over the area. The bridge was considered so important, Chassion chose the site for his command post and assigned two teams to the mission. The rest of the platoon was strung along the route doing the same thing at other vital points along the "Highway to Heaven," as it was referred to by some.

Each recon team sat up their M-60s at opposing ends of the bridge and placed claymore mines and trip flares at key points the enemy would have to travel either from the surrounding jungle or from the gorge in order to launch an attack. Sandbags had been filled and stacked to form fighting positions; foxholes were dug and sandbags reinforced on the flanks of each position, giving the two machine-gun teams added protection. Hand grenades and parachute illumination flares were placed in each position for quick access; radios were squelched down, and all was quiet as the sun faded over the western slopes of the mountains.

Then the longest part of the mission began: the long wait through the night.

Franklin and Dawes were together, hunkered beneath the west end of the bridge, when Chassion hurried across the bridge to check on their situation.

"Sit rep?" he whispered.

Dawes spoke softly. "Tighter than a frog's ass underwater, Plat."

Chassion was barely visible, his face painted in green-and-black camouflage. "Good. Keep your people alert. These little bastards want this place out of the action real bad."

"We're good for the night, Sarge," Dawes said.

Chassion whispered to Franklin, "Sharps, you got anything for the runs? I'm shitting like a goose."

"Got some paregoric. It'll tighten you up good, but it might make you drowsy."

"I'll stay awake. Give me some."

Franklin took his red-filtered flashlight and searched his medical aid kit. He handed the bottle to Chassion. "Don't take more than a couple of swigs every four hours."

Chassion patted him on the back. "Thanks, Doc. Damn, I got to go again."

He hurried toward the edge of the gorge. Moments later, they could hear the gurgling sound of his bowels emptying.

Franklin and Dawes chuckled. In the dark sky there was a loud "thud," then another, followed by the most brilliant illuminations the two had ever seen. Flares, fired from artillery or mortar coming from the direction of the Golf Course, exploded.

Franklin and Dawes looked toward Chassion, who was squatting, his pants down to his ankles, steel helmet cocked sideways, his M-16 resting on his knees. "Shit!" he yelled, and at that instant an artillery round crashed beyond him, the concussion pitching him backward. Franklin and Dawes watched in stunned silence as the platoon sergeant disappeared into the darkness below.

"Let's get the fuck out of here!" Dawes shouted to the team. "Under the bridge!"

Artillery rounds began crashing all around the bridge where the troopers, caught in the light of the magnesium flares attached to parachutes drifting to earth, could be seen scurrying for cover.

"What the fuck is going on?" Dawes was shouting into his radio within a heartbeat of him and Franklin rolling out of the foxholes for the greater safety beneath the bridge.

The radio crackled from the command post, but in the din of the artillery and mortar crashing around the bridge, and into the cavernous gorge, Dawes heard nothing he could understand.

Franklin looked toward the gorge, where approximately a hundred yards away, from deep within its darkened bowels, a plume of bright orange flame rose skyward, turning the gorge into a momentary inferno. The tongue of fire burned bright for a few seconds, then extinguished, returning the gorge to darkness.

More flares erupted overhead and Dawes, still on the radio and hearing nothing worthwhile, heard Franklin shout, "Charlie! To the front!"

Three Vietcong soldiers had been flushed from the darkened jungle by the rolling barrage. Their features were clear in the spewing magnesium flares drifting down, giving their shapes an eerie, ghostlike appearance as they ran forward in their familiar bandy-legged stride.

Franklin rose up with his M-16 when Dawes shoved the barrel down and said, in a near-crazed voice, "What's wrong with you, man! Ain't we got enough shit coming down on us without you adding to it!"

Franklin watched as the VC neared the darkness. "Oh,

God!" he said and pointed toward the fleeing enemy. In the flare light they saw Chassion had risen from the darkness of the gorge, holding his pants with one hand, his M-16 in the other. The platoon sergeant's helmet was missing, and he was cussing a blue streak.

Chassion and the fleeing Vietcong made eye contact at the same moment. The sergeant dropped his pants, triggered the M-16—but nothing happened.

"His weapon's jammed!" Franklin shouted. At that moment the VCs fired wildly at Chassion, as the tough plat daddy plunged over the gorge edge and again disappeared in the waiting darkness.

By the time Franklin and Dawes had snapped out of the shock, the VC had also disappeared.

There was silence, except for the furious Chassion, rising out of the dark cavern again, cursing a streak so blue even he couldn't understand it.

Dawes started to crawl beneath the bridge. "Where you going?" Franklin said.

"I'm going to hide in the fucking trees! Right now, I'd rather face a platoon of Charlie than Chassion. How about you?"

"I'm right behind you."

The two troopers stayed near the bridge, but out of sight, listening to Chassion bellowing into the radio until the sun came up.

The following day it was learned the "great attack" had been initiated by an overzealous and eager "brown bar" second lieutenant in the First Air Cav. Millions of dollars in taxpayer's money had been pissed away, troopers were terrified and terrorized, but the cav cattle trucks kept coming up the highway, carrying the young soldiers to the waiting battlefields of the Central Highlands.

22

As with all armies, the arrival of mail from home was always the most precious moment for a soldier. Mail call brought letters, "care packages" of nonperishable foods—the most treasured being Kool-Aid to put in the canteens, making the barely potable water tastier—needed items the army was slow on supplying, such as socks, undershirts, underwear, and even sunglasses. For Franklin, the arrival of a certain package from Saigon came to his great surprise: a portable tape recorder.

He read the return address—Brig. Gen. Samuel Sharps—and was tempted to throw it away, but upon seeing several cassettes, from his mother, his brother, and—to his surprise—his sister-in-law, Darlene.

He read the directions, inserted the batteries, put his mother's tape in, and sat back in his hooch and listened.

What he heard made him realize the tapes had not been censored, which was why his mother had sent the recorder and tapes to his father. A general carried more weight than a spec four.

"Hi, baby, it's Mom. I hope this finds you doing well. I think of you every day and pray you are safe. The news here is that more troops are being sent to Vietnam, which means the war is getting bigger. I have spoken to some of our friends who served with your father and their thoughts are that even more soldiers are going to be sent over there.

"I pray about this every day, hoping it won't be true. Back here we are having a sort of war of our own down South, where the civil rights people and a lot of black people are asking, 'Why should our people die for the freedoms of Asians when they don't have freedom in America?'

"It's the same question our people have heard since the end of the Civil War, but I guess you know that.

"Kevin is doing fine, and so is Darlene. She stays busy with the baby, and is nearly finished with her nursing degree at Arizona State. I hope she doesn't move away when she graduates."

His mother went on to talk about the ranch, local events, and other homey things. He rewound the tape and listened to it again, then the one from his younger brother, Kevin.

"Hey, bro, how's the hero doing? Hope this finds you well and safe. I've been following the war on the television and in the newspapers. Looks like you guys are in some pretty rough country. Not so rough here at Berkeley, unless you call getting the clap a hazard of education. Not me, bro. But a few of my dormies."

After a minute or two, Kevin's voice seemed to change, sounding more ominous.

"I don't know what's going on with Mom. Maybe it's just that she's lonely what with you in Vietnam and me in college. But I think she needs to hear from you soon. We sent some extra tapes so you can talk to her. She needs to hear your voice. You need to send them to Pop, so he can get them to her without somebody listening to them."

He talked more about music, summer classes at U.C. Berkeley, and the upcoming football season. Franklin rewound the tape and played it again.

Finally, he listened to the tape from Darlene. Again there was a foreboding concerning his mother.

"Hi, Franklin. Hope this finds you well. I'm here at Sabre Ranch, and Mom has left me alone to talk to you. I'm glad she did. I don't want to burden you because I know you have enough on your mind what with [long pause] . . . everything that's going on over there . . . but I think you should know.

"She's been to Doc Malone a few times and he is sending her to a specialist in Phoenix. She won't tell me anything, except that it's just old age. Maybe it is, I don't know.

"But there seems to be something on her mind and I think you can help. I think it would really help if you would try to make contact with your father. I don't think you know, but he was wounded in a bomb blast in Saigon a while back. He's okay, but the telegram had already been sent to your mom before he could stop it.

"She loves him dearly, as you know, and wishes that you would try to mend your fences, not for her sake, but for yours.

"I hope you will take care of yourself and write to me and send tapes if you can. You are one of the dearest people in the world to me and I can't wait until we can see each other when you get back here."

Darlene went on to talk about Argonne, her daughter, the child Adrian never lived to see or hold; she talked about her final year in nursing college, how the courses were more difficult, and that she hoped to stay in Arizona when she graduated. Franklin played the tape again; the voice of a beautiful woman made him forget, if only briefly, the horror that surrounded him and being so far from home.

In the box with the tapes he found a pint bottle of Jack Daniel's bourbon. Attached to the bottle was another tape labeled: "From Pop."

He snapped the cassette in half and tossed it into the garbage bucket near his bunk, rose, and walked outside to stare up at the sky. It was nearly dusk, overcast, and muggy, the taste of rain in the air. In the distance he could hear the sound of helicopters in the direction of the cav's Golf Course, and artillery and laughter coming from the hooches of headquarters company, where troopers read their mail for the hundredth time and shared "home life" with their buddies.

He really didn't have anything to share. What was there to say? That his mom may be having a medical problem? That black Americans were struggling for the simple decency of being treated equally? That his dead brother never held his child? That a beautiful woman he had loved secretly since high school was so far from his grasp that he may as well be on the moon?

He looked at the Jack Daniel's, cracked the seal, and took a hit from it. He saw one of the battalion cooks coming his way. He knew the "Spoon," as cooks were called, from pulling KP at Fort Campbell. In the moonlight, the Spoon looked angry. His features were tight, his hands moving nervously.

"Hey, man," Franklin said, "you look like you could use a drink."

The Spoon stopped, reached for the bottle, turned it up, and swigged, throat working, Adam's apple bobbing. Finally, he handed the bottle back. "Thanks, man."

Franklin watched him walk away, his M-16 slapping off his hip, going toward the latrine.

Franklin looked at the bottle: stone empty.

PART 3

OPERATION GIBRALTAR

23

In early September, after more than a month of deep patrols into the jungles of the Central Highlands, the First Brigade finally got a break. A patrol from the brigade made contact with a small enemy unit on Highway 19, killing one enemy soldier. The soldier was carrying papers identifying him as a member of the 95th Battalion, 2nd Vietcong Regiment.

It was no secret that the 95th was operating in the An Khe area, no secret especially to Major Joe Hicks, brigade S-2 (Intelligence) officer. Hicks was a solid soldier and savvy as they come. He had served with the Marines in World War II, the 24th Infantry in Korea—where he survived sixty-nine days, cut off and alone, behind enemy lines—and two Special Forces tours in Vietnam prior to the brigade's deployment from Fort Campbell.

He could smell the presence of the 95th and ordered patrol action to be stepped up, no matter the cost. Tired and pissed off, but smelling fresh opportunity, the brigade began pounding the bush. By day, patrols combed the mountains and sparse rice paddies; by night, ambush patrols set up in every imaginable place the brass suspected Charlie might move upon.

While on one patrol, a soldier from the 502nd Battalion, First Brigade, was scrounging for souvenirs when he accidentally stumbled upon what he thought to be a Vietcong. The soldier, who was actually a cook from Hawaii, had volunteered for the patrol to get a chance to see some action. While interrogating the VC, Hicks discovered he was a PAVN, another name for People's Army Vietnam or, to the grunts, plain old North Vietnamese Army!

The man had come from the north to get his ass captured in the south!

What Hicks and others learned confirmed suspicions that there was a major Vietcong unit in the area and at battalion strength.

All the bells starting ringing; all the lights started flashing.

The prisoner, fearing, no doubt, for his life, wanted to strike a bargain: his life and freedom, including joining the Americans, for information on the 95th. Hicks accommodated, and the man began chattering. Convinced the NVA was for real, Hicks had him put on an aircraft to fly over the area and get an exact fix. What was overlooked was that the man had never flown before and the experience scared him mindless. He recognized nothing from the air.

Hicks was livid, thinking the bastard was just buying time, when another stroke of good fortune surfaced. He picked up a radio intercept from a nearby Forward Air Controller (FAC), whose "bird dog" was taking fire from the ground by a .50-caliber heavy machine gun. The reported area of the firing on the FAC was the same area the NVA had designated to be the Vietcong 95th Battalion's command post.

The First Brigade had found Charlie.

The OPLAN—Operational Plan—was designated Operation Gibraltar, an assault that would utilize air strikes, artillery, and airmobile deployment of troops from the brigade's 2nd Battalion/502nd Airborne Infantry, commanded by Lieutenant Colonel Wilfred Smith, into the village of An Ninh, on September, 18, 1965.

The hardest part of the planning was selecting the unit that would lead the assault. The '02 was chosen because it had found the first hard evidence the 95th was in the highlands. Hackworth had argued hard for 1/327, since it was his opinion the "Above the Rest" battalion was the finest of the three battalions in the brigade, led by the most competent officers and noncoms.

As the word snaked through the brigade, there wasn't a "Screaming Eagle" that didn't want to get into this fight. The troopers were finally going to take it to Charlie and give him a taste of his own medicine, fight him in the open, shoot standing straight up, move forward, and take the enemy where they lived.

Spec Four Franklin Sharps wanted to get on with it and wondered how it was going to get done.

The word came down in whispers, mostly among the noncoms, who chewed hard on their cigarettes, stomped their boots, and wanted to scream to the heavens. Not a one could believe that the 1/327 would be left out of the fight.

Chassion looked like a man chewing steel and ready to shit nails, he was so angry. Trout was even worse, pacing about like a caged tiger, wondering what it had been all about.

"*Hell!*" one noncom from C Company cussed. "We all ought to be in this fight. The whole fucking brigade! Overwhelm the little fuckers and tear them out a new asshole!"

This wasn't the smell of mutiny. These were soldiers who had come to fight and found an enemy who wanted to toy with them. They had come to fight the war and go home. All the troopers had been getting since arriving was a lot of shit many were not prepared to accept in silence. These were paratroopers who had been trained to go behind enemy lines, suffer casualties, and hold their tactical positions, keeping the enemy occupied on more than one front, denying them the opportunity to consolidate their assets on one advancing force, until the infantry came in and mopped up.

Too many of the hardened veterans of Korea, most of whom had served in World War II as well, saw it simply: *"You might leave the dance with a fresh young whore, but while you're there . . . you two-step with the bitch you brung!"*

It wasn't vintage Darryl Royal, the University of Texas coach who coined the phrase, but it was close enough, considering this was war, not football.

The 1/327 had been the vanguard of the brigade and had earned the right to be the first to engage the Vietcong.

24

* * *

Franklin had a friend he'd gone to jump school with who was on a chopper with the 101st Aviation Battalion.

He collected up his gear and found Chassion. The platoon sergeant was sitting in his hooch, writing a letter home, using his flashlight to write by.

"Plat, I need a favor."

Chassion looked up, laid down his pen. "What's the problem?"

Franklin shrugged. "I need to get over to brigade HQ, I need to talk to my father in Saigon. I just found out that my mother's sick. I don't know what's going on, but I got a letter from my brother."

Franklin knew he was playing a long shot, but there was no other way.

Chassion nodded but looked suspicious. "I guess a general's son can ask for one favor. But don't ever do it again. Do I make myself clear?"

"Yes, Sergeant."

"How you going to get there?"

"There's a deuce-and-a-half hauling some equipment over to

the HQ in an hour. I'll catch a ride back somehow."

The platoon sergeant had a glint of doubt in his eyes. "Make damn sure you are. We're going to have everybody ready for tomorrow, in case we're needed."

Franklin turned and left, breathing relief as he walked toward the battalion command post, praying there was a vehicle going toward brigade headquarters.

At the CP, frustration was boiling over at all levels; even the cooks had a case of the ass. The brigade had not had a hot meal since arriving at Cam Ranh Bay, which meant the Spoons had pulled every shit detail imaginable since their feet touched RVN (Republic of Vietnam) soil. Except for that first day in the field near Bon Me Thuot, when they brewed up banana pudding from local banana trees. While their intentions were only for the men who'd been cooped up on the USS *General Eltinge* for weeks, the result was the largest number of the "toilet trots" in the history of the division. Since then they had probably forgotten how to cook, utilized instead to pull guard duty, unloading ammunition and the tons of C-ration crates required to feed a battalion. Even Colonel Timothy and the entire command staff had lived on C-rations, using their own diet as a means to gauge how the troops were feeling and to show the special leadership required in combat. If his men slept in the mud, "Gentleman Tim," the beacon that lit the path, was deepest in the muck.

At the Golf Course, where the 101st Aviation Battalion was based alongside the incoming First Air Cav. He found a CQ (Change of Quarters) at the command post and asked the whereabouts of one of the crew chiefs on a Huey.

"I'm looking for Spec Five Ronald Douglas," he told the PFC.

The CQ pointed over his shoulder. "You'll find him on the

flight line. If you can find him. The oh-deuce is staging, and it's crowded as hell."

The flight line was packed with troopers from the "First Strike" battalion. The mood was nervous as the soldiers, formed into their platoons and companies, were spending the night on the flight line in preparation for the airmobile assault the following morning. The men sat on the ground, using their packs to rest against, their weapons at the ready. Franklin could sense a mixture of moods as he walked through the area—nervous chatter, light laughter, some smoking, others eating C-rations—typical behavior in light of the upcoming assault.

The Hueys sat in a long line, including seven marine heloes brought in to assist, as well as Hueys from Lieutenant Colonel Cody's 52nd Aviation. But it was obvious there were too many troops for the helicopters to accommodate.

Franklin found Douglas, a strapping, redheaded twenty-year-old from Casper, Wyoming. The crew chief was sitting in the open door drinking a can of beer.

"Douglas! Hey, man, how you doing?" Franklin called out.

The man stepped onto the tarmac and stared warily at Franklin. When he recognized him, he stepped forward, his hand extended. "Sharps, my man. What the hell are you doing here?"

"Looking for a cold beer."

"Don't have a cold one. But it's wet."

"That's good enough."

The two drank their beer and made small talk for a few minutes; then Franklin got to the point of his visit. "I need you to get me on this mission."

Douglas stared at him for a moment. "Are you here on orders?"

Franklin shook his head, drained the can of beer. "No. My platoon sergeant thinks I'm over at the commo center at brigade HQ calling my old man in Saigon."

Douglas released a long, low whistle. "Man, you are one

crazy motherfucker. You know you're AWOL?"

"I know. But I'm a medic, goddammit. You know there's always room for another doc on one of these operations. Hell, this is the first major American operation to jump off in Nam and I want to be in on the hunt. I've been humping these mountains for weeks trying to rock with Charlie. Here's my chance."

Douglas shook his head and grabbed two more beers, opened them with a church key, and handed one to Franklin. "I don't know, man. You're only about the zillionth dude to pull this shit. Everybody's coming out of the woodwork trying to get in on this op. Personally, I think you're all insane."

"We've been out in the bush hacking away since the get-go, and now that we have Charlie fixed, I want in on the kill. You've been flying around while we've been humping. Walk the bush for three months and see how you'd feel."

Douglas understood. The 101st Av Battalion left Fort Campbell prior to the rest of the brigade. The helicopters were transported on the USS *Iwo Jima*, a helicopter carrier, and were waiting when the troopers arrived at Cam Ranh Bay. Since then, the Av had inserted and extracted the troopers after long-range and deep patrols and medevaced wounded, seeing the frustration the proud brigade was feeling.

Douglas crushed his beer can and threw it into the darkness of the Huey's hull. "OK. I can get you on board with the troops we're ferrying on the first lift—"

"First lift?" Franklin interrupted. "It's not going to be a total assault by the whole battalion?"

"Not enough choppers," Douglas replied. "It's going to be a piecemeal op. Three platoons at a time. We're scheduled for three ferries into an LZ near the village of An Ninh. All this starts after the Skyraiders soften up the area. There's not much room to land in that terrain. If we put troops in another area, they'll be outside the artillery fan, and that'll leave their asses hanging out big time."

Franklin understood. Tactical air support would come from

A1-E Skyraiders, a good, low-level air-to-ground support fighter/bomber. However, air support can only stay on station for a limited period of time, due to fuel and ordnance expenditure. No fuel, no bombs, no more air support without returning to base to rearm and refuel. But artillery would be on reserve should it be needed to support the troops once they were on the ground. Artillery operated within a "fan" for maximum firing distance and breadth. Once outside the fan, there would be no support and that could be disastrous.

Douglas hopped off the edge of the chopper. "Throw your gear in the bird and get some sleep. You're going to need it, my man. When the oh-deuce guys start loading up, just act like you're a medic assigned to the chopper. When they insert, go in with them. That's as far as I can get you. After that, you're on your own, good buddy."

Franklin watched Douglas disappear in the darkness toward a string of latrines where long lines were formed by the troopers of the 502nd.

As he loaded his gear into the Huey, he looked again at the lines and wondered how many of them would be dead by this time tomorrow night.

25

They were going to be the messengers. That certainty was clearly etched on their faces. As the oh-deuce recon team loaded aboard the Huey in total silence, each man carrying an array of weaponry similar to that carried by Franklin's platoon, Franklin sat up from a corner to the dismay of a hulking, tattooed sergeant. On his right shoulder he wore the patch of the 187th Regimental Combat Team. His face, like the faces of the others, was painted with camouflage.

The sergeant looked at Franklin and snapped, "Who are you? Mary fucking Poppins?"

"No, Sergeant. I'm a reporter with *The New York Times,*" Franklin said.

The man studied Franklin's gear, looking as though he'd figured it out, then took a bite from a plug of chewing tobacco. "I'd take a fucking medic with combat experience over your lame ass any day of the week. Get out your pen and paper, junior; you're going to war. But first, you might consider covering your family jewels."

Franklin slipped his steel pot under his butt just as the chopper lifted off and, staring past Douglas, who stood behind an M-60 in the open door, watched the darkened tarmac slip away as the chopper rose into the new dawn.

There was the sound of the air rushing through the doors, and the silence in the eyes of the other soldiers. But it was what they had waited for and now that it was about to arrive, there was evident fear. The men didn't look at each other; it was a thing men share in going to war. Don't look the other in the eye; you might see something you don't want to see—maybe your own reflection dancing off the eye of a man who will soon be dead. Maybe the man will be you.

The sergeant nudged Franklin. "What outfit are you with, boy?"

"Recon. First of three-two-seven."

The sergeant looked him in the eye. "Phil Chassion's outfit. You the medic for Recon?"

"Yes."

"I heard he had one. I wanted one myself, but they wouldn't give me one. How did you pull it off?"

"Sheer bravado, Sergeant, and a large measure of charm and bullshit."

"I hope you've got plenty of it, son. You might need it before this day is over."

"I won't let you down."

"That's good to know. When we get on the LZ, you hang tight on my ass and go wherever I go . . . do whatever I tell you. I don't like prima donnas, and no one hangs back."

Franklin stuck out his hand. "Spec Four Sharps. You can count on it, Sarge."

The sergeant shook hands and pointed out the door. In the near distance, an A1-E Skyraider was streaking past, traveling in the opposite direction. "Lock and load!" he shouted, "we're getting close!"

The men locked and loaded ammunition into their rifles. Face muscles were tight, eyes narrowed. Franklin's mouth was dry as salt. The fight was about to be joined.

26

An Ninh was a small village, of little significance in size and importance to the world except to the NVA, the VC, and the approaching First Brigade. The village was nestled at the base of tall mountains, and rice paddies flourished nearby; tall trees gave the hamlet the look of historical elegance.

It was also a staging area and training center, carefully secreted into the mixture of water, rice, and rock.

The most frightening—and ironic—aspect of a battlefield is the silence. The silence of the mind. One expects the noise that shatters the mind and sends courage forward, carrying on foot toward the glory of all that the challenge has created to confront, and turns a human being into an individual. All of which creates heroes and memories never forgotten. It even creates cowards.

But that's not how it works. Not in reality.

There's the silence that awaits the recon element. The point guard is there to ensure there is safety for those who follow.

Franklin stepped off the skids of the Huey and heard nothing except the rotor slap as the helo flew away. There were no birds chirping. There were no old men or women moving about. No one ran for the little shelter the village offered. The village was silent, desolate in appearance, except for a few drifts of smoke that came low, even, across the ground.

That's the warning. The mouth goes dry. The air stands still, even in a strong wind. It's as though nature—and God—has decreed, you're here . . . and there's no way back unless you carve a path through a hell you will never understand in your old age.

And the path begins where Hell opens up. Where youth becomes lost. Children are a dream of the future. That there are no more thoughts of family picnics, or cruising through town with your buddies on weekends. When the faces of pretty girls you've known become memories so distant, pictures carried in wallets, side pouches, or just in reflection, can no longer be brought to mind. When the taste of what once was—that was so wonderful—becomes so bitter you can only taste blood . . . and hear the cries of your comrades, and can't remember their names.

When you realize the ground around you is filled with people who want to kill you! And the fight you have dreamed of—and searched for—is about to become the nightmare you have longed to find!

That's when you know you've found what you've been looking for. That's when you know you're in the deep fucking shit!

And the only way to deal with shit is to put up with more shit than the enemy. You might have to eat some of it for a bit. But, if you can stand the taste . . . you'll survive the smell!

The teams inserted onto smooth, dry ground, as though it had been made especially easy. There was no elephant grass, only clean ground. The blades from the choppers whipped and turned up the surrounding trees, then the choppers pulled back hard and roared away.

Then, again, there was the silence, a sort of life of its own, but one new thing all recognized: the smell of smoke. Smoke has a sort of life of its own. Often, it can't be detected in the heights, for it dissipates quickly. In the trees, it's running away, like a bird fleeing. On the ground, it drifts, moving across the earth as though driven, but when it comes from *beneath* the ground, it has an odor of burnt dirt, acrid, despising to the senses.

Franklin and the others knew they had not landed at the base of a mountain that might hold the enemy in a tight position. They had landed right in their lap!

27

The recon sergeant took the mike. "Hold the second lift. We're in the deep shit. There's something wrong, bad wrong."

But it was too late. The recon unit had spread out on insert, taken position, and saw in front of them that Charlie had set the table and the brigade was the main course.

The first shot was fired, and another; though from a consolidated unit, one from the right, one from the left.

The recce team had landed fifty yards from the underground mess hall of a full regiment.

There is no greater confusion that will ever confront a soldier, no matter how well trained, than to be in a situation he cannot confront, control, or understand. This was the situation the first lift was now caught in.

Franklin saw the first major battle of the Vietnam War, between combined and well-entrenched NVA and VC and approximately thirty-six American soldiers, begin as a major cluster fuck on the American side of the field.

The enemy, who had laid tight during the A1-E bomb preps, taking few casualties, now appeared from nowhere, like the ghosts they had been called, moving low, easy, over ground they knew so well, as though it were a lawn they had mowed from childhood, to slots preselected, to drop in, fire, then move again.

The trees, soft and lush, turned into a fan of ugly gray as the bullets began to spray from the enemies' concealed positions; the crump of mortar fire mixed with the "slap" of the Hueys and din of machine-gun fire, preventing any single sound from being identifiable. Worse, the troopers were caught stone-cold in the open with nowhere to hide, their only hope to move forward and take ground that offered some form of protection.

Franklin saw the fire pattern: cool, calm, coordinated, like a prom night planned by a committee of old teachers who years before had been to the same dance. But now the ballroom was getting deadly.

He looked up and saw two helos take heavy hits of fire, tilt almost simultaneously, and pitch toward the ground. There were no explosions, only the sickening sound of steel scraping against the ground; the screeching of metal being torn from the fuselages as the skids were torn off and the rotors whirled crazily against the earth like eggbeaters, disintegrating in hundreds of deadly flying pieces.

Surviving troopers spilled from the choppers and began running in all directions, disoriented, without leadership, running straight toward the enemy positions, minds dazed.

"Evans! Jackson. Get the sixty trained on that tree line!" The sergeant roared.

The two troopers set up the machine gun and began firing. Red tracers spewed toward a tree line, answered by an equal hail of enemy lead.

The sergeant began organizing his men, pointed at Franklin, and shouted, "You get on my six, boy, and don't lose me for nothing!"

The sergeant grabbed two troopers and flung them forward. "Lay in fire onto that position. We've got to set up a perimeter! There's another lift coming in and we have to give them cover!" He took his M-79 grenade launcher and fired toward the trees. A deep, groaning explosion erupted, followed by a black-gray cloud of smoke.

Franklin looked to his right and saw a soldier running toward them, firing at the enemy from the hip. He was ten yards away when he suddenly stiffened and pitched forward. Franklin crawled to the wounded man, rolled him over, and saw a bullet hole above his right eye.

Along the forward edge of the battle area, the troopers were forming small pockets of resistance but were still trapped in the open.

The sergeant was on the radio, and Franklin heard him yell, "Where's the fucking artillery and air support!"

He could not hear the reply but could read the answer on the sergeant's twisted face as he began grabbing his men and slinging them toward the enemy. "Fire and move! Fire and move!"

Franklin wasn't sure if it was the training taking over or the sheer force of the sergeant's will, but the troopers began moving forward in small groups, one advancing and firing, another laying low, spitting out cover fire until the other team dropped and began firing. They rose and advanced, no more than thirty men, in teams, moving out of the open toward cover.

Not all of them made it. Screams of the wounded stretched from one end of the line to the other and the dead lay crumpled in thick mud, bloody heaps that suddenly took on new purpose.

"Use the dead!" the sergeant yelled. He dropped behind a dead soldier and began rolling the body, its arms and legs flopping crazily, across the open ground, using the corpse for cover while firing over the top. Suddenly a pack became a shield from incoming bullets, helmets a small defense against the enemy.

It was a horror Franklin could not have imagined as he

crawled behind the dead soldier and began rolling his body toward covered ground. Like the others he would raise, fire at the bright flash of an enemy rifle, then roll the body forward and repeat the maneuver. All along the line the troopers used their dead comrades to stay alive and try to take command of the fight. None stared into the dead faces; none recognized if their shield was that of a friend or stranger.

Charlie had played his cards right. The trap had not been sprung until the paratroopers were too close for the air support to be deployed without killing American soldiers.

The shouts and screams of the NCOs and the wounded, mixing with the stutter of the M-60s, began setting a rhythm that had something of a settling effect. That and the fire of the M-16s and explosions of grenade launchers were giving the battlefield a violent musical score all its own.

They pushed forward, inching toward the enemies' advance positions. Hand grenades starting flying, exploding, showering the sky with deadly shard. The troopers were so close they were protected from the shrapnel either by being under the mushrooming cloud of flying steel, or by their dead shields.

Finally, the soldiers reached the same terrain giving cover to the enemy. The fight was now going to be close in, each yard to be dearly paid for.

Franklin rolled over the top of his human shield and crawled furiously toward the sergeant, who was on the radio. The voice of Colonel Timothy could be heard talking to the battalion commander over the PRC-25.

"What's your situation?" asked Timothy.

Colonel Wilfred Smith, the battalion commander, shouted, "I'm pinned down on the back side of the landing zone. Behind a rice paddy dike. All my troops are pinned down. We've got a hundred and thirteen dead."

Franklin looked at the sergeant, whose face suddenly screwed up in confusion. Franklin understood: *How could the commander know, in such a short period of time, the number of*

*dead! Especially if he was pinned down behind the forward
element and wasn't really in the fight!*

"Shit!" the sergeant spit. "The BC's panicking!"

"Where's the artillery?" Franklin said.

The sergeant shook his head and pointed to a distant mountain range. "Stuck in the mud on the other side of that mountain."

Franklin knew a successful operation would have to rely on artillery, especially an operation like they were in now.

The sergeant snapped, "We're outside the artillery fan, son. So there never was any planned for this operation."

"What about more troops to come in and give us support?"

Again the sergeant spoke the words Franklin didn't want to hear. "We have another company about eight hundred meters from here. Judging by the sounds from where they're at, they're in just as deep shit as we are."

Franklin looked around. The troopers were digging in and were now engaging the enemy from more secured positions.

The sergeant slapped Franklin on the shoulder. "Welcome to the oh-deuce."

28

The morning wore on with the paratroopers gradually taking small bits and pieces of ground along the battle line, but paying for every bloody inch. Screams of the wounded gradually faded, as most had either died or simply lost the ability to raise their voices. Many of the survivors bore small wounds from shrapnel where grenades were used close in during the move out of the paddy area and into cover.

Franklin was amazed at how smart Charlie had played the Americans into this obvious trap.

What was being heard over the radio was not encouraging. A1-E Skyraiders couldn't provide further fire support due to contaminated fuel back at the airfield in Qui Nhon. All twenty-six troop-carrying helicopters designated for the operation were either destroyed or nonoperational. Most of the officers had been killed on the initial landings, including company commanders and platoon leaders. Then there was a voice over the radio, that of a lieutenant, who said, "We're outnumbered and surrounded. Cut off from other units. Running low on ammunition. We may be forced to go to escape and evasion, sir."

The angry voice of Colonel Timothy came on the radio, telling him, "You're United States paratroopers, Lieutenant. You're supposed to be outnumbered and surrounded, *and* cut off, *and* running low on ammunition! You will not—I repeat—you will not go to E and E! You will fight them, Lieutenant, you will fight them, take ground, and establish contact with smaller units and advance forward. Use the enemies' ammunition. Do I make myself clear? Fight back!"

There would be no relief for some time to come, if it came at all.

They were on their own, without officers, which, Franklin would soon learn, might be their only hope to survive.

The most incredibly hated, despised creature in any military in the history of warfare is without argument the noncommissioned officer. Until there's a battle. All around the village of An Ninh, where young troopers lay pinned down, fighting a well-entrenched enemy, taking acreage in small bits, the NCOs rose to become mammoths of the moment.

Most of the noncoms were combat veterans of Korea, some of World War II, and thus no strangers to the fierceness of fighting for survival. Along the line, the NCOs gathered the men into small fire teams, calmly giving the soldiers instructions on how to take the ground and hold on to it until the support elements could get their act together.

Through his cool professionalism, the sergeant organized a number of fire teams, some from Recon, others from A Company who had straggled into his domain. He pointed toward a hill commanding a superior position over the landing zone. Smoke from the assault rifles, machine guns, and mortar found the enemy positions but Charlie continued his relentless barrage.

"We're going to have to take that fucking hill. If we don't . . . we're dead." He shouted into the radio to other soldiers grouped along the line. His voice was loud, but not panicky.

Quickly, squad leaders or survivors from the company began checking in, requesting orders. The sergeant took inventory of the weaponry at their disposal.

"We've got two M-sixties," one shaky voice said.

"Good. I need them to set up on the flanks. Get one to the left of the smoke."

"What smoke?"

"The purple smoke I'm going to throw to my front. We have one sixty. That'll be the center of the advance. Get one to my left. Thirty meters to the left flank. Do you copy?"

"Yes, Sergeant."

The sergeant threw a smoke grenade to the front of their position. The purple haze drifted upward, then spread in the direction of the hill.

"Do you see it?"

"Roger that," the voice came back. "The sixty's on the way. . . .Wait!"

More gunfire erupted from the hill toward their position. "Go to single shot. Not automatic," the sergeant shouted. "Save your ammunition until you have a target."

The troops were settling down, firing smoothly, but ammunition was becoming critically low and resupply was unlikely for a long time.

Minutes later the radio crackled with the voice of a soldier. "Our sixty's on your left flank."

"Wait one," the sergeant barked as he motioned for Franklin, who slid beside the noncom and listened to his instructions. He nodded at a tall white trooper, a buck sergeant, and told Franklin, "Go with Bartholomew's team." He looked at the squad leader. "Bart, slip into the slot to the right and work forward between the gun on the right flank and ours in center. Watch for our people coming from the right flank to hook up with your team."

Bartholomew, using hand signals, pointed to the direction of their deployment. Heavy machine-gun fire crackled overhead

and explosions spewed dirt and debris into the air, but no one
was hit. Franklin knew the other team on the right had been
spotted. In what seemed forever, eight troopers suddenly appeared, dirty, some bloodied, their eyes sunken, but appearing
eager to fight.

Bartholomew called the sergeant and gave him the sit rep:
"We're hooked up on the right!"

"Sit tight!" the order came back. "When we're hooked up
on the left we'll open up from there. When you hear the sixty
on the left flank open fire, we'll start to swing from your flank!
Advance twenty meters and hold your position. When I give the
order, lay fire onto the hill to cover the left flank's movement."

"Roger!" Bartholomew yelled as he hand-signaled the others
with a balled fist, the sign to wait for his order.

Minutes later, the M-60 at the center opened fire; seconds
later, the '60 on the left flank began firing, along with the
M-16s and grenade launchers. At that moment the paratroopers, stretched along a seventy-meter line, began moving from
the thin cover at the edge of the landing zone toward the hill
where enemy fire punished the paratroopers and deprived a
landing zone for support elements.

The roar of the fusillade coming from the hill and the guns
firing from the center and the left flank of the American line
was furious. The right flank began moving fast, firing at VC
soldiers who suddenly popped up from concealment, now in
the path of the advancing paratroopers.

Franklin fired short three-round bursts, as he had been
trained. He heard screams from bushes where moments before
an enemy had been firing. Bartholomew, carrying a twelve-
gauge pump shotgun, ripped off three quick rounds, killing two
enemy soldiers manning a machine-gun position. The scene was
macabre, as more smoke was thrown forward to conceal their
advance.

Franklin charged over the dead body of a VC and realized
they had overrun that part of the Vietcong forward line.

"Down!" Bartholomew screamed. The right flank went down and, as the '60 opened up from the center, swung their line of fire onto the center and left flank of Charlie's front line to cover the advance of the Americans on the left.

Explosions from both hand grenades and M-79s vibrated the ground; heavy gunfire from automatic weapons joined; the air seemed to pulsate from the sound.

Franklin heard a scream from his right, turned to see a man writhing on the ground, holding his stomach. Blood filled his fatigue jacket to the waist. His hands were red, his face ashen. Franklin stared into his empty eyes and watched as his mouth froze open in death. He knew nothing of the man, except that he was white, a paratrooper, dead.

Franklin was not in the 502nd; he was in the 327th. He was among men who, back at Fort Campbell, he and his battalion comrades had engaged against in intramural sports, war games and barroom brawls. He knew none of them! But now, by God, he was one of them.

The battlefield transcends personal anonymosities, whether over sports rivalry or even a woman. Here they weren't fighting for a flag. Not for an ideal or principle. Not even a nation.

They were fighting for each other! For here they had no one else. Trophies in the battalion trophy case meant nothing. Which battalion had more battle streamers on their guidon meant nothing. Here, on the field of battle, the only thing that meant anything was one immutable fact: If the battalion loses . . . the individual will lose. After that, nothing would be significant.

"*Fight back!*" as the brigade commander had ordered, became the essence of every American at An Ninh. It became the lifeline to getting back to "the world." Back to Mom and Dad. Back to wives and children. Back to cruising the strip and arguing over music and sports. Back to hamburgers that tasted good. Back to cold beer.

Back to warm, moist pussy!

And fight they did. Like a cornered animal, fearing nothing, for they had nothing left to fear, for they were dead. They just hadn't stopped breathing. Or, as Charlie was now learning, fighting back!

29

By late afternoon, word had come to the beleaguered paratroopers that there were other assets now being brought into play. The First Air Cav had been contacted to provide assistance to bring 101st support troops into the fight via First Cav helicopters, since the 101st had no operational choppers. Falling back on the promise given their division that their troops would be allowed thirty days of preparation time upon arrival before their first combat campaign, the air cav's response was, "No way!"

Hackworth had gone ballistic. From brigade headquarters, he shouted to the cav officer, "An American battalion is fighting and dying, taking casualties, with support nil or nonexistent, so you bastards can sit on your asses at An Khe, eating hot rations and drinking beer in the whorehouses. It was the Screaming Eagles who cleared out your yard for you."

The officer responded with a weak reply, to which Hackworth responded, "I guess it's necessary to inform General Westmoreland that the Screaming Eagles—which he once commanded—are about to lose the first major battle of the war because you won't get your people into the fight!"

That was all it took to get the cav motivated. The word was sent to the troopers at An Ninh: Hold on. We're coming!

Fuck them all! was how the paratroopers felt. *We've come this far without them. . . .*

30

* * *

All along the line, fire elements from different sections were advancing in alternating corridors toward the base of the hill. What had begun as certain slaughter for the Americans hours ago was becoming a battle for survival on both sides.

Both sides! Now, Charlie was fighting for *his* survival. He might control the terrain, thought Franklin, but he was no longer dictating the day. Charles wanted to hug the belt? Wanted to sit in the audience and watch the play being acted out on the stage? Wanted to snipe from concealment? Wanted to booby-trap children to kill Americans?

Not on September 18, 1965.

Despite the fact there was little or no tactical air support, no artillery or heavy weapons support, despite being outnumbered and without further reinforcements, having taken heavy casualties initially and being pinned down in the open terrain and running low on ammunition, on this day, as it neared noon, Sir Charles was learning how to rock-and-roll with some very pissed-off American paratroopers, whose only dream for the past three months had been to go eyeball-to-eyeball with them.

What had started out as a nightmare for the paratroopers was turning into a dream come true. With smooth and precise overlapping fire deployment, the paratroopers, once in dire straits, were now taking command of Charlie's front doorstep.

The fighting decayed from modern military tactics to primordial survival tactics: hand-to-hand combat. Neither side could fire without the fear of killing their own. Even the enemy on the hill was denied the use of their mortar, heavy machine guns, and artillery, for fear of killing their own men. Their wounded were like the wounded trooper, without assistance, alone, and cut off from their element.

Franklin watched in awe as the soldiers charged into enemy positions, never stopping, pushing forward, the rage burning in their eyes. There was no time for chatter, only the raw, down-into-the-dirt killing that one man does to another when he's afraid of nothing. Not the Devil . . . or God Almighty! Neither was on the battlefield.

Especially God, thought Franklin. *If he had been here, He would have stepped in and stopped this shit.*

Every man knew that for a fact, even the Vietcong.

It no longer mattered how many enemy soldiers the troopers killed. That's never important. What mattered was simple: Airborne soldiers are inserted to take and hold ground. That's their job. If they have to kill, they will. The airborne soldier doesn't glorify himself by how many enemy tanks he knocks out. That's the job of the armor units. Enemy kills is the job of the infantry, coming in behind the Airborne in overwhelming numbers. The job of the Airborne soldier is to provide a point of reference, a "link-up," for the other units who would ultimately claim the victory.

Franklin watched in awe as one soldier charged toward a mortar pit, jumped inside, and with his bare hands ripped the metal sights off the tube and used it to crush the skull of the enemy mortar man.

Another soldier beat back three Vietcong with the remainder of his broken M-16.

Another ripped an AK-47 from a VC's hand, turned it around, and shoved the bayonet through his throat.

There was no quarter asked, none given, by either side.

Then the incredible happened, so inspiring Franklin could not forget if he lived a thousand years.

The sergeant staggered forward from the smoke and carnage, his body riddled with bullets. He pointed toward the hill and, with his last breath, ordered, "Don't pull back. Don't pull back!"

Franklin screamed, "Take the hill! Take the hill!"

Another trooper screamed, blood running from his mouth, "Take the hill! Take the hill!"

Fear was no longer present in the ranks of the paratroopers.

The Vietcong broke from the onslaught, their confidence overwhelmed by the bravado of the troopers, who breathed their fire of hatred like demons, using rifle butts when ammunition was gone. Helmets as bludgeons. Feet and fists. Knives and teeth. Not to be denied that this was now their moment!

Upward they moved, into a darkness that began to descend as the sun drifted behind the distant mountains, turning the blood-soaked ground from red to a dark purple, then black.

By the time darkness fell, the base of the mountain and its approaches were in the control of the survivors of the morning landing.

The 101st had lost the morning, settled scores in the afternoon, and was preparing to hold on to the night.

Overhead, the flare ships began circling, dropping the large drums of illumination that turned the sky into near-day. Drifting down on parachutes, the glowing canisters created eerie shadows on the terrain, macabre and frightening. The faces of the dead seemed to give off a brief look of surprise as the light touched their faces, then were darkened hulks until the light danced onto them again.

The fighting settled into other pockets the rest of the night, as it became obvious that help truly was on the way. Charlie had broken contact and was fleeing to other holes in the ground to hide to wait for another day.

When morning arrived, elements of the brigade began linking up with the troopers. Vietnamese Army Rangers were blocking one side of the mountain; 2nd Battalion of the 327th infantry—deemed Task Force Collins—was connecting onto both flanks of An Ninh. And the cav had arrived, ferrying in troops in their shiny new helicopters, experiencing their baptism of fire.

The fresh troops advanced past the worn-out troopers of the oh-deuce, in pursuit of the enemy. A young lieutenant stopped near Franklin and saluted him smartly.

Now relieved, the men sat, smoking, fidgeting with their weapons, staring down the hill at the carnage and wreckage spread everywhere the eye could see.

Gradually, those who could walk assisted the wounded toward the LZ, now busy with the arrival and departure of Hueys.

Franklin and the survivors loaded the wounded and the dead onto the choppers on the very LZ where they had landed. As they climbed aboard the choppers, bloodied, but unbeaten, the hills still looked surrounded, but the enemy was disappearing, back into their caves and tunnels.

· · ·

The brigade won the battle, according to the numbers: 257 dead VC and NVA; 13 dead and 40 wounded Americans. Franklin knew there was nothing really to cheer about, except the fact he was alive. For that he was grateful.

PART 4

★

QUI NHON

31

Tim's Traveling Trouble was given a new mission: to clear Qui Nhon province for the arrival of the elite Korean Capital Division. Much to the brigade's chagrin, the Vietcong had come out only once in regimental size to fight the Screaming Eagles. Except for Operation Gibraltar, Charlie had sat in the bleachers, watching the game being played by the American paratroopers, learning their strategy, remaining patient.

For the Screaming Eagles, the short journey to the rice paddies of Qui Nhon province was as different in purpose and terrain as a ski trip in the mountains of Colorado would be to an alligator hunt in the swamps of Louisiana. The First Air Cav would assume the mission of keeping Charlie's mountain sanctuary under constant threat and harassment, which included shutting down the Ho Chi Minh Trail.

The First Brigade's new mission was to protect the harvest in the vast expanse of rice paddies, which was vital to the national economy, the Vietnamese people, and the Vietcong. What met the troopers was a terrain as equally deadly as the mountains, though there were no tigers and monkeys; now there was simply nowhere to find protection from the Vietcong snipers, who could disappear without a trace. And of course there were the ubiquitous booby traps, more numerous, sophisticated, and well concealed than in the mountains, since they could be maintained more frequently and deployed over a larger area. Booby traps in the mountains were mostly along trails in the thick jungles, especially punji pits, and more easily detected.

That was not the case in the rice paddies, where every inch of the murky water could conceal punji stakes, poles entangled with rusty barbed wire, land mines, and unexploded artillery ordnance. Petrol was even effective; since gasoline weighs less than water, it floated on the surface and could be ignited, turning a paddy into a raging inferno, leaving a trapped patrol with no direction to run.

He also knew inserts and extracts, especially medevacs, had to operate on limited hard surface, giving the Vietcong more easily recognizable points of reference on where the Americans would land their helicopters. Graveyards were bracketed for artillery and mortar fire and often heavily mined and booby-trapped by the enemy.

Humping the mountains had been physically exacting, but the paddies were a natural nightmare, a place where soldiers would wade through water from their knees to their shoulders, each step forward wearing away their endurance. Under enemy fire, running with the burden of equipment made them easy targets for concealed snipers and automatic weapons crew. Not even the dikes offered a route through the paddies, since the narrow separations between the paddies could be easily mined or booby-trapped and were certainly monitored by enemy snipers.

Streams and rivers were just as lethal, constantly traveled by sampans carrying innocent-looking civilians who could suddenly open fire with a deadly fusillade and disappear into a shoreline of thick reeds, escaping along routes known only to the enemy.

Then there were the snakes, the mosquitoes, and the worst

aggravation to most of the troopers, leeches as thick as a man's thumb.

Mosquito repellent did little good to protect the skin since the water quickly rinsed it from the skin. The only alternative was to roll down the sleeves, button the blouse to the collar, and wear a towel around the neck. This added some protection from the leeches and mosquitoes, but not from the relentless heat of the scorching Asian sun, where shade was a luxury; groves of trees, where they existed, were prime zones for Charlie to zero in on with every lethal device at his disposal.

Villages were designed differently in the Central Lowlands, with the structural design mainly bamboo framework, mud siding, bamboo flooring, and palm fronds for roofing—where each bamboo shoot could conceal lethal explosives primed for easy demolition.

The establishment of base camps was made more difficult with limited areas of terrain suitable for a large force to set up a base operation. Vehicles were limited by the fact there were few—if any—passable roads, nearly eliminating the use of gun jeeps, supply "mules," and ammunition caissons. Artillery and mortar squads had to set up in mud and muck, which had a great effect on accurate firing. Patrols were forced to sleep in the paddies, knowing any suitable ground available would probably be mined and targeted by the VC.

Immersion in the water brought added problems for equipment; where clothing, boots, radios, and web gear rotted with such rapidity, the brigade supply officer was under constant pressure to replenish the basic rudiments required by a modern army. Most important, the M-16, already proven to be too delicate and inadequate in Nam, required constant maintenance from jamming, due to the mud and ammunition corrosion. Rifle barrels filled with mud often exploded in the troopers' hands when fired.

But protective cover was the greatest concern: There was simply nothing the soldiers could lie behind to return fire.

As the First Brigade troopers had learned in the Central Highlands, "walking fire" in the mountainous bush had been a bitch, but walking fire in the rice paddies was a motherfucker!

Where Franklin found the living conditions at An Khe had been at best difficult, Qui Nhon was nightmarish. The rain was endless, overflowing rice paddies, turning the plain into a giant lake that seemed to have no distinctive shores. Roads were nearly impassable, where there were roads; travel by vehicle meant an excursion into a no-man's-land.

The troopers of 1/327 were literally living in mud—if they were lucky. Otherwise, they often slept in water, their nylon camouflage poncho liners their only cover from the elements.

The base camp of headquarters company was a small fort surrounded by barbed wire, minefields, heavy machine guns, mortar, infantry positions manned by the platoons, and the command post at the center. Shade was impossible to find, unless beneath a vehicle or in the hot, steamy bunkers.

Midnight was guaranteed harassment time. One of Charlie's favorite tricks was to mingle with peasants, find a tree or bush, use a stick in the branches that pointed at a bunker within the compound. That night, he would return with a real weapon, place it in the precise branches, squeeze off a few rounds, then hightail it for home. There were few actual hits, but it wreaked havoc on the nerves of the troopers.

Patrols were running on a regular basis, stepped up to a higher level than at An Khe since the area was so vital to the economy.

Moments of respite were relished, although filled with the constant cleaning of equipment, personal hygiene, and perpetual refortification of the camp.

And then there was the thrill of mail from home.

The arrival of each new tape cassette was a joy for Franklin

Sharps, especially those from Darlene. He would sit and listen to her lovely voice and the sound of Argonne chattering in the background. The tapes gave him a sense of belonging to something good and wonderful that he could almost touch.

He had received several by the first week of October, playing them over and over, the voices carrying him to a place that seemed forever lost. The only sadness was listening to those from his mother. He sensed in her voice that something was wrong. She never complained, however, apparently not wanting to burden him with any problem she might have. His mother knew how to suffer in silence. How to endure in private. She was, he often thought, the toughest member of the family.

He was sitting in his hooch, listening to a tape from Darlene when Dawes exploded in, all excited.

"Come on, man; grab your mess kit!"

Franklin looked perplexed. "Mess kit? What do I need a mess kit for?" He wasn't even certain if he could remember where the kit was; they had eaten nothing but C-rations since arriving in-country.

"We got hot chow! Hackworth had hot chow flown in, man." Dawes appeared nearly delirious with joy.

Franklin bolted from his rack and began rummaging through his gear. "Yes!" he shouted, fishing the metal mess kit from his duffel bag.

The two hurried away, joining the swarm of troopers hustling toward the command post, the site of the mess hall.

A long line had formed at the entrance; the smell was nearly overwhelming. Porkchops were cooking on makeshift barbecue grills, as well as chicken, and there was beer. Not cold, but plentiful.

Franklin found himself drifting toward the smell with the others; there was laughter, chatter, jiving, and music blaring from a hundred transistor radios. Country and western, rhythm and blues, rock-and-roll. The only thing missing was an ocean with bikini-clad babes running along the beach, being chased by hundreds of hungry and horny paratroopers.

"That Hack is some dude, man," Dawes said.

"I wonder how in the hell he managed to pull this off. Hot rations in the bush is beyond belief," Franklin said.

Inside the mess tent, he could see the Spoons dishing out royal portions. They were finally getting to do a real job, and suddenly they were treated like royalty.

Franklin was just about to spear a thick, juicy chop with his fork when there was a flat bang of gunfire. Chicken, chops, mashed potatoes, gravy, biscuits, and beer went flying in every direction as the troopers dropped their mess kits and hit the deck and jacked rounds into the chambers of their M-16s.

From behind the mess tables came a shout: "Medic!"

Franklin stood and hurried around to the rear of the tables. Two Spoons were leaning over the body of a third, who lay on the ground, with a pool of blood forming near his head and his fallen M-16.

Franklin knelt and checked the man. He had a large hole in the top of his head; smoke from the discharged bullet wafted lightly from his mouth.

"He's bought it," Franklin said.

The mess sergeant stood and shook his head. "Poor motherfucker. He got a 'Dear John' this morning. His old lady run off with some college professor back at Fort Campbell."

Franklin looked closer at the dead man and recognized him. He was the cook who had emptied his bottle of Jack Daniel's up at An Khe.

"I never thought he would pull some shit like this," the mess sergeant lamented.

A voice from behind demanded, "What is going the fuck on here!"

Master Sergeant Charlie Musselwhite, from Cordele, Georgia, a tough Korean war veteran and maintenance platoon sergeant, stood over the tables.

Franklin said, "This man shot himself, Sergeant."

Musselwhite glared at the dead body. "Fuck him! Drag his dead ass out of here. Sharps, you can tag and bag him later." He was obviously outraged at the thought the man would commit suicide in front of his comrades while they were being served their first hot meal since leaving the United States. Musselwhite turned to the other men and shouted, "Goddammit, let's eat!"

The event was shocking, and ordinary people might have found the conduct of the men reprehensible, but the troopers were not ordinary people, and these were not ordinary times.

32

The recon gun jeep became instrumental in the Qui Nhon area. A standard jeep, designed for rugged or muddy terrain, it was equipped with radios and a pedestal in the rear. An M-60 or .50-caliber machine gun was mounted on the pedestal, which could hold a standard ammunition box. The man sitting in the right seat was the "scout observer." The driver drove, constantly trying to maintain control over difficult terrain; the observer watched for trouble, and the gunner behind the pedestal was on constant alert.

There was only one problem: the vehicle was road-bound in the Qui Nhon area, making it vulnerable to attack by either land mines or ambush by the Victcong.

With an operation apparently in mind, the recon platoon was dispatched to reconnoiter a village north of Highway 19, into what was considered known VC-controlled territory. Air reconnaissance—while effective to a point—could minimize the need to acquire more information, and it was always necessary to send in the grunts to root out the story.

Franklin was assigned to Dawes's team, and the group saddled up in three jeeps. Since they were short one man, Franklin was delighted to be given the role of gunner on the jeep with Dawes and Marion.

The small convoy rolled out of the base camp just after daylight and headed east, passing through several checkpoints before turning north, toward what was referred to as "Indian country."

The monsoon had begun, flooding the paddies over the edges of their dikes, making the narrow road, which was no more than a trail, barely visible. The recce troopers were now at full alert, knowing they were beyond the artillery and mortar fan and any tac air support needed would take a good bit of time to arrive.

The jeeps groaned and ground their way slowly, passing peasants knee-deep in the paddies, picking rice and placing it in wicker baskets that floated nearby, or strapped to water buffalo. Children worked alongside the women—there were mostly women or old men, a definite sign the countryside was ruled by Charlie. The younger men were off in other areas planning attacks, recruiting, and training in hidden enclaves.

Franklin tuned his transistor to Armed Forces Radio, transmitting from Saigon, and listened to music while scanning the terrain.

It took nearly an hour to reach the first ville, a hamlet of about one hundred Vietnamese. What they found waiting for them was shocking and appalling.

Huts were burning; children sat in the dirt crying; young women, mostly half-naked, were consoling one another. As the jeeps rolled to a halt, the villagers stared at the Americans with contempt.

Dawes stepped from the jeep and looked around, his face etched with disgust. "What in the name of everything holy has happened here?" he wondered aloud. Then he motioned for the others to stay mounted. "I'm going to see if I can find out what's been going on. You guys sit tight, and keep good eyes."

He walked among the villagers, all of whom appeared in shock and dismay. His Viet language wasn't very good but it was better than the others'. An old man suddenly appeared, his face bloodied, eyes blackened and swollen. He and Dawes spoke out of range of the others, but after several minutes the squad leader joined the team.

"What's going on?" Franklin said.

"Grab your aid bag, man. These people need some attention."

"What's going on?" Marion called from the rear jeep. "Did Charlie do this?"

Dawes motioned them to gather around him. "The village was paid a visit last night by a Korean patrol. I guess they enjoyed themselves with the women and beat the shit out of the old men when they were asked for information about the Cong. They pulled out early this morning." He waved at the burning structures. "They set the fires before skying out. The people were able to get most of them put out, but all their rice stores were destroyed."

"Those motherfuckers," Marion seethed. "From what we've been hearing, they're worse than the Vietcong."

That was the word traveling through the brigade. The Republic of Korea—ROK—army was patrolling the same province and in the short time they had been operational had made a savage reputation in the countryside.

Dawes looked at Franklin. "They need your help, brother."

Franklin grabbed his aid kit and M-16 and went to the center of the ville. Dawes spoke again with the old man—the village "headman"—who began talking to his people. Gradually, the injured began forming a line where Franklin had set up his equipment.

A young woman was first in line. She stood naked from the waist down, where blood ran along the inside of both her thighs. She had been horribly raped. She had her arms crossed over her breasts, and Franklin could see more blood soaking her black pajama top. Her eyes were vacant; she stared emptily at him. Gently, Franklin pulled her arms down and raised her pajama top.

"Those motherfuckers!" he yelled out. He felt the bile rising in his throat.

The nipples on the young girl's breasts had been cut off.

"Holy fuck!" Dawes said. "Look what they done to this child."

Marion started for his jeep. "Let's get those cocksuckers!"

"I'm with you, bro," Burkett said, starting for his jeep.

"Hold it!" Dawes ordered. "You ain't going nowhere."

"Bullshit," Marion said. "This ain't human, man. Those fuckers need to pay. They need to pay with everything they got."

"Right on," Burkett yelled. "Fighting the Cong is one thing. This is . . . man . . . I don't even *know* what this is."

"Goddammit!" Dawes said, "we're not vigilantes." He looked at Franklin. "What can you do for this baby?"

Franklin shook his head. "I'm not a surgeon. She needs a real doctor. In a real hospital." He looked at the others; all were injured beyond the realm of his skills. "I imagine there are others who'll need the same."

Dawes thought for a moment, then walked to his jeep. He radioed the headquarters command post. He spoke for several minutes, then returned to Franklin. "Do what you can for them, Franklin. What I need to know is how many of these folks need a real doctor. Headquarters is going to line up a Chinook."

"Chinook?" He knew an H-47 "banana boat" could carry half the village.

Dawes nodded. "It looks like there's going to be too many for a Huey. We'll set up security at the edges of the ville, just in case Charlie hears about this and takes it out on our asses. Can't say as I'd blame him much." He patted Franklin on the shoulder. "Do what you can. I'll need a count as soon as you can get it on how many we're going to medevac."

For the next hour Franklin did what he could, which amounted to administering morphine to the young girl, bandaging her breasts, and examining her vagina. She had been literally torn apart. There were others in equally bad shape. Dozens of broken bones. One girl had an ear cut off. A small boy had been stomped in the groin to the point his scrotum was so swollen, his penis was not visible. An old woman's nostrils had been slit.

When Franklin was done bandaging, cleaning wounds, and administering the last of his morphine, there were eighteen people in severe enough condition to be evacuated.

He walked over to Dawes, who looked like a man bent on revenge.

"What's the count?"

"Eighteen."

Dawes took the radio and reported back to headquarters. Franklin heard a voice reply, "The Chinook is inbound. Get the place ready. Pop smoke on the LZ."

Marion approached with the headman of the village. The old man's wrinkled face was as worn and weathered as old leather and what few teeth he had were bright red from chewing betel nut, popular among the villagers. There was nothing in his eyes but the look of ancient despair.

"What's up?" Dawes said.

Marion pointed to the old man. "The old guy has something to tell you. I can't understand much of what he's saying. Something about VC."

Dawes and the headman walked and talked. The combination of the old man's broken English and Dawes's fragmented Vietnamese allowed the two a limited communication.

"What did the old man have to say?" Franklin asked, taping a bandage over the eye of the last villager left to treat.

"The old man is showing his gratitude for our help."

Franklin could detect Dawes's excitement. "What did he have to say?"

Dawes took his map and pointed to a village ten clicks to the north. "He says there are beaucoup Vietcong in this village. He said the VC forced the young men to join their ranks, and that's where they take them for training." He tapped a spot on the map.

Franklin chuckled. "He's probably full of crap."

"We've heard all that shit before, man," Marion said skeptically.

"I don't think so," Dawes said. "The old boy's pretty pissed at Charlie right now. He sent a runner to the village to have the VC send help when the Korean patrol arrived. They didn't lift a finger."

Typical Charlie: Having a village wiped out by the Americans or their allies was more important than the people. The propaganda was priceless.

"You better get on the horn to base camp," Marion said. "Find out what they want us to do."

Dawes went to his jeep and spoke for several minutes with the platoon leader. When he returned he was smiling. "We're to get these people out of here and return to base camp."

That was good news to Franklin and Marion. If there was a large Vietcong force in that village—the next stop on their patrol—they didn't want to go in outnumbered.

"Right," said Franklin. "They're ready to transport." He pointed at the other villagers. "What about them?"

Dawes shook his head. "I guess they're on their own. But we bring the headman back with us."

Franklin knew there would be a Vietnamese interpreter waiting. If the old man was lying, the interrogator would have a better chance of finding out.

• • •

Thirty minutes later, in a cloud of red smoke, the Chinook landed in the center of the village. The prop wash swirled to the dirt, fanned burning embers, causing fires to rekindle. The villagers had to begin a fresh battle to save their village. They had nothing to fight with except buckets of water filled from the rice paddy.

The Americans jumped in to help, but there was little that could be done. What was left standing by the Koreans was now gone.

"Let's mount up!" Dawes ordered. "We can't do anything more for these people." He put the headman in his jeep behind Franklin just as the powerful blades from the helo began to churn up the power.

The Chinook lifted off, and the American gun jeeps pulled out to return to base camp as ordered.

The village was no longer in existence, except in the minds of the villagers, who had nowhere else to go.

The troopers left behind everything they had: three crates of C-rations, poncho liners, and all of the remaining bandages and antiseptic in Franklin's aid kit.

33

Two days later the battalion was gearing up to return to the area the village headman claimed was a Vietcong training and staging area.

A Company—known as the "ABU" Company—had been selected to lead the assault, with the Recon Platoon in the vanguard.

The mood around Recon was upbeat but not boisterous. The men knew the lessons of the past. Hopes had been raised too many times, only to see them dashed for one reason or the other. They would be landing in the open, moving in water up to their waists, and would be easy targets. The trick was to get in with the element of surprise on their side, take cover, and push Charlie back while the support troops rode to their assistance.

Franklin went to the medical platoon and resupplied his aid kit. He found several of his buddies, many of whom he had not seen since leaving the Nha Trang area.

Spec Four Eddie Carreon, from San Antonio, Texas, was cracking a beer when Franklin arrived. He tossed one to Franklin and said, "Come on, man. Grab some suds and shoot the shit."

Franklin dropped to the ground with the others, sipped his beer, and began listening to the stories they had to tell from the units they were assigned to as medics.

The story seem to be universal: slogging through the mountains, now the water, and no major operation with Charlie. Their blood was up; all were in good spirits. The troopers were eager for a good fight with the Vietcong.

"I just want to get my hands on one of those motherfuckers," said Carreon. He whipped out a switchblade. "Just for a few seconds. That's all I want."

"Bullshit!" said Warner, a young guy from Oklahoma City. "Charlie'll take that knife away from you and cut your dick off with it. Then what will the señoritas do in San Antone?"

"San Antonio will have a day of mourning!" Carreon said.

Everyone laughed. Carreon was so handsome, he was damn near pretty. When he went to combat medic school in San Antone, the telephone rang night and day in the orderly room. To say he was popular with the ladies was an understatement.

Franklin felt good being with the guys from Medical Platoon. Each platoon has its own persona, and the medics were a group of carefree, boisterous young men. They had to have bravado. They weren't there to be heroes, but when the infantry got their asses shot off it was the medics who had to rise to the occasion and go get the wounded, drag their asses to safety, and patch them up. They had earned the respect of every soldier in the battalion.

Franklin left at 2100 to the sound of trucks pulling into the battalion area. The troops would be ferried to the helicopter pads, where they would go through a final check, then mount up and ride.

The moon was full and the weather report solid for the morning assault, but he knew the men would get little sleep, if any. They would lie in their hooches, think about home, family, wives, children, women they planned to have in the future.

Each man would have a thousand things on his mind, but not sleep. Sleep was what a soldier thinks about after he's survived a battle.

34

The sun was rising over the Central Plains, a brilliant orange glow, except where dotted by tiny black specks on the low horizon. To the Vietcong soldier standing guard at the edge of the village, the specks seemed to grow in size until they began to take the shape of giant dragonflies. Within seconds he could hear the faint sound of the rotor whipping the wind echoing from the distance, and he knew what was coming and what to do.

The soldier began running through the village, sounding the alarm. Within seconds huts and other buildings were emptying of soldiers, women, and children, all racing toward their assigned positions. Mortars were uncovered, aimed on the only available landing zone near the village. Crews manned their Goryunov heavy machine guns, the equivalent to the .50-caliber, and the Dekteryovs, the Russian counterpart to the American M-60. Bells were ringing, pans being banged, turning the village into a frenzy of activity.

One young woman, dressed in black pajamas, wore heavy bandoliers of ammunition strapped over her shoulders; in her arms she carried a baby no more than three months of age.

RPG-7 rocket teams scurried through the village to their positions while infantrymen ran on foot to take up positions along the system of dike walls necklacing the ville.

"The Americans are coming!" Shouts rang out as the village suddenly turned into an armed encampment and prepared to meet the invaders.

A Company was inbound in heloes with the recon element at the point. Huey gunships flew at the outer flanks, providing air cover for the assault force. The Recon Platoon was at the lead of the assault. Their task: secure the LZ for the incoming company of Airborne infantry.

Franklin was riding with his favorite team, Dawes and the others he'd known since coming aboard back at Fort Campbell. They were all silent now, their butts puckered tight against their helmets, most of them chewing nervously on C-rat chewing gum. Each man carried rations for two days and their standard complement of weapons, ammunition, and water.

They felt the Huey bank sharply, then descend, and the door gunner shouted, "All right, heroes, get your asses ready!" He pointed to the distance.

A village could be seen in the early-morning light. It was a large village by normal standards. It appeared to be on a point of land with a river running through its center. Tall trees surrounded it.

Dawes reached over and high-fived Franklin. "Good luck, man."

"I'm with you!" Franklin shouted. He slipped on his helmet, leaving the chin strap loose, then jacked a round into the chamber of his M-16, checked to see the safety was on, and prepared for the assault.

The team threw their legs over the side and leaned back, their feet braced on the skids. The feel of the water racing past made it seem they were traveling at the speed of sound.

They heard the pitch change in the prop and felt the nose rise as the chopper slowed toward a momentary hover.

Franklin leaned forward and scanned the front. What he saw chilled him. "Damn!" He pointed at the paddies to the front.

Dawes leaned forward and looked. "We're into the shit, brother!"

Mortar fire began falling on the rice paddies selected for the landing. Geysers spewed into the air; tracers streaked long snaking paths of lead from the edge and interior of the village, where heavy machine guns were firing at the troops and helicopters.

The team dropped into the water, which came above even the taller men's waists, and began pushing their bodies through the paddy, their weapons held high above their heads.

Franklin could see Chassion motioning for everyone to move forward.

The Recon Platoon fanned out and charged toward the dikes, their only protection. They were caught in the open—again!— and it was starting to look like a repeat of An Ninh when Franklin heard the thunder of a 105 howitzer artillery round crash into the village.

He saw a ball of smoke and fire rush into the sky; then there was another explosion, then another, this one from an incoming flurry of rockets fired from a Huey gunship.

He looked at Dawes and shouted, "Yeah! This time we've got the firepower!" He raised his weapon and fired, not aiming, just in the direction of the enemy, letting them know life was about to become difficult.

Pushing on, he reached the dike, hugged it close for a moment, then rose up and fired at the muzzle flashes coming from dikes nearly one hundred meters away, near the edge of the village.

More artillery began to fall on the village. Smoke billowed and he could see black-clad VC running in every direction.

Franklin spotted one figure in particular in front of the dike, running from right to left of his line of fire. He took careful aim and squeezed off a round. The bullet cut the water a few feet in front of the target.

He fired a second round. The bullet cut the water short of the target.

He took a deep breath, released slowly, then squeezed.

The target pitched forward and disappeared beneath the water near the wall of the dike.

"Yeah!" he shouted. "Yeah!" It was the best shot he had ever made. And probably the luckiest.

The second wave made its approach south and east of his position, into another line of paddies. A third lift would land north and east, forming a horseshoe at the front of the village. Another element would land north, where they would set up a blocking position. The frontal assault would sweep forward, driving the VC—who would no doubt begin fleeing under the superior firepower—into the waiting guns of the blocking element.

That was the plan.

Chassion motioned the troopers forward, moving in fire teams. Mortar crashed and shook the surface of the paddies; bullets stitched crazy paths of tiny rooster tails across the surface. Miraculously, no one was hit as the team approached the dike wall.

Suddenly, to his right, a VC ran along the top of the dike, then dropped out of sight on the far side. Franklin took a hand grenade, pulled the pin, and lobbed it over the edge. There was an explosion, and in the air above him, framed against the sky, an object was floating down, as though from the heavens. Mud? Tree stump? What?

Only when the body impacted against him did he realize it was a human being. The Vietcong's weight, joined with the weight of his equipment, pushed Franklin beneath the water. He could feel himself drowning; he could feel the VC's body entangled with his, and he knew he was going to die.

There was only silence and, opening his eyes, the brown

muck of the paddy water. He was going to die. He was going to—

Then, it dawned on him: *Stand up, fool! You're only in water up to your fucking waist!*

He pushed upward and saw the sun. And the face of the dead man, whose leg was entangled in Franklin's harness. He pulled the leg free and threw the body off just as another VC ran along the dike. He raised his weapon and fired. There was a puff of gray smoke, a loud bang, and he felt something sting his side. He looked at the barrel of the M-16. The muzzle was parted like petals on an open flower. The bottom of the magazine was also missing. He could only figure the barrel was full of mud when he fired and when it exploded the back pressure blew the rounds out of the bottom of the magazine.

He was lucky. But he was without an M-16. He took his pistol and hugged the dike, watching the others as they pushed over it and began driving the enemy back toward the village.

He saw two feet sticking out of the water. The body was head-down. It was the target he had dropped from the first dike. He figured the VC had an AK and ammo strapped to his body and so reached down and felt hair and, as he pulled the VC up, said, "Come here, motherfucker."

The body came up easy, and he saw the bandoliers around the upper torso. He saw the face of a young woman and he saw a baby pop from her arms and bob in the water like a cork floating on a pond.

It was a moment when the sounds of baby Argonne, on the tapes, reached across from one side of the world to the other. When the shame of all that had been done to those children in the mountains surfaced with the same surprising suddenness as with this child.

The mother was the enemy, taking ammunition to those who would kill his comrades.

But the child was not part of the bargain.

He looked at the woman. His bullet had hit her in the right side of her back, come out the left breast, and damn near cut the child in half.

A sudden spray of enemy fire, kicking in the water, broke his reverie. *Grieve later, goddammit! Get your ass moving.*

He stripped off the bandoliers and pushed her body away. He took the towel from around his neck, wrapped the child in it, vaulted over the dike, and raced to a palm tree, where he laid the bundle down, then raced toward the battle.

35

The advance from the dike to the edge of the village, where Charlie chose to form a line of defense—again hugging the belt and denying tac air and artillery—was where the fighting grew intense. But it allowed the incoming lifts to move across the paddies with little resistance, since the VC heavy weapons assets had been abandoned. Now it was in-close fighting, nerve-wracking, but at least there was cover.

And for the first time since Franklin had been in-country . . . overwhelming odds in the Airborne's favor. At least it looked that way, from the mortar pit where he was hunkered beside Dawes.

The crackle of M-16 fire and AK-47 chatter, mixed with the deep stutter of the M-60s and the M-79 and hand grenade explosions, created an incredible, horrific noise, the sounds echoing off the hard mud huts and rustling the palm trees, at the base of each where Charlie had a bunker and a sniper at the top.

"Slow and easy, slow and easy. No telling what kind of shit Charlie's got hidden for our ass," Dawes warned.

Both ducked as a spray of AK-47 swept the front of their

position, kicking up dirt that flew over their heads.

"See what I mean?" Dawes said.

"Where's the rest of the platoon?" Franklin had been the last one over the dike and into the ville and was disoriented.

Dawes began pointing to where the recce troops were positioned. Chassion had set up a command post near a mud hut at the center of the leading edge of the ville. Three squads on his right flank, three on his left.

For the first time, they had the enemy boxed in, on their ground.

This is our ground, Franklin thought.

The recon troopers were the point of the bayonet, shoving it in, but going slow, decisive, making certain it would be a clean thrust. Each step calculated, calm, with precision. Forget about checking the huts. To hell with booby traps. Pull the pin, watch the spoon kick, then throw the grenade inside.

There was no time to check for civilians. This was a war zone. There were no civilians. If they weren't there to fight, they should be somewhere else.

Methodically, the platoon moved through the village, knowing that A Company was following close on their heels, taking out the flanks, shutting off the avenues of retreat.

Charlie was running now, but he was putting up a fight. Sporadic gunfire broke out as he left the house, not giving up an inch without a fight. "This is the way it should be," Franklin said to nobody in particular.

36

Her hair was gray and hung long and loose at her shoulders. Her hands were gnarled like twists of dry vine, her face pleasant, showing nothing of the horror she had known in her life or in her final moments.

She reminded Franklin of his grandmother in Arizona, lying asleep.

He had thrown a hand grenade into the hut, kicked back, waiting for the explosion. When the ground shook and the earth moved, he went inside, firing his rifle.

Then he moved on to the next hut.

He had a grenade, and was about to pitch it inside when he heard the sound of a child crying. He looked in the window. The child was sitting on a bamboo mat, alone, a small cook fire burning nearby. The aroma of the hut caught his nostrils and brought him back to reality. He leaned through the window and saw the door and the mousetrap. He knew there was a bullet beneath the tiny nail planted on the small piece of wood where the lever would strike.

He eased his M-16 through the crude window and fired. The mousetrap tripped and set off an explosion.

Not today, Charlie. We know your fucking tricks.

But the child was crying. Another of Charlie's tricks. Get the babies to distract the attention. Dumb-assed, good-natured GI Joe, the sentimental bastard from decades past, always a sucker for a baby. An old woman. Or a skirt.

Not today!

He carefully put the pin back into the grenade, securing the spoon. He moved on.

Not today. Not fucking today!

It was weakness Charles counted on.

A kid from Iowa with a big heart winds up with his guts in his hands.

Not today!

A dumb-ass bar bouncer from New York City—who's never seen trees except in Central Park—is fire-walking the bush. His ass is hanging out all over the place. He just wants to go home, but he's a killer now. A stone fucking killer. You want to bag him, Charles?

Not today!

A surfer from Malibu is coming off the paddies, getting his ass shot at, and learning a new 360 on the waves. He's carrying iron. Explosives. Think you can bring him down?

Not today!

Want to kill me?

Not today!

Franklin moved on, part of the sweep, hoping there would be something—someone—to fight!

"Watch your six!" Dawes shouted. He was at the next hut, and starting to go forward, when there was a single shot.

Franklin ducked instinctively, then looked toward Dawes.

Dawes was sitting by the edge of a hut with a distant look on his face, eyes vacant, as though something had been lost, and he was looking for it but couldn't remember what it was. He was dead.

Franklin realized there was no sympathy left in him. Like

Chassion said, "The only place you'll find sympathy in this world is in the dictionary, between suicide and syphilis."

He moved slowly from hut to hut, tossing in the grenades. Firing a killing side burst after each, then moving on.

As he reached the river dividing the village there was an explosion. "What was that?" he shouted.

A voice called back, "Charlie's blown the bridge over the river. Covering his retreat to the other side."

The village was now split into two enclaves.

On this day, Charlie was tough. He wasn't going to give up an inch of ground without a fight.

Franklin saw the figure slip from the side of a hut and start to make a run for the river. He was smaller than Franklin but deadly as a cobra. Franklin cut across his line of flight and dropped behind a well. He watched as the VC came forward, rushing hard, his eyes solid and straight.

He had that special look of fear on his face, the one that's visible on a trapped animal; he was caught, and he knew it. He had no choice but to fight.

Franklin rose up and leveled his M-16 at the enemy soldier. Their eyes joined for a split second, just before Franklin squeezed off a neat three-round burst. The bullets stitched the VC across the chest, sending him into a pirouette like a drunken ballet dancer. He didn't scream. He fell silently to the ground, clutching his AK-47, and lay still.

Franklin moved forward, not thinking or feeling. Move and fire. Reload. Keep moving. His world had been reduced to this tiny microcosm where strangers were joined in the ancient ritual of fighting to the death. He felt the hate boiling up from within his soul.

He had to be cautious, not careful. Careful creates a pattern the enemy can home in on. Cautious allows latitude while at the same time making one dangerous. They had Charlie on his front porch, and like Franklin's grandfather had said, "You can chase an old cur dog all over the town, but when he gets under his front porch . . . he'll bite your leg off!"

And that's what it came down to.

Overhead, the air whistled as the artillery streaked toward the opposing bank of the river. The sound of the incoming 105 round, followed by impact and a thunderous explosion, meant the howitzers were on target. This was not the time for short rounds.

The crackle of M-16s mixed with the explosions, and all was coming closer. When the troopers reached the river, there was a glorious sight. Approximately twelve Vietcong were swimming toward the far bank!

Franklin raised his rifle to fire, then stopped. He thought he saw what Charlie was up to: Children had been mixed into the group of fleeing soldiers. They were splashing and kicking to the other side, being dragged along by the struggling enemy.

"Hold your fire!" somebody shouted. "There's kids in the line of fire!"

The troopers had to stand helpless and watch as the enemy soldiers crawled up the bank, dragging the children along, using them as human shields.

Within seconds, the VC disappeared into the enclave of huts on the far side, taking the children with them.

Overhead, a gunship banked low, its guns blazing from both doors, bullets spraying the front line of huts facing the river. The mud-and-thatch structures seemed to melt as the gunfire tore at the walls and roofs, tearing huge chunks away with its vicious storm of firepower.

"Slick motherfucker." That's what Marion had to say as he knelt next to Franklin, near the edge of the river, sweat pouring from his face. "Motherfucker knows how to give up something . . . to keep something."

"They killed Dawes," Franklin said acidly.

"Yeah, I know. Guess it just wasn't his day." There was a long pause. "Why have we stopped? We ought to be going after them."

Franklin couldn't understand Marion's lack of compassion for Dawes. It was as though he had not existed.

"Dawes is dead, man, and all you can think about is Charlie."

Marion shrugged it off. "Who the fuck are you to come at me with this shit? You're the guy that wanted to kill Charlie. For your dead brother. That's all I've heard about from you. 'Kill. Kill.' Shit. You come here to kill; I come here to go home. To my wife, kids, my family. You understand the difference?"

Franklin didn't.

Marion went on. "I'm just some dumb-assed nigger from Mississippi that ain't never gonna have shit. That's been my life. I was drafted; I didn't want none of this shit. But there is a GI Bill. I can go to college, get an education, a good job, and buy a home." He waited, got no reaction, and went on. "Charlie ain't nothing but a step I got to cross along the path to where I'm going. He's in my way. You see, brother, the difference between you and me is real simple: You kill for the dead. I kill for the living."

Marion walked away to a position that gave a good view of the enemy on the far side of the river.

Franklin sat alone, listening to Marion's words echo in his brain. Remembering the look on the face of Dawes.

And for a while, the shooting stopped.

37

By late afternoon the fighting had settled to a stalemate. The concern for civilian casualties on both sides of the river had forced a lull in the conflict. Positions were taken up along the river by both sides, but except for sporadic sniping it was quiet.

Watching the dead Vietcong being counted and gathered made Franklin remember he had something to tend to. He walked to where the baby lay wrapped in the towel and dug a deep hole at the base of a palm tree with his entrenching tool. He placed the child in, covered it over, then patted down the dirt. He knelt, said a short prayer, then took the ET and his weapon and returned to the village.

There were more bodies to deal with, on both sides.

The dead enemy were searched, their weapons stockpiled, and the corpses stacked like cords of wood in a huge net attached to a helicopter. The chopper lifted off and flew away, to deposit the enemy dead in a government-maintained mass grave.

The back side of the village was cleared and used for medevac. Franklin tagged Dawes, stripped his gear from his body, and, with the help of another trooper, placed the remains inside and zipped the body bag. Dawes's remains were loaded up, along with two wounded troopers.

As he stood in swirling purple smoke, watching the Huey depart with his friend, Franklin felt nothing but emptiness.

He walked back to where a command post had been established and there found two nuns had just arrived to work in an orphanage on the other side of the river. He thought that's all the Americans needed, to bring carnage onto a home for victims of the war.

Then the rain began to fall; blinding sheets swept through the village, reducing visibility to zero. Franklin wondered if across the river the Vietcong were taking a break as well.

Franklin had set up a small aid station in a hut and was treating minor injuries suffered by the civilians. The medic from a platoon from A Company—who was now in the village—joined him and the two began treating minor cuts and abrasions. Two wounded Vietcong had been captured and were being interrogated. Information of the VC's position on the far side was critical.

It had grown dark when the most incredible event of the day occurred for Franklin. One of the nuns, plus an old mama-san and a young woman, showed up at the aid station.

The young woman, no more than eighteen, had gone into labor.

"You want me to what?" Franklin asked Chassion.

"You're the medic. You know how to deliver a baby, don't you?" There was a wry look on his face as though he were enjoying Franklin's dilemma.

"I don't know *anything* about delivering babies. Have the mama-san do it. She's probably done it a hundred times."

Chassion shook his head. "Do you know what a breech birth is, Sharps?"

Franklin knew. The baby was turned feet-down instead of head-down.

The expectant mother was doubled over; blood filled the crotch of her black pajamas.

"The baby's already coming out, goddammit," Chassion yelled. "You might not be much, but you're all she's got."

Franklin looked defeated. "Jesus, Plat. The father of the baby is probably across the river shooting at us right now."

"That's not the baby's fault," Chassion said. "I know this is tough, but you can do it."

"What if I screw up?"

"You won't. We're going to get Doc Benjamin on the horn. He'll talk you through it. Come on, let's get her in one of these hooches."

The woman was taken to a hut where two rough tables had been placed together. Poncho liners provided some comfort, but he doubted if she noticed the difference. She was crying, moaning, occasionally screaming.

He cut away her pajamas, and sure enough, there was a small pair of feet projecting from her vagina. First, he hooked her up to an intravenous solution and gave her an injection of morphine. The battalion surgeon was on the radio, instructing him what to do.

The woman was at full dilation. His hands trembled as he listened to Major Raphael Benjamin's instruction over the radio.

"You'll have to put your hand inside her and feel for the umbilical cord."

Franklin put his fingers inside; he could feel the baby's tiny shoulders and the cord wrapped around its neck.

"Tell him I feel the cord."

The word was passed, and the doctor replied, "Lift it over the baby's head."

The woman screamed and writhed. "Hold her, goddammit,"

Franklin shouted to Chassion. The burly sergeant clamped down on the woman's legs; another man pinned her shoulders to the table.

He tried again, felt the cord, then slid it over the child's head. "It's done. Now what?" Sweat was streaming from every pore in his body.

"Take the baby by the feet and pull it toward you. Try to help slip the shoulders and arms through the birth canal."

Jesus! This was like delivering a foal from a mare.

He began pulling the baby out. The mother was now going ballistic and nearly levitated just as the baby's shoulders became visible, but the two paratroopers pressed her back down.

Blood was flowing as he saw the head suddenly appear, and with a final, determined pull the baby popped out like a cork from a bottle of champagne.

Franklin fell back exhausted, releasing his grip on the child. It was a little girl, purple from the ordeal and covered with creamy and sticky film.

Chassion slapped him on the shoulder. "Way to go, kid. I knew you could do it."

There was a loud applause as the mama-san swept up the child and began cleaning her mouth and nostrils with a grimy towel.

Since the day began, he had seen the life of a friend come to a violent end, taken the life of other human beings, and brought a life into the world.

38

The rain continued to fall, turning the ground slick and deadly, especially for the soldiers who had to cross the open street. A young lieutenant, Harry "the Horse" Godwin, had his fill of the snipers as it turned dark. He was a former marine and a top athlete at Henderson State, and he took his best sharpshooters from A Company and positioned them to have a field of fire along the street and over the river to the Vietcong side. Then, stripped down like a fullback, he would charge across the opening to the other side, dodging and weaving as they tried to kill him. At the moment the enemy snipers fired, Godwin's sharpshooters would fire on the muzzle flashes. Time and again he raced across the street, until gradually the sniper fire stopped and both sides settled in for a long and nervous night.

The night was continually aglow from a combination of flare ships dropping their iridescent load from above, to the mortar squads firing illuminating rounds that aided in lighting up the night, to the individual soldiers shooting their handheld parachute flares into the darkness.

Despite the weather and the bridge being destroyed, the

troopers stood watch in case the VC sent a sapper squad or infantry probes across the river. And it still wasn't certain there weren't enemy hiding on the American side. It was that thought that had the nerve cages rattling the most during the night. The flares turned branches and pieces of rubble into human shapes. Each sound was enough to bring a weapon to bear.

Franklin rose from his bunk on the floor, grabbed his weapon, and left the aid hut and went outside to relieve himself. He stepped around the edge of the hut and had started to unbutton his fly when a sound deep and sinister snapped him to full alert. It was coming from the other side of the hut. He eased around the edge, but the darkness was too thick. Then, a flare popped overhead, and nearby there was movement, and a gnawing sound.

His eyes locked onto the creature. Ten feet away, a bamboo rat was holding a coconut in his front paws. The critter seemed the size of a bulldog and, rearing up on his hind legs, grew to an enormous proportion. Franklin had seen bodies the rats had devoured, even dismembered, dragging limbs off to feed on.

He was so scared, he couldn't pull the trigger. All he could do was backpedal, pissing his pants all the way to the inside of the hut. He broke down one of the tables, used the wood to build a small fire on the floor, and climbed on top of the smaller one. *Tonight I sleep off the ground.*

He lay there all night, listening, jerking up at every sound. He stayed on the table, except when it was his turn to pull guard duty with Marion.

The morning brought more disappointment. The weather had broken and a Huey was sent to check out the situation on the opposite side of the river. The sniper fire had stopped. There was no movement. Nothing.

Then a child—a boy—appeared on the bank. The nun was

summoned and given binoculars. She recognized the child. A sick feeling began filling everyone's guts.

The chopper didn't take any ground fire, and the scenario was starting to look all too familiar. In less than half an hour, the fear was confirmed. Somehow, Charlie had managed to slip out of the village during the night. There was no known figure on how many had been in the enclave on the other side of the river, and now they were gone. They had even managed to take their dead with them.

A patrol, under the cover of the Americans from their side of the river and the gunship in the sky above the village, crossed toward the debris from the bridge.

The children in the orphanage were safe. What the patrol discovered to be the answer lay in the small building used for the school.

Chassion stood seething at the blackboard, where a crude drawing of a helicopter was still scrawled on the slate.

"The little bastards used this as a classroom, Sarge," Marion said. "Look at all the shit." Human excrement was on the floor.

"The little fuckers kept us busy on the river while they planned their getaway," Chassion said.

Franklin studied the room, scanning the interior for any sign of how the Vietcong might have escaped. There was a fireplace in the wall, which seemed out of the ordinary. More important, there was nothing in the recess to suggest it was recently used for a fire. He took his bayonet and carefully scraped at the front edge. "Look at this, Sarge."

Chassion examined the fireplace for a moment, then ordered, "All of you . . . clear out. Get outside." He took a hand grenade and pulled the pin. There was an open window beside the fireplace; he threw one leg through the opening, then tossed the grenade into the recess.

Chassion rolled out of the window and raced to a tree. The explosion blew the back of the building apart, but not even the rubble could hide the hole that was revealed by the detonation.

The soldiers came back inside and saw how the Vietcong had eluded them. "A tunnel," Marion said angrily. He cleared away rubble with his hands, discovering a larger hole leading into the darkness below.

Chassion got on the radio and called the company commander. He explained the situation, then walked outside. The others followed, and he told them, "They're sending over a tunnel rat. He'll be here in a few minutes. Take a break and have a smoke." He looked at Franklin. "Come with me. Let's check out the orphanage."

The two moved cautiously across the street to a building where children could be seen through the structure. There was no door and no glass on the windows. Inside, nearly two dozen children sat on bamboo mats lined neatly along each side of the wall. It was heartbreaking.

"Poor little bastards," Franklin said.

"Yeah. Life's a bitch. They'll probably grow up to have to kill American soldiers." There was a hard glint in Chassion's eyes; he fidgeted at a grenade on his harness, and for a moment Franklin was scared of what the man might do. Then he said, "Check them out. Do what you can for them."

Franklin gave the children a quick examination. Except for being terrified from the noise and the fighting, none were injured. The nuns arrived a short time later and he went back to the school.

The "tunnel rat" was there, a short, wiry Mexican who looked no bigger than the kids. These were the men who had two primary attributes that allowed them to go into the tunnels and see what Charlie had beneath the ground: they were small and had ice water in their veins.

A rope was tied around his waist, and with a flashlight in one hand, a .45 pistol in the other, he was lowered, headfirst, into the tunnel.

The only way they could tell his progress was to watch the line play out. Gradually, it would move at different increments, mostly slow, sometimes in quick bursts of footage. Franklin helped on the rope and thought he could feel the "rat's" pulse beating from below into the palm of his hands, but knew the pulse was his own. If something happened, he might have to go down and bring him out.

When he thought of the bamboo rat, his skin crawled again; sweat beaded on his forehead, especially when there was a long run on the rope. Whatever was down there was known only to the "rat" and whoever might be lurking in the darkness.

He knew the design of the tunnel: sharp turns and angles, and probably deep, carved-out spaces serving as surgical rooms or barracks, often with shelves carved above the pathway to give a guard a small niche to hide and wait for the "rats."

The tension fell off the rope; it went momentarily slack, and a tug on the line followed. He would back out now, slowly inching his way in reverse to the light.

When the tunnel rat emerged, he was slick with sweat. He sat on the floor for a moment, untied the rope, and lit a cigarette. He didn't say a word for a long time. "It's empty, but lots of sign of activity. They left in a hurry. Blood trails lead toward the north. Then it gets slick and muddy."

"They came out near the bank of the river on the edge of the ville," Chassion said.

"Yeah," the rat replied. "Probably at the tree line to the north. Right under our noses."

Chassion reported to the command post and received orders to return to the other side of the river.

There was nothing but frustration on their faces as they crossed, to return to base camp with little to show for the effort.

PART 5

SABRE RANCH

39

The ringing of the telephone jerked Shania Sharps's attention from the television set, where she was watching a political speech by Arizona senator Barry Goldwater, giving his support for President Johnson's decision to commit more troops to Vietnam. The country was beginning to show strong signs of division over the war and now the government was fueling the flames by sending more soldiers, ships, and aircraft.

This is crazy, she thought.

The voice was familiar, that of Dr. Jessie Malone, a family practitioner in nearby Willcox. She had been nervous for several days, awaiting tests Malone had made the week before. When he finished giving her the report from a specialist in Phoenix, she cradled the receiver and walked onto the porch. The sun was setting and the sky clear, pristine, and clean, the faint image of the moon already visible overhead.

The world seemed to have gone insane. Vietnam. The Civil Rights Movement in the South. Barriers against Supreme Court–mandated desegregation of schools, restaurants, and public facilities. Social and economic bankruptcy in Negro communities throughout the country.

It is all so insane. She went back inside to get a shawl.

In her bedroom, for some unexplained reason, she found herself opening a cedar chest, where she thumbed through thick packets of old letters written by Samuel to his family and to her during his years overseas.

When her fingers touched one particular envelope, she smiled, feeling the love and history that lay within. The letter sent by Samuel to his parents on his first day upon arriving at Tuskegee.

The day they first met.

40

He arrived in Macon County, Alabama, on a hot afternoon to the sound of thunder. The sky was cloudless. He noticed a flash of sunlight streak across the horizon and a moment later watched an airplane appear overhead. Samuel pulled off the road as the airplane—it was an A-6—snapped onto its back, then rolled back to straight and level flight. He watched breathlessly; then the A-6 disappeared over a tree line. He took his map and confirmed that he was north of Tuskegee, close to Tuskegee Army Airfield.

He drove for twenty minutes until he came to what looked like a sentry booth. A Negro military policeman stepped out and saluted smartly.

"Can I help you, sir?"

"Is this the airfield?" Samuel stammered.

The MP smiled. "Yes, sir. This is Tuskegee Army Airfield."

"I'd like permission to come onto the field."

The MP straightened. "No, sir. Unless you have official business, the field is off-limits to civilian personnel."

Samuel looked beyond the MP and saw two airplanes circling in the distance.

"Anything else I can do for you, sir?" the MP asked with an obvious impatience.

Samuel shook his head, backed up, and drove toward Tuskegee. During the drive he made a promise aloud. "The next time I come back I will be on official business."

He couldn't get the roar of that A-6 out of his mind.

Since first telling his family he was going to Tuskegee Institute despite the railings of his grandmother and mother, Samuel had often asked himself, "Why was Tuskegee selected to be the army's training center for Negro pilots?" He knew the hatred that existed in the South. Why, then, did the military select a location in the Deep South? The Negro press claimed it was to guarantee the failure of the program; supporters insisted it was because Tuskegee was a shining example of the Negro's opportunity to succeed in the South.

The campus was smaller than he had imagined; buildings stood in neat rows, their red-brick structure gleaming in the sun. He parked his car and strolled along the campus, stopping at the statue memorializing Booker T. Washington, who had founded the institute in 1881. He stood for a moment staring at the statue, trying to imagine the strength and courage it took for the man to defy so many odds arrayed against him.

He found the administration building and saw a sign directing him toward Admissions. In a tiny office bulging with stuffed bookshelves, he walked up to a small man with wire-framed glasses perched on his nose, sitting at a desk.

"Can I help you, young man?" There was an amused smile on his face, making Samuel uncomfortable as he removed his Western hat.

"My name is Adrian Samuel Sharps. I've been accepted into the fall semester."

The man rose and extended his hand. "My name is Professor

LeBaron. I assist with admissions this time of year, but my primary position is professor of agriculture." He scanned a ledger in front of him. "I see you're majoring in agriculture. No doubt you'll take one of my classes."

Samuel nodded. "No doubt." He fumbled with his hat.

LeBaron knew what was going through his mind. "We need to get you enrolled and get you a class schedule figured out." He stopped and looked again at the ledger. "There is one problem—"

"Samuel," he interrupted. "People call me Samuel. What problem is there, Professor?"

LeBaron tapped the ledger. "In your initial application you didn't request dormitory facilities."

"Why is that a problem?"

"Limited facilities, Mr. Sharps. Now that the army has begun training young Colored men to become fighter pilots, our dormitories are overflowing."

Samuel looked dejected. "I never gave it a thought." He looked around, feeling foolish. "I guess I can find a place in town."

LeBaron laughed. "This is Alabama, young man, not Arizona. A young Colored man can't just go and 'find a place in town.'"

For the first time Samuel began wishing he had gone to the University of Southern California.

But LeBaron wasn't a man to let opportunity slip through his fingers. "May I make a suggestion?"

"I'd be grateful."

"I have a place outside of town that I'm preparing for young men in your situation. There're four rooms, two beds to a room. It's clean and away from folks in town. I have one more vacancy. If you don't mind living in the country."

Samuel beamed. "Not at all. I grew up on a ranch in Arizona. I know all about living in the country."

"Excellent. I think you'll like the accommodations. You'll

receive breakfast and supper seven days a week as part of your rent. My daughter will do the cooking, but you'll have to share household chores with your roommates."

"That sounds fine with me, Professor."

They worked together on determining what classes he would need: biology, English, mathematics, and others, until Samuel said, "I'd like to take ROTC."

LeBaron looked at him with surprise. "You want to become an army officer?"

"No, sir, I want to become an army aviator. That's why I chose Tuskegee Institute. I can do both while going to college."

LeBaron sat back. "Do you have a pilot's license?"

"Not yet, but I intend to take primary flight instruction from a man named Charles Anderson." He handed LeBaron the letter he had received from Sparks Hamilton. "I set aside enough money for the training."

LeBaron shook his head gravely. "There's thousands of young Colored men trying to get into the flight program. Most have been rejected for one reason or other. Most all are college graduates and have pilot licenses."

"I think that will change when we get into the war, sir. I want to be ready to do my part."

"You think there will be a war, Mr. Sharps?"

"I do. Our country can't stay out of it much longer."

LeBaron said nothing more. He filled in the last blank with the words: "Reserve Officer Training Corps."

LeBaron handed him the form. "Classes start on Monday," he said, and wrote down the directions to his home. As Samuel left, LeBaron reflected that he had filled his boardinghouse with eight tenants in the last two days. Each one was an agriculture student, all were strong and had worked on farms, and now the last one was a rancher.

Only two were pursuing the ridiculous notion of becoming army aviators.

. . .

Samuel followed the directions to the house, only a few miles from the institute. He parked in front where two other automobiles sat, both with out-of-state license plates. He took his suitcases and had started up the steps when he heard the sound of voices near the side of the house. Two men in their early twenties appeared wearing work clothes. Samuel stood on the porch, saying nothing as they saw him.

"Good afternoon," said one of the men. He was tall and lanky and had a thick mustache. The other nodded, a heavyset man with a shaved head.

"I'm Willis Reeves," the tall man said, offering his hand. "Are you a new tenant?"

"Yes. My name is Samuel Sharps." He extended his hand. "Professor LeBaron sent me here. I'll be bunking with you fellows."

"Daniel Cook," the heavy man said as he shook Samuel's hand. "Looks like you and I'll be sharing a room." Without asking, he took one of Samuel's suitcases and went into the house, with Samuel and Reeves following.

The smell of fresh paint and fried chicken greeted Samuel inside the front room of the boardinghouse. He looked around, pleased with what he saw. There was a parlor, and a hall that led to the bedroom. He put his suitcases beside an empty bed and looked around. He was about to say something when he glanced through the window and saw a woman walking through the backyard carrying a chicken, freshly beheaded and neatly plucked.

"Does she live here?" Samuel said.

Reeves laughed. "You'd think she owns the place. Her father is Professor LeBaron. Her name is Shania."

Samuel whispered her name to himself. She was the most beautiful woman he had seen.

"We better get back to work," Cook said.

Samuel turned to them. "Do you need some help?"

Both smiled at him. "We're digging a hole for the outhouse. You sure you want to help?"

"I've dug plenty of outhouse pits in my time."

The two left while Samuel put on his work jeans and boots. When he was dressed he went through the kitchen and saw the young woman standing at the sink. She looked up from the chicken she was preparing. "I hope you like chicken. Poppa called and said we had a new tenant for supper. He said you were a big man and I should prepare another chicken. You look like you could eat a whole fryer by yourself."

Samuel felt his stomach groan; he had eaten little since yesterday morning.

"I could eat a horse."

Shania laughed. "I hope chicken will do."

He took off his hat. "I'm Samuel Sharps."

She wiped her hands on a cloth and shook his hand. "I'm Shania LeBaron. Supper is at six. I hope Poppa told you that he and I take our meals here. It's easier than cooking here and at our home."

"That makes sense." He stared at her for a long moment, still holding her hand. At last, he released his grip and clamped his hat on his head. "I better go help the fellows with the digging."

He found Reeves and Cook digging the trench; a small wooden house stood nearby, the white paint still drying in the heat. A zinc-lined vat lay on the ground. That would serve as the septic tank, preventing contamination of the ground.

The three worked together. Cook dug with a pick while Reeves shoveled the dirt into a wheelbarrow, and Samuel hauled the dirt to a nearby mound. After two hours of digging and shaping, the three hefted the zinc liner into the trench. Finally, the small outhouse was placed over the hole and the three stood looking at the structure with wonderment.

Cook said, "I've never used outdoor facilities before. We had indoor toilets on our farm back in Virginia."

Reeves laughed. "I grew up on a tobacco farm in Kentucky. All we had was privies. You'll get use to the smell. It's the winter that makes you miserable."

"I wouldn't mind the cold right now," Samuel said, wiping the sweat from his face. "Is the humidity always this bad?"

Reeves nodded. "It can even get worse. But in the winter it'll sink into your bones and freeze you half to death."

So many new things, thought Samuel.

"You boys done a good job."

Samuel looked up to see a young man in an army uniform. His hat was cocked to the side and he seemed to swagger as he stepped off the porch. A patch on his left shoulder was that worn by ROTC. He had light skin for a Negro, a thin mustache, and stood as tall as Samuel. "Afternoon, gents. I'm Thomas Guillard, your new roommate." He shook hands with the three and looked around the place. "Reminds me of home back in South Dakota."

"South Dakota?" Reeves said. "I didn't know there were any Negroes in South Dakota."

"Lot of Coloreds have lived up there over the last seventy years. My granddaddy served there in the army."

Samuel looked at him curiously. "Was your grandfather in the cavalry?"

"The Ninth Cavalry. Fought at Milk River along with the Seventh Cavalry. That was the last big battle of the Indian campaigns. There weren't any more threats from Indians, so when he retired he married a Sioux woman, bought a piece of land near Belle Fourche, and started farming."

Samuel felt a bond with this young man. "My grandfather retired a sergeant major with the Tenth. Our family lives in Arizona and raises cattle." He looked at Guillard's uniform. "You're in ROTC."

Guillard grinned. "Just picked up my uniform this afternoon." He straightened in military fashion. "How do I look?"

"Great. You look like the grandson of a soldier," Samuel said.

They heard Shania's voice. "Better wash up, fellows. Supper will be ready in thirty minutes."

The diggers washed while the soldier inspected the outhouse.

The remaining roommates arrived just before supper was served. During the meal LeBaron suggested, "Why don't you gentlemen tell us a little about yourselves?" He looked at one of the new arrivals.

"I'm Delbert Hughes, from Pennsylvania. I'm an agriculture major."

They listened as the others introduced themselves. Austin Braxton from Tennessee, Fillmore Hall from Indiana, and Terrence Spann from Illinois. All raised on the farm.

LeBaron looked at Guillard. "What about you, Thomas?"

Guillard shrugged. "I grew up on a wheat farm in South Dakota. My grandfather was Colored, my grandmother a halfbreed Sioux. Her father was a white man." He could see they were curious, for his complexion was almost too light for a Negro. Then he chuckled, adding, "My mother is a white woman. That's why I'm not dark-skinned."

The forks stopped in midair.

"Your mother is white?" asked Reeves.

"White as winter snow."

Cook shook his head. "Down here a white woman seen with a Colored man would be jailed."

"Or lynched," Braxton added.

"Wasn't it difficult growing up with a white mother and Colored father?" Samuel asked.

Guillard shook his head. "Folks in South Dakota aren't prejudiced against Coloreds. Just Indians. They hate them so much they don't have any spare hate or time to use it on Coloreds. We get along just fine."

LeBaron asked Samuel, "What about your family, Mr. Sharps? Are they still living?"

"Yes, sir. At least my mother, father, and grandmother. She's getting old, but she's still spry." Then he told them about his family and the part the Sharps family played in settling the Western frontier. Buffalo Bill Cody. The Rough Riders. His father and uncle in the Great War. He even told them about him beating a tank on a mule.

"Sounds like you gentlemen have already had interesting lives," LeBaron said.

"Wait until classes begin," Shania said. "Life will become very boring."

That night Samuel sat on the front porch oiling his Sharps rifle. He sat looking at the moon, rubbing the stock and barrel, summarizing the day's events. Afterward he wrote a letter to his family, telling them about the trip from Arizona. The best part was the last half of the letter telling them about his first day in Tuskegee: He had seen an army airplane, enrolled at the institute, signed up for ROTC, helped his new roommates dig a hole for an outhouse, made new friends, and eaten dinner with a cultured man and his beautiful daughter.

"Except for the digging and the humidity, I consider my first day at Tuskegee as being perfect," he wrote at the end.

41

Such a beautiful day, Shania thought, when she returned to the front porch. Too beautiful to be ruined by tragic news. She sat there for a long time until the darkness and the slight desert chill drove her inside, again to the telephone.

She dialed a number and waited until she heard her son's voice. "Kevin. Hi, baby; it's Mom."

The reply of Kevin's voice gave her sudden comfort.

An hour later, in his dormitory at Berkeley, Kevin Sharps suddenly felt weak as he hung up the telephone. At nineteen, he was shorter than his brothers, and his skin darker, which he figured was inherited from a branch of his mother's genetic tree.

He sat on the edge of his bed and stared at the wall for what seemed an interminable time until his roommate walked through the door carrying a placard that read: STOP THE WAR!

Desmond Sedgwick, a WASP raised in the San Fernando Valley of Southern California, was a scrawny kid with long, stringy hair to his shoulders and a scraggly, reddish beard. But he was a friend and a fellow member of the local antiwar group raising hell on campus in protest of the war. He propped the sign against his study desk. "What's happening, brother?"

"I'm going to have to go home, Sedge."

Sedgwick detected alarm in his voice. "Problem?"

Kevin's gaze was fixed on the protest sign.

"Not your brother or old man, is it? Nothing's happened to them, has it?"

"They're fine. I guess." He walked to his desk and picked up a letter. The envelope had been made from the sides of a box of C-rations held together by strips of adhesive tape. In the corner was the word FREE where a stamp would normally be placed. Soldiers in Vietnam were allowed free mail service to the United States. He chuckled at the thought of the government's generosity and removed the letter, written in pen on toilet paper that he figured accompanied the C-ration unit, and read the words from his brother again.

When finished he contacted the international operator. It was time to get a message through to his father.

An hour later he had finally reached Saigon Headquarters, Military Advisory Command Vietnam. His father wasn't there, so he left a message to contact him. He made certain the secretary understood the message was marked: URGENT!

Then he contacted the American Red Cross in Oakland and spoke with the night receptionist.

When finished sending a message to his brother in Vietnam, he sat on the bed and cried.

42

*   *   *

General Sharps was furious when he came out of the MACV briefing. *More American troops to be deployed to South Vietnam?* He couldn't believe the rush to decision-making that was going on at the higher echelons. He believed the first step should be to shut down the Ho Chi Minh Trail and train the Army of the Republic of Vietnam to defend itself properly. Continual buildup would create more pressure on the country and delay that training. Added pressure would undoubtedly come from the deployment of more troops from North Vietnam. It was becoming Korea all over again.

When he arrived at his office there was a message waiting for him.

PLEASE CONTACT DR. JESSIE MALONE AS SOON AS POSSIBLE. VERY URGENT. CALL ANY TIME NIGHT OR DAY.
LOVE, KEVIN

It took nearly an hour to get through, and the time difference didn't help. Finally, he heard the sleepy voice of Dr. Malone answer from Arizona.

"Jess, this is Samuel Sharps. What's up?"

Malone's voice was fraught with concern. "Samuel, I assume you've heard from Shania?"

"No, I was contacted by Kevin. He said it was urgent that I contact you."

"I'm glad you did. There's something I need to discuss with you."

"Is it about my family?"

"It's about Shania."

Sharps sat down and listened. The physician spoke for nearly fifteen minutes without interruption. When Malone finished, the general returned the telephone to the cradle, went to the liquor cabinet and uncapped a bottle of Jack Daniel's, poured three fingers from it and downed it quickly, then poured another.

He sat for a long while sipping the whiskey. He wanted to get drunk, but he had to stay sober. At least until he made the call he dreaded to make.

Finally, he contacted the MACV communications center and ordered, "Patch me through to the First Brigade commander of the One-O-First Airborne. Colonel James Timothy."

It took some doing, but he finally reached the brigade commander.

"Colonel Timothy, this is General Sharps at MACV. I need a personal favor. . . ."

When he hung up the telephone a few minutes later, he realized that not only was his wife's life in jeopardy in Arizona, but also his son's life was in jeopardy in South Vietnam.

43

*   *   *

Franklin was stretched out in his makeshift bed in his bunker at the Screaming Eagles base camp near Qui Nhon. Music played softly, and the rain had stopped, releasing the swarms of malaria-carrying mosquitoes that plagued the camp. His muscles still ached from the long recce, scratches had turned into infected pustules on his face, and his neck still burned from leech bites. What bothered him most were his feet. His soles were wrinkled and cracked, toenails soft from constant immersion in mud and water, and each toe throbbed as he dried them. His ankles were swollen, too, and felt numb.

But his gear was STRAC ("Skilled, Tough, Ready, Around the Clock" or "Shit The Russians Are Coming") clean, his LC-1 harness scrubbed and dried out, jungle boots rinsed and ready, and most important his weapons were spotless and oiled.

He had time to think. Mostly he thought about the last mission. Big-time disappointment. Not much to show for the effort, considering Dawes was dead. The enemy body count was not that high but they did shut down a training facility, at least for the time being. He figured if every search-and-destroy mission achieved that level of success, the war would be over somewhere near the turn of the century.

"Specialist Sharps," a voice called from the entrance.

Franklin looked up to see platoon leader Lieutenant James Gardner.

Franklin snapped to attention and saluted. "Above the Rest, sir!"

"Get your gear and turn it in to Sergeant Hughes. Then report to the command post," Gardner said.

"But, sir, I—"

"Just do as you're ordered, Specialist Sharps." Gardner's voice suddenly took on a gentler tone. "There's someone here from Saigon to see you."

"Yes, sir." He knew his father had finally come to visit.

Franklin reported to Hughes, carrying his M-16, .45 automatic pistol, machete, six hand grenades, four white phosphorus (Willie Peter) grenades, and a twelve-gauge sawed-off pump shotgun, along with his medical aid kit.

Franklin asked Hughes, "Is something wrong, Sergeant?"

Hughes's mouth tightened. "Go on to the CP, son. You'll find out what's going on."

He reported to the CP, a bunker made of railroad ties and sandbags, guarded by machine-gun emplacements. The moment he entered he knew something was wrong. Standing beside his company commander, Captain George Shevlin, was an air force officer.

The grim look on First Sergeant Leo B. Smith's face, coupled with Major Leif Svenson's drooped shoulders and sad face, was all Franklin needed to know. "Is it my father?"

Svenson stepped forward. "I'm Major Leif Svenson. I'm your father's aide at MACV. Come on, son. You're going with me to Saigon."

"Is my father dead?"

The major shook his head. "No. It's your mother. She's very

ill and she's requested the Red Cross to have you and your
father sent home on emergency leave."

Franklin stared at him a moment, anger building. "So he sent
you? Why didn't *he* come?"

The place fell quiet as Svenson's eyes narrowed and he leaned
into Franklin's face. "How you feel about your father doesn't
mean a fiddler's flying fuck to me, soldier. Hell, without your
father's rank and privileges you wouldn't even *see* your mother
until after it's too late. So, I suggest you tighten down that
smart-ass mouth of yours and follow me to the chopper or I'll
have you arrested for insubordination!"

Franklin straightened, his eyes locked to the front. "Yes, sir!"

"Move it out, soldier!"

Franklin stepped smartly toward the chopper, his face burning with anger.

44

General Sharps heard his name called over the public-address speaker in the VIP lounge at Ton Son Nhut Air Base, picked up his service hat and briefcase, and threaded his way through the throng of American military personnel in the transient section. He was amazed at how young they looked, mostly kids of eighteen a year ago, now older in experience but still young, though haggard and gaunt in expression with empty eyes that reflected the "tour of horror," as so many referred to a year in the Vietnamese bush.

He was tired but felt a rush of excitement as he stepped from the air-conditioned building into the hot June sun, where the tarmac seemed to boil beneath his feet. In the distance sat a Boeing 707, where beautiful young stewardesses waited at the top of the steps to welcome each passenger aboard.

In the first-class section, he found his seat near the window and opened his briefcase and removed the message sent by Kevin. Odd, he thought, how urgent messages usually bring tragic news from the war zone to home; it seemed out of the natural order of things for it to be in reverse.

He returned Kevin's note to his briefcase as a colonel sat

down beside him. His uniform still smelled new. *Fresh from the bush?* Sharps wondered. He noted the ribbons covering the man's blouse were brightly colored, his combat infantryman badge and parachute wings appeared to have been minted that morning.

Soon enlisted personnel began to board, most wearing khaki's, some still in their jungle fatigues, having only had hours to get from the battlefield to the airport. They could change later, Sharps supposed. Didn't want to miss the bird taking them back to the *world*!

They were of all sizes, shapes, and colors, as different as people could get with the exception of one common denominator: They were going home.

Their faces reflected the emotions of the moment, most of them trying to laugh or smile, others lost in thought, moving past him in slow, funereal fashion, their eyes making momentary contact with his, then turning away quickly, or avoiding him altogether. He knew it was his rank. Most of them probably figured he didn't deserve such a comfortable seat in first class. Why not them? They had suffered the most. He could see their contempt.

Then he saw the soldier he had waited for and stiffened as the face clarified with that special look of the lost returning from war. The young soldier moved aimlessly a few feet, stopping, then continuing down the aisle.

When he stopped next to the general's row, Sharps wanted to reach out and touch his hand, but the soldier said nothing, and his straight-ahead stare signaled Franklin's refusal to give his father the slightest notice.

The captain seated beside Franklin sat up quickly as the general leaned over. "You mind exchanging seats with me in first class? I'd like to ride back to the States next to my son."

The captain nodded, then looked at the soldier sitting beside

him, who had already fallen asleep. "My pleasure, General."
He rose and with briefcase in hand walked forward as Sharps
stowed his briefcase, coat, and hat in the overhead luggage com-
partment, then paused to remove a blanket. He leaned over his
seat and spread the blanket over Franklin.

"What the fuck!" Franklin exploded from sleep, throwing his
arms out as though fending off an unexpected attack.

For a moment Samuel saw fear etched on his face. "Easy,
Son, easy."

Surprise replaced Franklin's look of momentary fear. He
studied his father for a moment, then huddled beneath the blanket as though it were a shield.

"Good morning, sir."

Sharps couldn't hide the indignation he felt at so cold a greet-
ing. " 'Good morning, sir.' Is that any way to greet your old
man after all this time?" He extended his hand, which Franklin
shook with obvious reluctance.

"Pop, how you doing?"

"You're looking good, Franklin. The bush seems to have
toughened you up."

Franklin turned and stared through the window. On the tarmac beneath the wing, a military policeman patrolled with a
German shepherd. For a moment he thought of the Kit Carson
and his dog and wondered if the Kit was home with his family.
If he had a family. If he had a new dog.

"Yeah," Franklin said to his father's image reflecting off the
window, "the bush toughened me up. Amazing what a little
time in hell can do for a person."

The air was thick enough to cut with a bayonet. Sharps put
his hand on his son's arm. "How have you been, Son?"

Silence.

"Talk to me, Franklin. Let's not fly home treating each other
as strangers."

"We are strangers, Pop. Have been most of my life."

"You've changed."

Franklin looked at him incredulously. "What did you expect? One of the Hardy Boys? I've been killing people and living in crap. Yeah. I've changed. Or maybe you've changed—forgotten what combat does to men."

The general's face saddened. "I haven't forgotten. Believe me, I haven't forgotten."

That said, he straightened, tired of his son's belligerence. "What I expect is for you to display some respect. If not as a son, then as a soldier."

Franklin raised his left hand and mock-saluted his father. "Yes, sir . . . General Sharps, sir."

In the seat across the aisle, a lanky white Marine sergeant major had been observing the younger enlisted man's disrespect to the general. He leaned across the aisle. "Is there a problem, sir?"

Sharps was embarrassed. "No, Sergeant Major, just a family discussion."

Reluctantly, the Marine leaned back in his seat, but not before giving Franklin a scathing look.

Silence followed for what seemed an interminable time. Finally Sharps said, "I'm sorry about your mother, Franklin."

Franklin pulled the blanket over his shoulders. Since his father had sat down, he had barely looked him in the eye. Was it anger? Hatred? He wasn't sure. Yet now there was something to discuss. His father had answers he needed. He lit a cigarette. "What's the situation?"

The general pointed to the overhead NO SMOKING sign. "When did you start smoking?"

Franklin butted out the cigarette. "After my first combat patrol."

"You know it's very bad for your health."

"So are combat patrols. Look, Pop, cease fire for a few minutes. What can you tell me about Mom?"

"I called home last night, spoke with Doc Malone, then called Kevin. Later, I called your mother."

"And?"

"She is dying of brain cancer."

Franklin sank back in his seat. "I knew there was something wrong. Especially in her voice on the tapes. She never mentioned anything about her health."

"I'm sorry I couldn't come up to the highlands and bring you here personally. I had to arrange matters for our trip to the States. That's why I sent Major Svenson."

"Yes, sir," Franklin said. "But there's something I need you to explain."

"What is that?"

"Why are you here? Why are you going back after all these years? You've only been back once in the past five years. When Adrian was buried."

Sharps's tough veneer seemed suddenly fragile. "She's still my wife, the mother of my children." He sighed "She's dying. I have the right to be there. To see her one last time. To be with you and Kevin."

"To ask her forgiveness? Or to soothe your conscience? After what you did to her? Bullshit! She won't forgive you. Kevin won't forgive you. And I sure as hell won't."

"I regret what happened, Franklin. It was a terrible, shameful mistake. Men make mistakes. You'll learn that as you get older."

He could hear his father's words, but the voice sounded different. A voice laccd with pain.

"She chose to go back to Arizona and take you and Kevin with her. She said she wanted a home, not a military base to live on. I had my career. Whether you believe this or not, your mother understood. She recognized I had my duty."

"Duty?"

Sharps pointed to the two rows of ribbons on his son's army

blouse. "Yes, duty. I'd say you know something about it."

"I'm twenty years old. I've been in combat and seen more shit that I ever imagined possible. And there's more to come when I come back. That's not duty. That's a fucking waste of youth."

At that moment the stewardess's voice came over the intercom as the Boeing began taxiing to the runway. "Welcome aboard Flight Nine-Nine-Nine. Please fasten your seat belts and prepare for immediate departure from the Republic of South Vietnam to the United States of America. You're going home, guys!"

At that moment, the inside of the Boeing shook as the applause and shouts erupted.

Several hours later, Franklin looked through the window and saw that it would grow light soon, as the Boeing flew toward the sun. It was dark in the cabin, but not quiet. The voices of men happy to be alive spoke in low laughter; music purred softly from a hundred transistor radios. They had survived. What waited was not completely certain, but it was better than the uncertainty they had left behind.

He even felt a certain admiration for his father, whom he had worshiped until the terrible day his betrayal to his family became known. How could he do that? How could he rip the hearts out of his wife and children?

He rested his head on his pillow and stared through the window at the stars, at the bright moon, then closed his eyes and fell to sleep.

45

* * *

Franklin found himself in the water, the night as black as tar, except for the occasional flare lighting the sky, drifting slowly to the rice paddy. He was alone, separated from the others, trying not to make any noise. He carried a baby in each arm; they slept, though their bodies trembled from the coldness of the water. He had forgotten what cold water felt like. How it tingled the skin, sank into the bone, and sent a rippling charge of exhilaration through his body.

He was lost but could hear voices. The words were in English, so he knew he was heading in the right direction.

A thick mist had formed on the water's surface; rich and heavy, unlike any fog he had ever seen. He tried to be quiet, but that was not possible. The weight of the two babies was becoming a burden and he began to stumble forward, splashing, nearly falling, as the muddy bottom pulled at his feet.

One of the babies began crying, and there was gunfire coming at him, tracers leaving their red signatures only inches from his body.

He turned, as though to shield the children, but meat and bone could not prevent a bullet from harming them. Another flare and one of the babies had been struck. The sky became bright and he could see the child's mouth open, as though yawning.

The baby . . . a bamboo rat! Teeth like daggers, mouth seeping blood. The monster had bitten him in the chest. His left nipple was gone. It sank its teeth into his neck, its feet thrashing, clawing at the other baby.

Argonne! The baby in his other arm, her face shredded by the razor claws of a beast that was growing by the second, becoming stronger with each slash and tear at his and Argonne's flesh.

He tried to rid himself of the creature, to fling it away, but now it was too big. With a violent swing of one of its front legs, it ripped open the belly of . . . the baby . . . Argonne. . . .

Sharps jerked awake as a stewardess leaned across to Franklin, who was thrashing and screaming, still locked in the throes of the nightmare. He reached up and turned on the overhead light. "Franklin, wake up, Son. Wake up. You're safe."

Franklin began to come around, mumbling like an incoherent child lost in a dark place. Gradually, his voice trailed off and he fell asleep again.

General Sharps sat back in his seat and whispered to the stewardess, "It's over."

46

* * *

The 707 landed at Travis Air Force Base, California, where the servicemen were processed through Customs and transported to local bus and train stations and to the airport in San Francisco. It was at the airport that Franklin received his first taste of the welcome antiwar demonstrators had for servicemen returning from the war.

Standing behind police barricades, demonstrators carried antiwar placards, shouted obscenities, and jeered at the men who only a few days before had been risking their lives for flag and country in Vietnam.

Franklin carried his duffel bag on his shoulder, trying to ignore the throng, but felt his blood boiling as he entered the terminal.

A fat young woman in a garish muumuu broke past a policeman and swung a placard, hitting Franklin in the back. "Welcome home, hero. How many kids did you kill?" she shouted.

Franklin's arm shot out, as with a life of its own, and his hand smacked her loudly on her face. The placard fell from her hand, and she seemed to dance lightly above the ground, her arms flailing to keep her balance.

"You need a bath, you filthy bitch," Franklin said.

The crowd had grown quiet. A voice shouted, "The motherfucker's crazy!"

Franklin shoved his face close to the woman's. "What's the matter, you ugly bitch? Fly too close to the flame?"

She stared at him, paralyzed with fear. One side of her face bore a scarlet mark. More shouts followed from the crowd, who were stirring from their shock. Franklin ignored them but from the corner of his eye saw a policeman advancing toward him. The woman stumbled backward, then ran drunkenly toward the crowd of demonstrators as the general dragged Franklin toward the entrance, ignoring the shouts of the demonstrators. Just as they reached the open door, Franklin felt something hit his back. He smelled the putrid odor, looked at the sidewalk, and saw the sack of excrement lying at his feet.

They walked into the terminal and Franklin went directly to the men's room, where he stripped off his uniform, his Corcoran jump boots and black beret, and threw the entire ensemble into the garbage can. After changing into his only set of civilian clothes—Western shirt, jeans, and cowboy boots—he tossed the duffel in the trash barrel and walked back into the terminal concourse, where he found his father sitting at a table in the bar.

The general was trembling. "You OK, Son?"

Franklin shrugged. "Yeah. The flower bitch caught me off-guard. I should have knocked her fucking head off."

"You can't let those people get to you so easy," the general said. "Hell, boy . . . they're everywhere. What are you going to do? Attack the whole peace movement? You've got to learn to ignore them."

Franklin's fist crashed onto the table. "Christ! Seventy-two hours ago I was in the bush, where all I had to worry about was staying alive. Since then I've been told my mother was dying, reunited with a father I haven't seen in years, flown halfway around the world, and spit on by some scuzzy flower bitch who smelled like my old jungle boots. Now, you say I should lighten up?"

The waitress appeared, pad in hand. "What would you gentlemen like to drink?" She studied Franklin warily.

General Sharps ordered a Rob Roy.

She looked at Franklin.

"I'll take Johnnie Walker Red—a double with water back," he said.

"May I see some identification, please?" she said.

"Identification? You must be kidding me."

"Miss?" Sharps said. "He's just returned from Vietnam."

She shook her head. "The law requires any patron who purchases alcoholic beverages in the state of California must be twenty-one years of age. That's the law. Please show me your identification if you wish to be served alcohol."

Franklin was seething. He looked at his father. "Old enough to die for my country, but not old enough to buy a Johnnie Red. Welcome back to the real world."

He walked out of the bar and did not look back to witness his father giving the woman a withering lecture on giving a soldier a break.

47

The pair arrived in Phoenix late that night, their conversation still trapped in the void created by the many wedges that had driven them apart over the years. Franklin realized that had it not been for their common mission—his mother—they would have journeyed together as strangers. This didn't bother him since he was not there to be a benevolent, grateful son. He wanted nothing to do with his father, saw him as just another general, a lifer, not a father who had been there for his family. He had been there mostly in memory, rarely in actuality, arriving for Christmas or an occasional birthday. Now, they were both soldiers, and he was reminded of a time when he was in a park and stood at the feet of a statue of a great general mounted on a charging horse. That's how he viewed his father: the horseback general, sabre thrust forward, dashing toward glory. He saw himself and the other "grunts" as the horse; metaphorically considering himself one of the "stone ponies," the soldiers who took the generals to glory on their backs.

That, as much as anything, angered him. Granted, his father had served his country bravely. But what about his family? On that point, he had never shown up for roll call.

. . .

Dr. Jessie Malone was waiting for them at the arrival gate, wearing a somber face, looking disheveled and tired from the drive from Willcox; he also seemed like the Grim Reaper, bearing the burden of news that no one wanted to hear but must be shared.

"Franklin, how are you?" He offered his hand to the general, then wiped his handkerchief at his sweating brow. Overweight and nearly bald, he had known the Sharps family for as long as he could remember. His father had treated the family before he was born.

"How long has it been?" General Sharps said. He held the handshake as if calculating the time.

"Adrian's funeral," Franklin said.

"Of course . . . Adrian's funeral. Seems like ages," Malone said. "We seem to be drawn together by tragedy."

"Too often the case, Jessie. Too often."

Franklin, impatient for the amenities to end, asked, "Dr. Malone, how is my mother?"

The physician motioned toward the BAGGAGE sign. "Let's get your luggage. I'll explain everything on the way to Sabre Ranch."

The drive began with Dr. Malone shifting constantly in the driver's seat of his station wagon. The general sat silently beside him while Franklin sat in the back, aching for answers. Once out of Phoenix, Sharps rolled down the window and said, "My God, smell that sweet desert air."

"Hell, Samuel," Malone said, "that's Fillmont's stockyard. You have been gone for a long while."

The general pointed toward the stockyard, its outline marked by fluorescent lights burning in the rich desert darkness. "My father once did business with the Fillmonts during the Second

World War, along with Joaquin Samorran, that Mexican bandit from Hermosillo. What a pair they made. My grandmother was convinced Pop had climbed in bed with the devil."

"Yes, I remember his reputation," Malone added, "Samorran and your father made a lot of money selling beef to the government during that war."

The use of the term "that war" struck Franklin as curious. As though there had been so many, each no longer had its own identity; rather, they were mustered together like apples in a barrel.

"What about my mother, Dr. Malone?"

He saw Malone's eyes in the rearview mirror. It was obvious it was a subject he preferred to ignore. "She has a geoplastoma, Franklin."

"What is that?"

"It's a form of cancer; a brain tumor, to be precise."

"Is it operable?" Samuel asked.

Malone shook his head and again looked at Franklin through the rearview mirror, then to the general. "No. She and I both agreed it would be best for her to spend the rest of her days as normally as possible." He paused and wiped his handkerchief at his forehead. The heat spilling in from the desert was almost unbearable. "She's going to die. That's why I requested the Red Cross bring you both home."

Samuel looked toward the darkened desert flashing by the station wagon. "How long . . ." His voice trailed off.

"No way to know for certain," Malone said. "Two days . . . two weeks . . . two months. Definitely no longer than two months. I have prescribed pain medication, but that's only to keep her comfortable. She's lucid but there are times when she simply cannot get out of bed."

"Will it be quick?" Franklin asked.

"Quick, when it finally comes. She has all her faculties, but she'll sometimes appear confused. She won't wither, but . . ." He appeared to be searching for the right words.

"But what?" Franklin said.

Malone glanced to Franklin through the mirror, and spoke to both of them. "She must not be excited. I can't emphasize this point strongly enough. I know you have a tenuous relationship with your sons. That has to be put aside. If she gets psychologically distressed it could kill her like a bullet." The discomfort in the station wagon was palpable. "I know you two have had a tough time in Vietnam, especially you, Franklin. I was opposed to her requesting that both of you return at the same time. I told her it might be disastrous. But she was insistent. She said she had to have her family together . . . one more time. She said there was something important she had to accomplish. That you both had to be there. You know Shania. She's a fighter . . . and a charmer. He looked over pointedly at the general. "I'll hold you personally responsible at the first sign of conflict between you and your sons."

"She'll not be distressed. I give you my word." Sharps turned to Franklin and offered his hand. "Despite what you might think, my word is good."

Franklin ignored the hand. "Yes, sir," he said.

The rest of the trip was spent in silence.

48

It was nearly midnight when the station wagon eased through the narrow gate at the family ranch outside Bonita. On the arch above the metal cattle guard at the entrance, three cavalry sabres—joined at the fulcrum—hung beneath a sign that read: SABRE RANCH.

Franklin felt a sudden rush of relief as he stared at the sabres, gleaming in the brilliant moonlight as though branded against the stars. "Kevin put a nice spit shine on the sabres."

General Sharps nodded approvingly. "They never looked better."

The wagon eased through the gate and made the short drive to the house. Flooded in the headlights, Kevin stood waiting for them.

Franklin bolted out the door and bounded onto the porch into the waiting embrace of his brother.

"God, it's good to see you, S-Three." That was one of the nicknames the general had given his sons. "S" for Sharps and a number designating order of birth.

"Welcome home, Franklin." He stood at arm's length and studied his brother. "Man, you look great."

"See what a healthy diet and plenty of exercise will do for you! Makes for a—"

Kevin joined in the chorus. "Lean . . . mean . . . fighting machine!"

At that moment the general stepped onto the porch. Kevin eyed him warily. "Hello, Pop. Welcome back to Sabre Ranch."

Sharps was nearly speechless as Kevin suddenly embraced him. Taking a moment to recover, he returned the vigorous embrace. "Hello, S-Three. How's my young man?"

"Just fine, Pop." Kevin's eyes drifted to Franklin, motioning him to join the embrace. Doc Malone stood on the front step, his head motioning Franklin toward the pair. Franklin shook his head and turned toward the door and saw an image in the bedroom window.

Shania Sharps stood there, wearing her housecoat, watching the reunion. Despite the darkness, Franklin could see the sadness in his mother's eyes. As he crossed the threshold into the house, he heard Doc Malone call aloud, "Good night, fellows. Tell Shania I'll stop by tomorrow. And by the way, welcome home."

Franklin stepped inside and paused momentarily in front of the fireplace. Above the mantel, on wooden pegs embedded in the wall, hung the Sharps rifle carried by his great-grandfather.

He knocked lightly at the half-opened door and heard his mother say, "Come in, Son."

Franklin saw his mother reclined on what appeared to be a hospital bed. He sat down beside her. "Hi, Mom. How's my favorite lady?"

There was a quiver of apology in her voice. "I'm sorry your homecoming has to be so unhappy. It's not what I had planned." She glanced at the door, where the general now stood, looking uncomfortable.

"Don't apologize, Mom. We're all here. Together." His eyes drifted to his father.

She touched his cheek lightly, looking toward the door. "How are you, Samuel?"

General Sharps came to the other side of the bed and kissed her lightly on the mouth. "Franklin and I flew together from Saigon." He sat on the edge of the bed and took her hand. "It was a long journey, but we survived."

"Surviving is all that matters." She glanced at Franklin. "Frankie, may I speak with your father . . . alone? We can sit in the living room a little later."

"No problem. I'll check on S-Three." He leaned over and kissed her on the forehead, then rose and left the room.

When they were alone, Shania said to Samuel, "You look splendid. I never saw a more handsome man in uniform than you. Except for our sons."

He kissed her hand. "You look beautiful."

"You always know the right words, but I never knew you could lie so gallantly."

The general caressed her hands. "I could never lie to you—" He stopped; as a bolt of shame threaded through his body.

Shania smiled. "Oh, Samuel, how could two people have been so wrong? To have wasted so much life?"

"Wrong? You? You're the only right person I've ever known. I was the one who was wrong. Now I have to pay."

She shook her head. "No more. You've already paid dearly. We all have. You. Me. Franklin. Kevin . . . Adrian." She sat up, grimacing in pain.

"Shania, my dear, you mustn't upset yourself. Doc Malone said—"

She sounded strong and reassuring, trying to be resolute, as she always had in crisis. "Please, Samuel. Let's not avoid the truth. I'm dying. Oddly enough, I find consolation—even contentment—in that reality."

He looked at her incredulously. "How?"

"It brought you and Franklin home. I realize you'll both have to go back to Vietnam, but at least we'll have this time together." She sat upright and cupped his face in her hands. "There's a lot that must be accomplished in this short span of time. There's no time to be wasted. This must be a time for healing."

Samuel felt small in the presence of this remarkable woman. "You're incredible; your strength makes me feel embarrassed and ashamed. But mostly, you make me feel proud. I'm the one who committed the wrong to this family, yet it's you . . ."

"No, Samuel. As your mother always said, 'Life treats us all the same. We're all born . . . and then we die. Somewhere in between we're bound to have our hearts broken.' " She took a deep breath. "Now, let's have no more talk about the past. Let yesterday stay where it is. You had your career and I needed a home, where the boys could have stability."

She thought for a moment. "I tire easily, Samuel, but there is one thing I would like to do while we're all together."

"Whatever you want," he said.

"A trip."

"A trip?"

"Yes, all of us together."

"To where?"

"To Quimas. We can rent a villa for a few days."

"Mexico?" He nearly shouted the word and thought she had taken leave of her senses.

"Yes, to Quimas, a place filled with wonderful family memories. We can spend some time there, fish, swim, watch fireworks. Remember, we used to spend Fourth of July in Quismas. We'll celebrate early. You can rent an airplane and fly us there."

He could only smile and nod at her in sheer amazement. "If it's Mexico you want . . . it's Mexico you'll have."

He embraced her gently and could only wonder why he had been so foolish all those years to cause him precious time lost.

· · ·

In the living room, Franklin was standing in front of the fireplace, looking at a framed photograph above the mantel of his
late brother in his West Point uniform. A black ribbon was
attached diagonally across the frame's right-hand corner.

Kevin stepped to his side. "I still can't believe he's dead."

"They've paid for it, Kevin. I made them pay for killing him,"
Franklin said.

Kevin put his arms around his brother. "What price have you
had to pay, brother?"

"It doesn't matter. They paid for the Sharps they killed."

The sound of their mother's voice drew their attention away
from the photograph. "Come on, boys. Let's go sit on the
porch. Kevin, bring your guitar."

Assisted by Samuel, Shania went onto the porch, followed
by their sons. She sat in a swing, where Samuel draped an af-
ghan around her shoulders. He sat beside her while Franklin
sat on the other side and Kevin knelt on the steps and began
playing "Where Have All the Flowers Gone?"

Samuel looked up at the stars and put his arms around
Shania, saying, "My God! What a night." He looked at Franklin. "But a little chillier than what we're used to, isn't it, Son?"

Franklin nodded. "Yes, sir. It feels good." His eyes searched
the rich darkness beyond the spray of the porch light.

Shania saw him and understood. She whispered, "There's
nothing out there but Sabre Ranch. You're safe at home, Franklin."

When Kevin began singing "Where Have All The Flowers
Gone?" Franklin chided, "You still can't sing worth a hoot,
little brother."

Shania said, "Beautiful words sung by a beautiful son."

When Samuel rose and stepped off the porch to the edge of
the darkness and stared up at the stars, Shania took advantage
of the moment and whispered to Franklin, "Kevin's been
drafted."

Samuel turned back and saw the look of surprise on Franklin's face. "What are you two plotting?"

Shania said, "I was telling him we're going to Quimas. We'll have a wonderful time. We'll celebrate a real family gathering. Darlene is coming and bringing the baby."

At that, Samuel realized for the first time since arriving that his daughter-in-law and granddaughter weren't at the ranch. "Where are they?"

"In Willcox, at her mother's. They'll be here in the morning."

"You're right, it will be wonderful."

49

At Sabre Ranch sunrise was Franklin's favorite part of the day. Sipping coffee on the front porch, he was moody, even though he was home, because his instincts made him feel like he was still in the bush, keeping him alert and alive. He looked up when he heard the door open and saw Kevin wearing his scrunched-down cowboy hat and boots.

"Want to go for a cavalry charge?"

Franklin jumped to his feet and hurried into the house, returning minutes later wearing his hat and boots. "Let's do it, little brother."

They went to the stable, where three horses were stalled, and saddled two of them. Kevin went to a tack box and pulled out two old cavalry sabres. Unlike the one that usually hung over the fireplace, the blades were scoured, blunt, and chipped along what had once been a sharp edge. These were practice sabres their father had found in an old gas station one summer and used to teach the boys how to ride and fight on horseback.

After attaching the sabres to their saddles they rode a few hundred yards west of the ranch to a stand of cottonwood trees where the family picnicked. A soft breeze blew, and the heat wasn't yet boiling as they spurred their horses and charged through the brush, dodging and ducking branches until they reached an opening where a single tree stood like a promontory.

The "sabre tree," it was called, and for good reason, since it bore more sabre cuts and gouges than could be counted. Franklin spurred his horse and charged, stood in the stirrups, and reached for the blade. He drew it smoothly, extended it over the horse's head, and as he neared the tree brought back his arm and slashed with all his strength. He felt the numbing thud rush up his arm as the blade cut into what was left of the scarred bark. He whirled for another charge.

At the moment he spurred the horse he saw Kevin watching him, both charging at each other like mounted cavalry from an ancient day. Both leaned, extended, then slashed, only the tree separating—and protecting each of them from the other's blade. Splinters of wood flew and both riders wheeled their horses and made another charge.

The air rang with each bite the blades made into the tree, followed by the pounding of hooves and the kicking of dirt with each new attack.

Again and again they charged until the horses were slimy with a white sheen of sweat. Both young men breathed heavily as they brought their horses to a halt, dismounted, and tied off the reins to the tree.

They sat facing each other on the ground, now soft and churned from their horses' hooves, and each stared past the other. Some time passed before Franklin finally spoke. "Mom told me you've been drafted."

Kevin continued to evade eye contact. "I've got to report in two weeks."

"And?"

He shrugged. "And what?"

"Come on, Brother. Play it straight with me. What in the hell are you going to do? Mom's dying . . . you've been drafted . . . we're going to Mexico. What I don't understand is why not Canada?"

"Canada is where I'll probably eventually go. I have friends in Mexico in the peace movement. They'll get me north in due time."

"Due time? Jesus. Mexico to Canada? You're going to be more traveled than me by the time you get to wherever you're going. Does Pop know you've been drafted?"

"Hell, no. Mom wanted to tell him, but I said no. It's my decision. My duty. I'll tell him once we get down there . . . where he can't turn me over to the law."

Franklin nearly laughed. "Duty? You don't know the meaning of the word if you're skying out for Mexico."

"I haven't forgotten. Duty doesn't mean doing something even if you believe it's wrong. Duty means honoring what you believe is right."

Franklin stabbed at the dirt with his sabre. "What the fuck do you know about what's right? You're talking about running away—to Mexico—like the rest of the draft dodgers."

"Don't call me a draft dodger." His fists were balled and he looked ready for a fight. "What about the brothers in Nam? Aren't they part of the program? The white man's program that drafts black kids and uses them as tools of political policy when they can't even vote in some states without bullshit Jim Crow laws stopping them! Shit, man, don't you know about Watts?"

"I know about Watts. A lot of the brothers in my brigade were pissed. Some come from Watts and a helluva lot of them believe that's just the beginning. But, goddammit, man, they didn't run away."

"How do they feel about fighting for a government that still treats them like second-class citizens?"

"Ask yourself that. You were in college. You had a deferment. What happened?"

"Conscience. I couldn't sit in class while our people were

being slaughtered for foreign policy. I joined the movement and my grades suffered."

Franklin listened in disbelief. "You are one self-righteous son of a bitch. And a fool to match. You can avoid all this shit and not become an outcast."

"Oh, yeah. How?"

"You can get Pop to help. He's a general. You can join the fucking Coast Guard. All they do is ride around in boats here in the states and chase pussy."

Kevin didn't find this humorous. "You don't understand. I don't want any part of a military establishment that oppresses our people."

"I'm not the enemy, brother. I want to help you with this problem."

"You don't sound all that helpful. You sound pissed."

Franklin slashed at the ground with the sword. "I am pissed. Pissed that you're running out while other guys—most of them white guys—are dying in that shit. Maybe that's why I'm willing to help. I've been there. I know about duty. Duty doesn't mean standing by with your dick in your hand while your kid brother gets tossed into a meat grinder."

Franklin whistled. "The old man's going to have a case of the ass like we've never seen. He'll go out of his fucking mind. And he's going to fly you there!"

Kevin laughed until tears began to roll.

When they both calmed down, Kevin asked, "What's the war really like?"

His brother looked to the clear sky and with his arms outstretched said, "We were bad to the bone, walked the bush like fucking gods, decided who lived and who died. Man, it was some kind of righteous trip."

His eyes had taken on a shining that suddenly made Kevin uncomfortable. "They say you go crazy after you kill another human being."

"Human being?" Franklin grinned. "They weren't human beings. They were targets. And you don't go crazy afterward, little brother, you go crazy just before you make the kill, just the split second before you come to grips with the fact that it's either that motherfucker or you." He looked around at the pristine beauty and sucked in a lungful of air. "Man, what a place."

Kevin did the same. "Mom used to say this is where God stopped to rest after creating the world. She said He saved the best for last."

Franklin nodded. "He did a helluva good job."

"I'm going to miss her, Franklin. Christ, why her? Why not me? Or you? Or the old man?"

"I don't know. Guess it's her time. I used to wonder the same about guys getting zapped in Nam. Good guys. I always wondered why them and not me. She's a helluva lady. I used to hear her every night in the war. Even felt her right there with me. Looking over my shoulder like some Guardian Angel."

Kevin turned away to wipe at tears. "I know what you mean. The way I still think of Adrian. Always there. Just a step beyond. Like they're waiting, or walking ahead, keeping an eye open for me."

"Like they're covering the point on a patrol. Covering your ass. Not like the old man. Hell, he's never around when you need him."

"He's here now." He patted the horse's neck. "You didn't see him in Nam?"

"Didn't want to. Fuck him."

Kevin sighed. "That's what he'll be saying about me soon."

"Thought about what you'll do when we get to Mexico?"

"I have the phone number of a guy in Cabo San Lucas," Kevin said. "He can get me on a fishing boat to Vancouver. Once there, there's other people who'll help. I'll find a job, get a place to live. I would be there now if it hadn't been for Mom's illness. I was supposed to leave the next day and just drive north. Can't now. Have to stay with Mom to the end."

"Maybe he won't find out."

"Bull. He'll find out. You know Pop. He'll find out. Besides, like I said, I'll tell him. I owe him that much."

"Shit, we don't owe him anything. And don't forget, there's the Coast Guard, the navy, even the air force. Hell, none of those guys actually go to Nam."

"It's not Vietnam. It's the military. I'm no coward. I'll die for my country, but not for this fucking war in Vietnam."

The brothers unsaddled their horses and put away the saddles, sabres, and tack and started for the house. The sun was blistering, the air dry enough to suck water from the body. Franklin wanted a cool drink and knew it was time to pay his respects.

He started around the edge of the house, paused to look back, and saw Kevin step onto the porch. "Aren't you coming with me, little brother?"

Kevin's face was etched with sadness. "No, big brother, you go ahead. All things considered, I don't feel I have a right any longer."

Franklin understood and continued to the back, pausing momentarily when he saw the wrought-iron archway of the family cemetery.

The graves were freshly tended as always, flowers trimming each plot, a gray marker at the head of each, silent sentinels marking the family's passage through time.

He whispered to himself, "The sergeant major, Selona, Grandma Hannah, and all the rest. Heroes all."

He walked directly to a particular marker, whiter than the others.

Lieutenant Adrian David Sharps
Born May 2, 1943
Died July 2, 1964, Republic of Vietnam
Graduate of United States Military Academy—Class of 1964

Over a year since he was killed, thought Franklin, as he stood at attention and saluted. "Good morning, sir. Specialist Franklin Sharps, reporting, as promised."

He slowly lowered his hand, then knelt beside the stone, and noting a weed, plucked it from the ground and whispered, "Guess Mom missed this one, big brother."

Tears filled his eyes as he read the headstone over and over. "It's been a long time, big brother. A long time. He wiped at his eyes and continued, saying, "But I made it back. I still have my legs. My hands. All my parts. I took a few hits but nothing serious. I guess you were there looking after me."

He took a deep breath and felt something break away inside like a tree shedding its bark. "I hurt bad, Adrian. Feel empty, alone. I feel like my guts have been ripped out. Sometimes I wish I had come home like you."

He ran his fingers through the soft grass, laid back, and searched the sky as though searching for strength. "I've come home to nothing. Everybody's leaving me! I don't want to be alone. I've been alone for so long. You know what I mean—in the bush. I don't know if I can stay here alone. There'll be no one . . . but you."

He felt his stomach tighten and he thought he would vomit. He felt so weak; so helpless. "Kevin . . . he . . . Oh, Adrian, if you could only hear me . . . tell me what to do."

Franklin fell slowly onto the grave; his lips touched the grass, and though he was joined to the ground he felt a thousand feet above the earth.

He lay there for a long time, the memories of childhood—when it was good, clean, and simple—rippling through his mind. After a time he felt a hand touch his shoulder.

"Don't do this to yourself," Kevin said. He knelt by his brother and they embraced, their bodies trembling, tears mixing at their cheeks.

They did not see their father and mother standing at the corner of the house, both holding each other. Tears streamed down

Shania's face; Samuel wore a mask of pain as he stood helpless.

Shania turned and walked to the front of the house; moments later, shoulders stooped and wiping at his tears, Samuel turned and followed his wife.

50

* * *

That afternoon, Samuel found Shania sitting on the living room sofa, staring through the window at Franklin and Kevin, who were repairing shingles on the roof of the stable. He sat down and took her hand and held her for a moment. "Does Fred Turner still have his flight service at the airport?"

She knew what he was up to. "Of course. The man practically lives there since Alice passed away and his son went into the army."

"Excellent. If we're going to Mexico, we're going to need an aircraft. I'll make the arrangements. We can leave tomorrow. Will Darlene and Argonne be going with us?"

"Of course. They'll be here later this afternoon."

"Then I better get busy. Is there anything you need while I'm in town?"

She handed him a list of things. He read it and smiled at her. "You've got everything all planned out, haven't you?"

She flashed her mystery smile. "The keys are in the truck."

At the garage he opened the door and froze. Sunlight filled the garage, where a sedan and truck sat beside another vehicle covered with a tarpaulin. He walked to the vehicle and lifted the tarp, ignoring the dust that had collected since the vehicle was last driven.

"Oh, my Lord." He looked at a green MG sports car and ran his finger along the polished hood. It was just as Adrian had left it before going to Southeast Asia. He sighed, re-covered the MG, and got into the pickup and drove away.

Samuel drove down the long road he once drove in his new DeSoto back in 1941 when he made his journey to Tuskegee. He thought of sleeping on the prairie between Bonita and Fort Davis, Texas, where he visited the graves of his ancestors and where he met another descendant of a Buffalo Soldier who had served with his grandfather Sharps in the 10th Cavalry.

When he turned onto the main road that led to Bonita, his thoughts were so full of that long-ago journey he didn't notice another pickup parked alongside the road. Nor did he notice the driver—a white man in his early twenties, with long, straggly hair and hippie beads—who eased his pickup onto the road and drove in the direction of Bonita.

The main street of Bonita always brought back fond but embarrassing memories for Samuel. It was on that street in 1941 that he saw a column of tanks roll past on the way to an area north of town where the unit bivouacked and began military maneuvers. He chuckled at the thought, recalling how he supplied fresh game for the unit with his Sharps rifle and wound up in a race with a tank on the Fourth of July. The whole town laughed as he rode up on the critter his father selected for him to ride against the Sherman tank—a mule!

He made quite a piece of money that day, crossing the finish line a few yards ahead of the armored challenger.

His first stop was the small airport where he took his first airplane ride in a Stearman, flown by a black aviator named Sparks Hamilton, a veteran of the 92nd Division and of the Great War in France. It was from Hamilton that he learned of the Civilian Pilot Training Program at Tuskegee Institute, in Alabama, where young Negroes were training as pilots in hopes of becoming aviators in the Army Air Corps.

Samuel parked in front of the hangar and walked inside, where he saw an aircraft sitting half-assembled; beneath the fuselage, a pair of legs jutted.

"Are you sleeping or working, Fred?" Samuel called out.

Fred Turner crawled from beneath the aircraft wearing oil-covered overalls. The moment he saw Samuel he started wiping his fingers with a grimy rag. He was in his sixties, tall, with thinning gray hair, deep blue eyes, and a ready smile. He had been a fighter pilot in World War II and nearly lost his leg when hit by a Japanese fighter in the Pacific.

"I'll be damned if it ain't Samuel. How the hell are you, General?"

They shook hands warmly, not just as friends but comrades of a great war.

"I'm fine, Fred. And you're looking fit."

Turner grinned. "The secret is hard whiskey . . . and soft women." They made small talk for a few minutes before Turner got down to cases. "Shania called the other day and said you'd probably be stopping by to talk about renting an aircraft. Christ, Samuel. I'm sorry to hear she's feeling so, so poorly."

"She wants to spend a few days in Mexico. What have you got that'll haul a family of six to Quimas and back?"

Turner, still wiping his hands, said, "Come with me."

They headed toward a lone hangar, the type used to store a single plane.

"This baby belongs to Taylor Carpenter."

Samuel knew the man; they had attended high school together. "Well, well, banker Carpenter."

"He has me rent it out when he's not using it, which is generally most of the time. He doesn't fly much and is a lousy pilot, anyway. It's a repossession he decided to hang on to."

Turner unlocked the door and slid it open. Samuel saw the

aircraft and let out an admiring whistle. "What a beautiful sight."

A Cessna 410 Golden Eagle sat within the shadows of the hangar, gleaming where the sunlight danced off its brightly colored fuselage and polished metal.

"Shania called and said you might need a bird with some room."

"She's thought of everything."

"She usually does."

"Do I need to take a check ride?"

Turner frowned. "I doubt that'll be necessary. You still remember how to fly?"

"I think so. Ain't it like riding a bike?" He let that sink in. "By the way, how's Michael?"

A proud smile filled Turner's face. "He's still flying gunships with the First Air Cav."

Michael Turner was a year older than Franklin. The two had played sports together in high school and joined the army on graduation. A rated pilot, he was accepted into the army aviation program while only nineteen.

"He's a fine young man, Fred. I saw him a few weeks ago. He stopped in at my office in Saigon."

"I know. He wrote all about it. Said his squadron commander was scared to say diddly to him for a week, what with him knowing a general and all." His eyes brightened. "I can't wait until he gets out, Samuel. It'll be just like we always planned . . . the Turner Flying Service. God, he's all I've got, and that's more than enough to make my life complete."

Samuel checked his watch. "Better be going. Lots to do. We'll be here at zero-seven-hundred tomorrow morning."

"She'll be waiting."

Turner went back to the hangar and was surprised to see a young man standing by the airplane he had been repairing. He took one look at the long hair and beads and decided he didn't like the looks of the fellow. "Can I help you?"

The hippie turned and pushed back a long, dark wisp of hair. "Wasn't that General Samuel Sharps?"

Turner picked up an oily rag and looked warily at the man. "That was him. Why?"

"I'm just passing through and thought I'd stop and see his son, Kevin."

"You know Kevin?"

"Yes, sir. We both go to college at Berkeley." He stuck out his hand. "My name is Desmond Sedgwick."

Turner shook hands. "You better call quick. They're all leaving in the morning."

"Oh? Where they going?"

"Mexico. Quimas. Having a family reunion."

"Well, thanks. I guess I'd better get in touch with him soon. Like I said, I'm just passing through."

Turner watched the young man walk away. He had been polite and well mannered, and Turner at least liked that in the young man.

At the ranch, Doc Malone was in Shania's darkened bedroom, where the only light glinted from a penlight he was using to check her eyes.

"Well?" Shania asked, after he opened the curtains. She was seated in a chair near the bed.

"No change for the present," Malone said. "What about the headaches? More frequent? More intense?"

"No worse than usual," she said.

"What about this fool notion of a trip?" he said pointedly.

"What about it? We're going to Mexico."

Malone handed her a bottle of Demerol pain pills. "Have you given any thought to the possibility of a serious attack down there? The consequences? You'll be in an isolated part of Mexico. Medical attention will be limited at best, maybe nonexistent."

Shania smiled in appreciation of his concern. "Would it matter if I was in the parking lot of the UCLA Medical Center?"

She had him there. "No. But there's always the chance—"

"The chance I might die? Jessie, I am going to die. I have this final chance to be with my children and my husband."

He said cautiously, "What about Samuel and the boys? Any problems between them?"

"No, they're perfect gentlemen. Very civil." She took in a deep breath. "That's what worries me. They're keeping their emotions all shoved deep inside. It's like waiting for an explosion."

Malone closed up his medical bag and sat on the edge of the bed. "If you need anything you know how to reach me." He patted her hand and left.

When she heard Malone drive away, she went to the desk in the study and began writing. She wrote three letters and sealed each in a separate envelope and placed them in her jewelry box.

In her heart and mind she knew her life had finally reached the threshold of the end and she felt helpless—but not because she was dying. That, she believed, was God's will. What tore at her the most was the heart-tearing reality that when she was gone, her beloved family would disintegrate.

She allowed herself a luxury thus far denied: She lay on her bed, head on her pillow, and had a good long cry.

Samuel was coming out of a store in Bonita when he stopped, recognizing an old friend across the street. "Carson!" he shouted as he hurried across the street to greet two high school classmates. "How are you, old friend?"

Carson Johnson was the same age as Samuel, as was his wife, who stepped close to her husband and glowered at the general. She looked hardened and bitter, as though time had eroded her. Johnson didn't look much better, his face reddened by what appeared to be what Shania called "whiskey blossoms."

"Hello, General Sharps," Johnson said. His voice had a hardened edge impossible to miss.

Samuel stiffened; he nodded at Johnson's wife. "Hello, Carson, Carol."

She said nothing but grabbed her husband by the arm and through clenched teeth hissed, "Come on. We're in a hurry."

Johnson ripped away from her grip. "No! I want this black son of a bitch to know what he's done!"

A small crowd was starting to gather by now, and Samuel was burning with embarrassment—and rage. "Carson, I—"

Johnson's voice roared along the street. "Shut up! Damn you, just shut up. You owe me this. You owe me this for Danny."

Samuel looked puzzled. "Danny?"

"Danny! My son, goddammit. I wrote you about him. When he was sent to Vietnam. I begged you to use your position . . . your rank, to keep him out of combat. To find him a safe job where you were." His voice quivered and nearly broke as he sputtered, "You refused!"

Samuel's eyes narrowed. "I couldn't do that for my own sons, Carson."

Carol pulled again at his arm, but he wouldn't be moved. "You killed your son . . . God only knows what that war has done to Franklin. And you killed Danny!"

Samuel was numb. Johnson was shouting, "Danny. They sent him home in a rubber bag!"

Samuel managed to whisper, "I didn't know."

Johnson shrieked, "Pieces of him . . . what pieces they could find."

His wife dragged at him now. She would not allow this to go further. "Carson!" she yelled in his face and yanked him down the street. But as she was leading her husband away, she paused long enough to give Samuel a hate-filled look. "Welcome home, Samuel," she said. "I hope you burn in hell!"

He stood motionless, his head swirling, as he watched two

old friends walk away, carrying their mutual misery. Finally, he turned and started for his truck, stopped, and stared at a sign in a store window: PROUDLY DISPLAY YOUR PATRIOTISM— AMERICAN FLAGS SOLD HERE.

51

All those medals. Franklin stared at the rows of decorations displayed in a large, glass-covered shadow box hanging from the wall of the study encasing row upon row of the decorations awarded to his father. He respected the man as a soldier and pilot; however, what once was respect for him as a father had now turned to anger. He recalled what Sergeant Hughes had said: *"Boy, you got a lot of hate in you."* Hardly room for anything else, since he had more than one target. Vietcong. His father. Difference was, he had never loved the Vietcong. They only tried to kill him.

He rubbed harshly at his face, trying to wash away the memory.

The door opened and he turned to see his father. His old man looked shaken. He hadn't seen that since Adrian's funeral.

Samuel walked to a cabinet and poured a large scotch, tossed it down, and poured another. "Care to join me?"

"Sure. Why not?"

Samuel handed his son the drink, raised his glass, and said, "To the profession of arms."

Franklin proposed his own toast. "To the living . . . and the dead."

Franklin raised his glass. "Now that I'll drink to."

Both downed their drinks with one blast. Samuel poured himself another, then—suddenly—threw the glass against the wall.

Instinctively, Franklin's hands went to his face to protect himself from the flying shards.

Shania's voice suddenly exploded from the door. "Samuel! Franklin! What in the world is going on here?"

Samuel walked to a tall gun case, removed an M-1 rifle, sighted down the barrel. Never saying a word, he returned the weapon to the case and removed a Thompson submachine gun. He examined the weapon carefully, as though looking for imperfections. "Carson and Carol Johnson. I ran into them in town."

Shania looked at Franklin, who appeared perplexed. "I see." With an understanding voice, she said, "I thought you knew."

"Thought I knew? That's one of the privileges of rank, my dear. Generals send men into battle; they don't have to review the dead." He bent down and started picking up the broken glass and, looking embarrassed, mumbled, "Waste of damn good scotch."

Franklin goaded him by saying, "Waste of damn good young men."

Samuel roared toward Franklin, his fists balled, his face filled with anger. He stood over his son and said gutturally, "Go ahead, Franklin. Take your best shot. Find yourself someone to blame. The Johnsons did. I'm convenient. It's not a new experience for me. I've buried more good men . . . written more letters to wives and parents—"

Franklin roared back with his own salvo. "But it's the first time you got spit on. Right? Now you know how I felt in the airport." He raised his glass, saying, "Welcome home, General Sharps. Airborne! Above the Rest!"

Franklin walked from the room, feeling the searing heat from his father's angry eyes. Shania walked out knowing her husband's pain.

Later that afternoon Shania was in the kitchen preparing rack of lamb for the evening meal, the favorite of her husband and two sons. She looked up as Franklin came in, walked to the refrigerator, and took out a bottle of beer.

"Smells good, Mom." He took a long pull at the beer. "How do you feel?"

She wiped at a wisp of hair hanging into her face with the back of her hand. "I've felt better."

He leaned against the counter. "Can I do anything?"

"Yes, you can."

"Name it."

"You can treat your father with more respect. This situation is difficult for him, too. It's difficult for all of us."

He shrugged unsympathetically. "Why should he have it easier than the rest of us?"

She looked at him sternly. "Easier? I'm not talking about easier. I'm talking about not making it more difficult. There's a difference. I saw your face and I saw your eyes. You delighted in what happened with the Johnsons."

He sipped from the bottle. "Somebody has to pay."

She slammed down her knife. "The Johnsons have to pay, not your father. He didn't kill Danny Johnson. They have to pay like we have to pay for Adrian, in our own private pain. They have no right to blame your father. He didn't kill Danny Johnson."

Franklin walked to the window and stood staring out at the cemetery. "Everybody has to pay, Mom. Everybody."

She came to him and cupped his face in her hands. "No,

Franklin, you're wrong. Everybody has *paid* and the whole country is still paying. The Sharpses, the Johnsons, every person in this country pays whenever one of our boys dies over there."

Franklin had to move into a very delicate area of discussion and wasn't sure how except to forge ahead. "What happened with Kevin?"

"He became involved in outside activities and lost his deferment. Now he's being drafted. Simple as that. He made his choice, just like you."

That wasn't good enough for Franklin. "You mean Pop couldn't—"

"No. He doesn't have that kind of power and even if he did, he wouldn't."

"Yeah. Not for Adrian . . . or Kevin."

"Adrian was his own man. Like you. Kevin is his own man. He knows what his decision will do to the family—to himself."

There it was, he thought. *She knows!* "You know what he has planned?"

"I have a pretty good idea."

"How do you feel about it?"

"I'll support whatever decision he makes. I'll expect the same from you. They'll both need your support."

"Support? For Pop?"

"Yes, for your father. He'll be furious. The humiliation will be unbearable. But that's between Kevin and your father. It's you and your father that worries me. You have to settle your differences."

"How can that happen?"

Shania, her eyes tear-filled, said, "Find a way, Franklin. Find a way. It begins here. Now. With you. He's waiting. He needs it. He needs you. It starts with you taking the first step. He'll take the rest."

"What if I can't?"

She went to the cupboard and took down several plates and glasses. "Then your world will be lonelier than any jungle you've ever seen. Someone has to hold this family together when I'm gone. You're the only one who can. I've been the link between Kevin and your father. If you don't take my place, quit acting the martyr and fool, this family will be destroyed." She stood, hands on her hips, glaring at her son. "I'm not saying it will be easy. It won't. I'm not saying it'll happen overnight. It may take years. But it will never happen if you do not take on the responsibility of keeping the Sharps family . . . a family."

"I don't know if I can. If I can forgive him."

She pointed to the cemetery. "Don't tell me that. Tell that to your family buried out there. They'd forgive anything to hold together what they've fought and sacrificed for. Do you think the sergeant major would have turned his back on his son— forever? Would Selona not have tried with her last breath to find a way? You think about them. And who you are. What you are. And what got you here."

"You might be asking too much of me, Mom."

"Then go ask Adrian. Be the kind of man your brother would have been. He would never have let this family be destroyed by what happened to him. Or for what your father did to me. Besides, that is between your father and me. It's our business. If I can forgive him—and I have—so can you."

There was the sound of a woman's voice calling from the front of the house. "Hello? Are we late for dinner?"

The two walked into the living room and found Darlene standing at the open front door, suitcase in one hand, and holding baby Argonne in her arm.

Franklin hurried forward and hugged the two long and lovingly. "Let me have her." He took the baby and held her high. "Mom, she's got your eyes and mouth."

Darlene hugged Shania. "Not to mention her temper."

Shania looked at Franklin with a raised eyebrow. "All Sharpses have a temper, my dear. It's a genetic thing."

Franklin picked up the suitcase. "I'll put this in Adrian's . . ." He stopped, then carried the luggage to the back bedroom.

Darlene's eyes followed him until he left the room. "He looks well, Mom."

"He's doing well on the outside. But there's a lot of demons on the inside."

"I would think that's to be expected."

Darlene took Shania's hand and held it gently. "How are you doing?"

"I'm doing fine. I just pray that Franklin and Samuel can find some way to settle their differences. It would mean so much to me."

"They will. I have faith in them, their love for you, and the Good Lord. That's a lot of support and strength to count on."

"Let's hope so." Shania stood. "Feel like helping me with dinner?"

That evening, for the first time since Adrian's funeral, the Sharps family sat down together at the dinner table.

52

* * *

Country music blared in the bar in Bonita where Franklin and Kevin found themselves among old friends. Billiard balls cracked, laughter throbbed, and both young men felt good being together again. They found a table in the corner, kicked back, and, like all cowboys, kept their cavalry hats clamped tightly on their heads.

A pretty waitress took their order. "What you guys want to drink?"

"Pitcher of beer, and a shot of whiskey," Franklin replied.

"Make that two shots," Kevin said.

The waitress hurried away just as Franklin heard their names being called through the swelling crowd. "Franklin! Kevin."

They looked up to see a young man easing his way toward them through the crowd.

"That's Dave Jessup!" Franklin said.

Jessup was Franklin's age; he wore a Marine Corps blouse, and as he drew closer Franklin could see the war in Vietnam had not gone well for his Indian high school classmate. He wore a black patch over his left eye, and a shiny steel hook protruded from the right sleeve.

Jessup threw his arm around Franklin. "Damn, man. You made it."

Franklin looked at him, a painful look on his face. "I have to go back, but I've made it this far, I'll make it the rest of the way." He looked at Jessup's obvious losses. "I'm sorry, Dave. I didn't know."

Jessup was an Apache Indian who grew up in Bonita and had been sent to Vietnam earlier in the year with the first Marines deployed to the war zone. "Fuck it! I'm alive, brother. That's all that matters. Hell, I just got out of the hospital. Home on convalescent leave from the VA hospital in Dago."

They sat down as the beer arrived. Jessup poured, then raised his glass. "Welcome home, brother."

They all took a long drink. "How did you get hit?" Franklin said.

"Land mine. Got hit on my first patrol. Hell, I wasn't in Nam two weeks and I'm on my way home. Didn't see much of anything except the navy hospital in Da Nang."

Franklin thought about that for a moment. Jessup was in and out before he knew what hit him. "In a way, that might be for the best, man. You didn't have to put up with all the shit before getting the million-dollar wound."

"That's what my uncle told me. He was wounded on D day at Normandy. First time in combat. Out of the landing craft and *zap*! On his way home. War hero and all. Guess that sort of luck runs in the family." He looked quizzically at Franklin. "How does it feel to be back?"

"Don't really know. Just got here last night. Haven't had much time to think about it. Maybe I don't want to."

"You will," Jessup said. "You will."

That sounded odd. "Why's that?"

Jessup poured another glass of beer. "War is hell, son, but the coming home is a motherfucker. You survive the war; then you got to survive the surviving."

"Has it been rough?" Kevin asked.

"Not too bad so far. Most of the guys at the hospital say they just quietly slip back home. Like coming in from a night patrol. The home folks don't want to know where you've been, what you've done, what happened. For the most part you're politely ignored. Except by the war protesters. They want you to join up with their side."

Franklin glanced at Kevin, a slight grin on his lips. "I've been told that by somebody I met." He took another sip of beer. "What're your plans now?"

"College. I'm going to be a big-time Indian. The Vocational Rehab dude at the Phoenix VA told me a grateful nation is going to 're-ha-bil-i-tate' my young ass. Rehabilitate. Shit! I looked it up in the dictionary. It means 'to restore to good or previous condition.' I asked the dude if they were going to give me back my hand and eye. . . . He said I had a lot of attitude. Said a lot of dudes got it worse than me."

Franklin couldn't imagine how, short of being dead. "Do they?"

"Without a doubt. They can't find a job because their brains are full of worms, their hearts full of pain and just plain out of hope. At least I have some money coming in from Uncle." He paused, then tapped the table with his hook and said, "I heard about your mom. I'm sorry, man. She's a great lady."

"Yes, she is."

"She came to the hospital and visited me when she was in the Los Angeles area seeing another doctor about her condition. Brought flowers, fruit, all that good stuff. The guys loved her."

This surprised both of the Sharpses. "I didn't know that."

"Oh, yes, and your old man, too."

This really surprised Franklin. "My dad?"

"In Nam. He came to the field hospital with General Westmoreland and some other big brass. Your dad told the medics they better take good care of me; then he pinned on my Purple Heart. Crazy times. Your mom and dad were the only two people who cared about me."

"What about your family?" Kevin asked.

"Down on the rez!" He laughed sarcastically. "The Indians on the reservation think I'm crazy for fighting the white man's war. They say we fight, then can't find a job. But a lot of Indians are in the service. Volunteers. Draftees. Lot of them getting hit in Nam, too. Just like the black soldiers." He looked at Kevin. "What about you?"

"I've been drafted. I have to report in two weeks."

Jessup stared at him with his one good eye. "So, what are you going to do?"

"What do you mean?"

"When are you booking for north country? Nothing but fools going to Nam. I told my brother the same thing, what the guys in Nam say—'they got me, but not my little brother!' " He downed his beer in two gulps. "Having one fucked-up dude in the family is enough. You better talk to him, Franklin."

Before they could go on, a young man stepped to the table. He was tall, lanky, wore Western clothes, and looked mean. "Howdy, hero," he said to Franklin. "Heard you was back in one piece. Your buddy here wasn't that lucky."

Franklin knew and disliked Bill Taylor. He was the super jock of the area, football scholarship to Arizona, and a righteous pain in the ass. "Hello, Bill, how's the throwing arm?"

Taylor snickered. "Better than your Injun buddy." He looked at Jessup. "Damn, Chief, you look like you tangled with a wildcat."

Jessup rose. "Get the fuck out you Jody fuck son of a bitch. You weren't invited."

Franklin stepped between the two. He stood close, inhaling Taylor's beer breath. "Bill, you haven't changed a bit. You're still the slimy little sack of shit you were in high school."

That's when Taylor's fist came up, slamming into Franklin's face. He reeled backward from the punch, and through glazed eyes saw his attacker closing in.

Taylor threw a wild roundhouse punch that hit only the air

above Franklin's ducking head; another punch was blocked. Franklin stepped inside Taylor, drove a knee to his groin, then slammed his fist against the back of his neck. Taylor went down like a fallen tree. Moments passed, and he rose, gripping a broken beer bottle in his hand. "I'm going to cut your fucking nigger head off!"

Taylor lunged with the jagged glass extended. Franklin kicked out, driving his hand to the outside, then threw a fist from center field into Taylor's belly. There was a rush of air as the jock was hurled backward into the table and chairs. He rolled on the ground, moaning and clutching his middle, and when he got to his knees, Franklin nailed him behind the ear with the heel of his boot. Only seconds had passed. The football star lay unconscious in a pool of blood, puke, and beer.

In the background, a single loud Indian war cry rose up from the silent, stunned crowd.

An hour later, the telephone rang at the Sharps Ranch. Samuel was sitting at his desk when he answered, listened for a moment, then said, "I'll be there in fifteen minutes." He hung up and sat there shaking his head when Shania came into the study.

"Is something wrong?"

He pushed himself away from the desk and hugged her. "The boys had a little engine trouble with the truck. I better go help them out. Go on to bed, sweetheart. I won't be long."

The parking lot of the bar was lit by the strobing lights of a local ambulance. Samuel could see two attendants wheeling a gurney toward the vehicle. He walked past and recognized the battered face at the bar entrance; he saw a man who resembled the Marlboro cigarette cowboy, Sheriff Wilson Prentice, a tall, burly man who looked tired and irritated.

"Prentice, what the hell's going on here?"

Prentice allowed a slight smile and extended his hand. "I heard you were back in Bonita, Samuel." He looked around, then waved his hand toward the bar. "All hell broke loose in there. According to witnesses, Bill Taylor started throwing punches at Franklin, and got his ass whipped for the mistake." He took a deep breath. "But goddamn, your son near killed that boy. Knocked him flatter than piss on a plate. And they tore the living hell out of the place to boot." There was an uncomfortable pause. "Samuel, I know you've got some personal problems out there at Sabre Ranch. I know about Shania, and I don't want to arrest Franklin, what with him still being in the service. Just do me a favor: Get him the hell out of here. I'd appreciate it if you'd stand for some of the damages, and my report'll show it was started by unknown causes."

Franklin appeared in the custody of a deputy. He was wearing handcuffs and a bruised face. Samuel said to Prentice, "Get the cuffs off. Have the owner send me a bill. I'll stand for all the damages. I don't want his mother to know about this."

The deputy removed the cuffs and Franklin started to say something to his father, but before the words issued Samuel pointed a hard finger at Franklin, saying, "Not a word! Not a goddamned word. Get your ass in that vehicle."

On the drive home, not a word was spoken between Samuel and Franklin. At the ranch, the two walked in acting as though nothing had happened. Shania asked her son, "What happened to your face?"

"I was checking the engine. You know how that hood doesn't stay up. It slipped from Kevin's hand and caught me on the face. Don't worry, Mom. I'm not hurt." At that moment Kevin came through the front door, looking sheepish.

She kissed them good night. She could smell the beer on their breath but chose not to comment. "You better get some sleep. Tomorrow will be a long day."

. . .

Franklin couldn't sleep. It was nearly one o'clock when he went onto the porch and sat watching the full moon. The desert shimmered; he heard birds flitting through the air and reptiles moving about the hard ground, and heard the door open. He figured it was Kevin and said over his shoulder, "We really got our asses in the sling tonight, little brother."

He was surprised at the voice that answered. "Your father said you only had car trouble."

Franklin looked up to see Darlene standing in the moonlight. She was wearing a robe and standing near enough for him to catch her fragrance. "Pop did a good job covering for us but I don't think Mom was fooled."

She listened to him explain and thought the whole incident was childish. "I would think you've had enough fighting to last a lifetime."

"I didn't start it."

"You have to learn to control your temper."

She had him on that point. "I'm trying to fit back in and it's harder than I thought it would be."

"Why? All you have to do is come back to the person you were. A good man with a bright future."

This took him by surprise. "I'm not Adrian. We were two different people. Always were. Even as kids."

"I know. I'm not expecting you to be like him. Just be the person I know you can be." Unexpectedly, she took his hand, and this made him uncomfortable. "What do you think of your niece?"

"She's beautiful. You've done a great job as a mother."

"Sometimes I feel very inadequate." Her eyes drifted off to the distance, a look he recognized. It was one of longing, of not quite understanding how things turned out the way they did.

"Adrian would be very proud." He was looking at her differently now. Not just as his sister-in-law, but as a woman. They were only a year apart in age, but he felt like a fumbling teenager in her presence.

"Do I make you uncomfortable?"

He shrugged. "Darlene, you scare the living hell out of me. You always did. From the first day Adrian brought you home."

Her fingers laced his more tightly. "I never meant to do that."

"It wasn't your fault. There just weren't many black girls around." Which was true. Most of the black people of the area were descendants of military families from the Old West years. Her father had been a porter on the Santa Fe Railroad between Los Angeles and El Paso.

"I'm sure you've had plenty of girls chasing after you."

"Not as many as you might think."

"I find that surprising. You're a very handsome man."

Jesus! What's going on here? His brother—her husband—lay buried in his grave not thirty yards away and here he was sitting with his widow and feeling . . . urges . . . that made him ashamed.

"He wasn't supposed to get killed. He was a general's aide. He was on a fact-finding mission, for God's sake. Two months out of West Point and he's killed by a land mine while driving on the outskirts of Saigon." He felt her tremble and put his arm around her. He could only sit helplessly while listening to her sob. "Nobody had even heard of Vietnam this time last year."

"That won't last much longer. Before it's over, the whole world is going to know about Vietnam."

She dabbed at her eyes. "How long do you think it'll take us to win the war?"

"I don't know. Back in July we were thinking we'd all be home for Christmas. I don't think that's the way it'll work out. Now that the North Vietnamese are into the fight, I expect it'll go on for quite awhile."

Darlene shuddered and laid her head on his shoulder. "I

watch the news and see so many young people opposed to what's going on over there. Young men are burning their draft cards, leaving the country. It's dreadful."

He thought about his buddies, on patrol this very minute while he sat in the darkness with a beautiful woman. "Can I ask you a favor?"

"Of course."

"Will you keep on sending me tapes when I go back?"

"Yes, I will."

Without knowing what he was doing, he kissed her. He was helpless. She smelled so wonderful, felt so good in his arms, and for the moment he forgot who she was.

53

He couldn't be certain of his feelings when he awoke later that morning. He felt ashamed for not controlling his temper at the bar and his feelings for Darlene. It would have been easy to write both off as combat stress. But the truth was, he enjoyed the fight and especially liked being with Darlene.

With sunrise came preparations for the trip. Samuel and Franklin were loading luggage into the back of the family car when they saw a car approaching. Neither had mentioned the events of the night before, both figuring the less said the better. The sun was barely above the eastern horizon, but there was plenty of light to see the dusty rooster tail of the approaching vehicle.

"Looks like someone is up earlier than we are," Samuel said.

Franklin lifted a heavy suitcase into the trunk, then stepped beside his father.

The car stopped and two men got out, both wearing uniforms, one an officer, the other an enlisted man. They approached and saluted.

The officer said, "Good morning, General Sharps. I'm Major Daniel Swopes, Army Security Agency, Fort Huachuaca." He motioned to the enlisted man. "This is Specialist Harold Townes. He's one of our ASA field operatives."

Samuel said, "Look, Major Swopes, my son got into a fight last night. No charges were filed by the sheriff and the damage was paid for. I don't think it's necessary for the ASA to get involved in this."

Swopes shook his head. "I know nothing of a fight, sir. I am not here regarding your son who's in the army."

Samuel was now more perplexed than before. "If not Franklin, then—"

"Desmond?" a voice interrupted from the porch. All turned to see Kevin standing there, a strange look on his face. Shania and Darlene stood at his side. Both looked confused.

Desmond Sedgwick—Specialist Townes—no longer wore his hair in a ponytail; it was cut military close, and he quickly averted his eyes from Kevin.

"General Sharps," the major said, "is there somewhere we can talk in private?"

Kevin stepped down from the porch and started toward the group, staring at Townes.

Samuel said, "Do you know this soldier?"

Kevin stopped beside his father, the stare unrelenting. "Yes, sir. He was my roommate at Berkeley. But he said his name was 'Desmond Sedgwick.'"

Major Swopes stepped in. "Specialist Townes was assigned to the Berkeley campus for field intelligence purposes, General Sharps. I've been sent here to handle this matter personally—and officially."

Samuel was thunderstruck; Franklin glared at Townes. Kevin had told him of his "roommate" and how he offered to help him avoid the draft.

"This doesn't concern my son Franklin?" Samuel asked.

The major removed a letter from the inside of his uniform coat and handed it to Samuel. "This matter concerns your son Kevin Matthew Sharps. He has been drafted into the army, and the ASA has reason to believe he intends to avoid the draft by going to Mexico. Ordinarily, the army wouldn't get this involved. However considering that he is the son of a general officer, the army has ordered me to intervene—to avoid personal embarrassment to you, and political embarrassment for the United States."

Before another word could be said, Kevin lunged forward, crashing his fist against Townes's jaw. The ASA agent flew backward, landing on his back, and stared up through glazed eyes.

"You treacherous son of a bitch!" Kevin shouted at Townes.

Townes started up but met Franklin when he reached his knees. "Stay down, motherfucker," Franklin snarled, his fists at the ready.

Townes slumped back, looking scared and beaten.

Swopes intervened. "Return to the vehicle, Specialist Townes." He looked at Franklin and snapped, "Do not interfere, soldier."

Franklin started to say something, but his father admonished him. "You'll do as you're ordered." To Swopes, he ordered, "Follow me!"

They marched briskly toward the house.

Franklin stepped beside Kevin and said in a low voice, "Well, little brother, I guess Mexico's out of the picture."

Kevin stood silent.

In his study, Samuel sat at his desk, Swopes across from him in a chair. "Now, Major, I'd like a full report on this situation." He watched Swopes take a file from his briefcase; then he sat for fifteen minutes listening to the officer share every detail of the matter.

Samuel twisted anxiously in his chair, but he wasn't totally convinced. "You have offered a pretty good case for your suspicions, Major, but suspicion is all you have. My son has a report date. Until that time he is not in violation of the Selective Service law.”

“I realize that, General Sharps. I’m here to inform you of what we believe to be your son’s intentions—to avoid the draft by seeking refuge in a foreign country. If he does, it will be a tragedy for your family, and for the rest of the country. The United States is under a great deal of pressure at the present on the issue of draft evasion. Should the son of a General officer evade the draft, it could have monumental ramifications. Hell, every draftee in the country could point at your son and use it for their personal benefit.”

Samuel could feel the tide coming in. “And the army isn’t prepared to allow that, I assume.”

“No, sir, the army is not prepared to allow that. It is clear from Specialist Townes’s reports that your son intends to evade the draft by not returning from Mexico, and that he intends to seek refuge in Canada.”

“That’s speculation on Townes’s part.”

“No, sir. We have hundreds of undercover agents throughout the United States, on campuses, in political groups, gathering intelligence. A complete network has been established to identify those who intend to evade, and to infiltrate the apparatus for evasion. We don’t have the manpower to contact every family of the individual evader, but your case is special.”

“You have army personnel spying on the college kids of America?”

“Yes, sir.”

“What about active duty personnel?”

Swopes nodded. “We have agents assigned to units for the specific role of trying to identify personnel who might desert before shipment to Vietnam. In this case, Townes happened to be roomed with your son.”

Samuel gave it some thought before saying, “When Kevin came home to visit his mother, Townes assumed he was going to use this opportunity to evade the draft.”

"Yes, sir. Townes indicated that was Kevin's purpose."

"What else did Townes report?"

Swopes looked at Samuel directly. "That Kevin was going to tell your family of his intentions."

Samuel stood and walked to the window. He gazed at the luggage sitting beside the car. A few feet beyond the glass, Shania sat in a chair slowly rocking the baby. "Major Swopes, this is a family matter. I appreciate your concern, but I'll handle it from this point."

Swopes stood and gripped his briefcase. "If I can be of help, please don't hesitate to contact me."

The general stood at the window until the officer got into his vehicle and drove from sight.

He went to the porch and stood by Shania. A hundred thoughts swirled through his head. He looked at Franklin. "Find Kevin and meet us at Selona's Bench in the cemetery."

A white wooden bench sat just beyond the entryway of the cemetery, built by Samuel's father for his grandmother decades before. A "place to come to," she would always say; a place to sit and reflect. The paint was cracked and needed sanding and repainting, Samuel thought as he stood by the bench staring at the tombstones.

When all were gathered he came directly to the point. He asked Kevin, "Do you intend to report for your induction?"

Kevin answered nervously, "No, sir. I do not intend to report for induction into the army. I was going to tell—"

His father's features hardened. "When? How? By postcard from Montreal?"

"I was going to tell you in Mexico."

"You miserable coward. You can stand here in this sacred place and speak those words? These people fought—and some died"—he pointed at several graves—"and some were born into slavery, yet they served this country, never enjoying the wonderful bounty you've known because of their sacrifices."

It made little impact on his son. "The war is wrong, Pop!"

"What the hell do you know about what is right or wrong? The very words that come out of your mouth were paid for in blood. This is not about your young, mystic notions about right or wrong. All wars are 'wrong' by definition. Right now we don't have time for philosophy One-O-One; we have a situation we have to deal with head-on, and running away will not solve the problem."

The line drawn in the sand could not have been clearer. Shania watched two men she loved take a stand for their beliefs and felt her heart breaking with every word that passed. It was like watching a battle unfold, one side firing a salvo, the other answering with equal force. But this was not a battlefield. This was her family, and there could be no winner.

"Please, both of you, stop," she pleaded. "Please stop before this goes too far."

Samuel looked at her. "Too far? It's already gone 'too far.' Our son is talking about deserting his country; he's talking about destroying his life and everything we've built. How far is 'too far?' " He looked at Franklin. "You're a combat soldier. How do you feel?"

Franklin was ready for the question; he had been since the night he returned and learned of Kevin's intentions. "I'll buy him the plane ticket with my combat pay. We don't want anybody in the bush who's not willing to be there. They'll get us all killed. If he wants to sky out . . . so be it."

Samuel realized something important. "You knew about this all along."

"I knew. If your family was as important as you say it is to you . . . you'd have seen it coming. But not you. Not the great black general. You have to prove to everyone that you're special. Shit! You're nothing but a nigger with a star on his shoulder." He pointed at Adrian's grave. "My brother is dead for no good reason at all. You pushed him all his life to go to West Point. He never had an option. Kevin does. Now you're not listening to him."

Darlene suddenly began weeping. "Franklin, don't talk like that."

"Why not?" He looked at his father, then his mother. "A few weeks ago I killed a fourteen-year-old kid. He had an old bolt-action rifle with the breech rusted shut. But that didn't matter. He attacked me. You don't know who we're fighting. None of the brass in Saigon know who this enemy really is, how determined they are. They are not going to quit. We are going to lose thousands because we are invading *their* country. Do you think America is the only country that will fight to the death against invaders?"

At that moment, something inside Samuel appeared to snap. His eyes hardened like nothing they had ever seen in the man. He started toward Kevin, as though mechanical, his hands rising up. "You! You're the cause of all this!" His voice was evil, guttural.

Shania had never seen him like this. "Samuel!" She shouted.

Just as Samuel's hands neared Kevin's throat, he was suddenly knocked sideways as Franklin threw his body against his father. They both went down in a tangled heap, thrashing and rolling on the ground shared by their dead family.

"Franklin! Samuel! Please!" Shania shouted. Kevin stood looking shocked; Darlene raced through the gate toward the house.

Franklin rolled Samuel onto his back, pinning his shoulders to the ground with his powerful arms. "He's my brother! Damn you, he's my brother!"

Samuel, wild-eyed, screamed, "He's not my son!"

Franklin shook him. "Why? Because he doesn't want to die in your war?" Franklin shook him again. "That's what we've been fighting for! Goddamn you! His right to make his own choice—right or wrong. My God! I've killed people for his right to make that choice. He'll pay—for the rest of his life—he'll pay! But he has the right—the right to choose!"

"You're wrong." Samuel gurgled. "You're both wrong. This isn't about choice. This is about honor!"

Franklin was now wild in the eyes and heart. "Who do you think you are? God! That's my brother—your son! Haven't we lost enough? How much more do we have to lose before you stand up and say 'no'! How many sons do you have to bury before you say 'that's enough'!"

Shania spoke; the words were barely audible. "Franklin . . . Samuel . . . Kevin . . . please. No more. Please."

"Mom!" Kevin shouted.

Shania, her hands over her ears, stumbled slightly, then slumped to the ground. She lay staring upward, her eyes appearing fixed on the sabres suspended from the archway.

All three men scrambled to her side. Samuel took her in his arms, lifting her head until he was looking into her eyes. "God, oh, God," Samuel muttered, "what have I done to you?"

She seemed to hear him; her eyes fluttered as she gripped his hand. "Don't let me die like this, Samuel. Not like this."

"Call Dr. Malone," he said to Franklin.

"No, Son," she pleaded. "Stay here with me. I'm sorry, Samuel. So very sorry." At that moment she appeared to draw a renewed strength from some inner source. "Don't hate your sons. Promise me . . . you won't hate *our* sons."

He kissed her lightly on the lips. "Not now, my darling. We'll talk later."

She smiled. "There won't be another chance."

Franklin looked sick at hearing his father's words; Kevin could only shake his head in sheer disillusionment.

Shania reached deeper, searching for the words. "You're a father who has sons who will be left alone. They will have to carry their pain without anyone to care. Franklin will have to deal with his sorrow alone. Kevin won't have a father to help him understand there is a proper—and noble—time for war. A time to die, if need be. Without you he will become an outcast. Without family. Without country. For God's sake, he'll have no meaning."

Samuel pulled her close and whispered, his voice sounding full of plea. "What can I do?"

She looked up at the swords. "You are the weld that holds them together. Like those sabres. Give them strength. Without you they will rust beneath the tears of hatred. Loneliness. And ridicule."

Samuel shook his head. "You ask too much. I could not forgive a son who would betray his country."

She mustered all her strength, and spoke forcefully. "You must help him. I can't, or I would."

Samuel's eyes filled with tears. "That's impossible."

Shania would not give up the fight. She knew she was dying. She knew there would be the living left behind. "I know it's unfair to plead from my position and to use this moment against you. But I have no choice."

Samuel's chest was heaving. In his heart, he could not let go of a lifetime of purpose. "I can't. My son, a draft dodger? Defiling the honor of men who've died? His brother? No!"

"Yes, you can," Shania insisted. "His brother cries from the grave to help the ones alive. I hear him, Samuel. In my sleep. On the wind. Now, at this moment." She paused, collected herself, then continued, her voice now serious and severe. "Why did you come home, Samuel? In search of forgiveness? Or to stand beside your family before what's left of it is destroyed? If so, it doesn't come without a price."

"I came because of you, and the children."

She shook her head, but now she was gentler; forgiving, but still imploring. "No: you came for yourself. Not to ease our pain and suffering, but to ease yours. For once in your life can't you put your family ahead of all other matters? Franklin needs you—he needs someone to help him through the bitterness that's tearing at his soul. Kevin needs you to understand—to be there through this difficult decision and what follows. If you don't, you'll lose everything. You'll die alone, without tears or children and grandchildren to marvel at your achievements. You'll be alone, Samuel."

Tears began to stream down his cheeks. He felt the remaining strength begin to drain from her body. "God, Shania. No. Not like this. Please, dear God, not like this."

"Shhhhhh. I'm so sorry, Samuel, but I must die knowing my family is again joined like those sabres. Please, I beg you, don't let me die a failure."

He sobbed openly now, his body trembling. "God, no, Shania. I won't." He struggled to sit upright. "Tell me what I should do."

Her words were growing fainter. "Hold on to them, Samuel. Find a way." She looked at Franklin and Kevin. "Help him. Please help him."

The two boys sat beside their mother. Franklin said, "We will. We promise."

Her eyes widened, and she reached beyond the three men she loved most on the earth, toward a grave marker, to another she loved, and with one final burst of breath said, "Adrian!"

Shania LeBaron Sharps slumped into her husband's arms, and there was silence beneath the sabres.

54

Four days after her death, Shania was buried beside her first-born child. Unusual for the time of year, a soft rain had fallen. A thick barricade of clouds hid the sun, and everywhere he looked Franklin saw darkness.

But the darkness of nature was brilliant compared with the darkness he saw standing between his father and brother. Since the moment of her death, neither had said a word to the other.

The following day, Samuel was kneeling at her grave when he heard Franklin's voice. "You're really blowing it, Pop."

Samuel remained silent.

"I expected as much," Franklin went on. "You made a promise to my mother. On her dying breath you made a promise you knew you wouldn't keep."

"People often say things in those moments they know aren't true."

"You are really one self-righteous son of a bitch."

His father turned and walked away.

Kevin was watching from the window. He went to the study and poured a glass of whiskey, his third in less than an hour, and raised it to the shadow box on the wall. "To the profession of arms," he said with a guttural voice, "and the honorable men who fight for duty, honor, and country." He downed the drink, stepped back and saluted with the glass, then threw it against the wall.

Samuel drove away recklessly and uncaring, swerving toward the highway as though drunk. He needed air. Not air in his lungs, air under his body. He needed to fly. To find a private place in the sky, as he had done so often when in need of solace.

When he arrived at the airport, an odd scene awaited him. A sheriff's car sat beside an ambulance. Two attendants were loading a body into the rear of the vehicle.

Doc Malone came out of the hangar. "What's happened, Jessie?" Samuel said.

"Fred shot himself." He handed over a telegraph. "This arrived this morning."

Samuel quickly read the telegram. "Dear God, Michael's been killed in Vietnam."

Malone shook his head sadly. "He was all Fred had. I guess he just couldn't live with the idea of being alone. He climbed into the cockpit of his airplane, stuck a pistol in his mouth, and blew half his head off." Malone put his hand on his old friend's shoulder. "I've got a bad feeling about this war. Is it ever going to end? Or is it going to just keep destroying people's lives?"

Samuel shook his head. "I don't know. It may only just be the beginning."

"I pray that's not the case."

Franklin was packing his suitcase when he heard a strange sound from beyond the house. A hard rain was falling when he stepped onto the porch and saw Kevin near the stable, wearing an old cavalry hat and holding a rusty sword. He was obviously drunk.

"What are you doing?" Franklin shouted.

"Going to the canyon!" Kevin yelled back, spurred the horse, and rode away.

It had been a family tradition, almost a rite of passage, for the Sharps children to make the dangerous ride down the steep canyon not far from the house. Franklin had made the ride, as had Kevin. It was the place where Sergeant Major Augustus Sharps broke his back, lingering several days in a coma before dying. Samuel had made the ride down the precarious slope to test his shattered leg after returning from the war in Europe.

The ride was dangerous to the strong and sober, deadly for someone drunk.

Franklin ran to the stable and saddled a horse; as he mounted up he heard the sound of a truck pulling into the yard. He started to spur the horse when his father rushed toward him and gripped the reins.

"Son, I need to talk to you." There was a desperation in his voice Franklin had never heard.

"I don't have time to hear your confession. Kevin's in trouble."

"What kind of trouble?"

"He's drunk and he's going to ride the canyon."

Samuel reached and grabbed his son and with a quick movement jerked him from the saddle. His eyes blazing, face streaked with rain, he shouted as thunder crashed from the sky, "We don't have time to play any more games. I was wrong. I had to lose my wife and see another man lose his son to understand what your mother tried to spare me. It's not like Adrian. He wanted to serve. Kevin doesn't." He pulled Franklin toward him. "I'm going to keep my promise to your mother."

Franklin could see in his father's eyes he spoke the truth. "I'll saddle you a horse."

Samuel went inside and slipped on his Western boots. On the way out he saw Darlene standing in the living room. He stopped long enough to kiss her on the cheek and say, "I'm going to get this situation straightened out."

He hurried toward the saddled horse.

Echoing in his ears was Shania's final plea: *"Find a way."*

55

He rode with the wind and the rain tearing at his face and, as when he was a boy, with his father riding beside him. But this time, unlike before, his father did not hold back on the reins and let him appear to win the race.

They rode with a vengeance, as their father and forefathers had ridden, heads bent low into the manes, looking neither right nor left, driving the animals with unforgiving harshness to the place all the Sharpses one day had to face. They rode to the canyon and Franklin could hear his father tell the story about when he was a lad sitting by the fire and Sergeant Major Augustus Sharps remembered testing himself when asked by Buffalo Bill Cody to join the Congress of Rough Riders. . . .

After receiving a request to join Cody's Wild West show, Augustus knew he had to face a test if he was to ride with the greatest horsemen in the world. He saddled up and rose through the early-morning darkness and minutes before sunrise sat at attention on a roan stallion named Shiloh. The horse showed a momentary restlessness, throwing his great head forward, then tried to rear up until he was settled by the tightening of the reins. Shiloh snorted and tried to crane his head away from the empty air beyond the rim of the deep canyon.

"It's almost time," Augustus whispered to him.

Augustus sat watching the eastern sky as the sun began to filter through the crackback ridges of the mountains northeast of Bonita. He wore a short-sleeved riding jacket and crisply starched pants that blossomed above his knees before disappearing into tall, highly polished cavalry boots. The dark blue cavalry hat he wore over his close-cropped hair was pulled down tightly at the brim, just above dark eyes that seemed to shine from within the brim's shadow.

The saddle on Shiloh was a McClellan, which he still preferred, what with the open slot in the seat that brought the horse's backbone against his tailbone, giving him the sense he and the horse were melded to each other physically. His Sharps rifle rested in the carbine boot on the right side of the saddle tree; on the left was his three-foot-long sabre.

The sun broke over the horizon; a red flood of sunlight swept the land and flooded into the canyon, running like fast water across hard ground. A narrow trail could be seen in front of Shiloh, a path that disappeared over the rim.

Suddenly, Augustus's arm flashed up; his fingers touched the edge of the brim in a sharp salute. He spurred the horse, stood in the iron stirrups, and leaned back as the stallion bolted over the edge into the redness of the canyon.

Down the stallion plunged, speed building as Augustus's right hand held firm to the reins, checking the power of the animal, while his free hand drew the steel sabre rattling against the saddle. With a smooth movement he extended the blade toward the imaginary enemy that lay waiting at the bottom. At that moment the sun flashed off the burnished blade and he felt the tightness of fear when he realized he was leaning dangerously far over the neck of the charging Shiloh.

He pulled the reins taut, sat back as far as possible, and distributed his body weight evenly, winning for the moment against the forward pull of the horse and gravity.

Down they drove, leaving a spray of dust too heavy to rise in the hot air. The deeper rider and horse descended, the thicker the sheen of the red dust collected, until the two appeared as flaming apparitions. It was only in the final moments of the descent, when the horse dived over the last ledge and he heard Shiloh's hooves crack against the hard floor of the canyon, that he yelled, "*Charge!*"

The canyon came alive with the sound of the stallion's pounding hooves and the rattle of the empty sabre scabbard. Augustus stood in the stirrups, leaned forward while extending the sabre beyond the stallion's rising and plunging head, preparing to receive the enemy charge. At the precise moment he and the enemy would join in battle, the sword flashed forward, narrowly clearing the head of the stallion; then he pulled on the reins, wheeling the horse into the opposite direction.

A scream burst from his lungs as he spurred the animal to full gallop, again stood in the stirrups with the sabre extended. He slashed and cut, parried, and thrust the blade at the enemy as though he were fighting a legion of demons, unaware that he was not alone.

On the ledge above the canyon, another rider sat on a horse, watching the mock battle as she had many times. Selona knew that he came here, to the edge of her small ranch, and made this ride whenever he needed to feel young.

Finally, Augustus drew the horse to a halt and, sitting at attention, saluted smartly with the sabre, then returned the blade to its scabbard with one crisp move.

On the canyon floor, except for man and beast taking in lungfuls of air, there was only silence.

• • •

A legion of demons.

His voice came calmly over Kevin's shoulder. "Kevin, Son . . . look at me."

What Samuel saw was a young man astride a horse at the edge of a path, his face tear-streaked, and his eyes fearful.

"I'll make it easy on you, Pop." Kevin's voice was calm, respectful. He took the rusty sword and placed the tip of the blade against his heart. Then he calmly planted the hilt against the saddle horn. "I'll just ride down, at full charge. You'll be proud of me. I'll let you off the hook."

Samuel dismounted. "Trust me, Son. You have to trust me. We're going to find a way out of this situation." He reached up and took the reins and felt the bit tighten in the horse's mouth. The front hooves were close to the edge.

"Easy, Son," Samuel said.

General Sharps put his hand out to Franklin, behind the two and just dismounting, a signal to hold his ground. He released the bit and ran his hand along the horse's neck, over the mane, into the saddle. He touched the rusty sabre, felt its cold steel. He looked up at his son, who sat looking into empty space.

He reached, gripped the sabre, and tore it away from Kevin's chest. At the same moment he pulled a .45-caliber Colt from his belt, laid the muzzle to the horse's head and fired.

Then the blade flashed beneath the sun and horse and rider went to the ground. To Franklin it was all a blur, but he heard Kevin scream and saw the sabre protruding from Kevin's leg just above the kneecap.

Kevin rolled from the saddle, his scream of pain more than his father could endure. "You bastard!" the boy yelled.

Franklin dropped to Kevin's side. "Don't you know what's happened?"

Kevin, wild-eyed in pain, couldn't answer.

Franklin put his hand on his father's shoulder. "You're Four-F, Brother. Can't be drafted. Not with that knee." He shook his head in amazement. "You might walk with a limp for a few years. But I'll swear that you fell on the sabre and I'm sure Pop will do the same."

Samuel said, "We need to get medical attention for him. You're a medic; what's your call?"

"Don't take out the sword," Franklin said. He took off his belt, tightened it above Kevin's knee. "He won't bleed to death before I can get to the truck. I'll call Doc Malone." There was a slight grin on his face as he mounted his horse and rode off.

Franklin had only one thought: *The son of a bitch did it!*

56

* * *

Following three hours of surgery, Kevin was rolled out of the operating room in the hospital at Willcox. Franklin, Samuel, and Darlene sat in the room waiting.

At last the surgeon came to them.

"The tendons were severed and have been reconnected, but I'm afraid there are many months—perhaps years—of rehabilitation facing that young man. I'll be honest with you. He very likely is going to be walking with a cane from now on."

When Kevin came out from under the anesthesia, the three were allowed a brief visit. They held his hand and tried to comfort him, but Kevin did most of the talking; apologetic and grateful. "Pop, I understand what you did. I know what all this has done to you, and I'm very sorry for the trouble and pain I've caused you. I hope you're not too ashamed of me."

Samuel gripped his hand. "Don't ever speak to me of shame again, Son. If anyone here deserves to feel shame, it is me. I'm a father who didn't listen to his sons, or to their mother."

After Kevin drifted off to sleep they found a Mexican restaurant and had a quiet dinner. During the drive back to Bonita, Franklin and Darlene sat in the back while Samuel drove, glancing from time to time in the rearview mirror, not oblivious to the affection he saw they had for each other.

It made him feel good. Maybe that was what Franklin needed, he thought. It was what Shania had been to him: a source of personal purpose, someone to come home to. He found a sense of pride in knowing he had changed in so many ways in recent days. *God! If Shania could only have lived to see it.*

What had he learned? That a man is no greater than those who surround him? That he does not have all the answers and will learn few unless he asks many questions? And, most of all, that he must question himself? He had not done that in so long he could not recall the last time. It was as though he suddenly awoke one day knowing everything, and, in recognizing that, knew that for so very long he had known very little about life.

For some strange reason the words of Abraham Lincoln's Gettysburg Address came to mind. Especially the part where he said ". . . *Today we are engaged in a great civil war . . .*"

In a way, America was engaged in a great civil war. Testing whether one part of the nation, or the other part, would prevail or whether the nation could bind itself together.

He thought that impossible in the present. There were too many battles yet to fight, on too many battlefields, both abroad, and, perhaps more important, here at home. The nation would survive the battles abroad, for it was supported by the force of the nation.

The military could not survive battles abroad if there was no nation.

He had learned the importance of a "house divided against itself."

He had no house only a few days ago, and his family had been losing all the battles.

But not anymore! He had made a decision, and by the time

they reached Sabre Ranch, while he did not have the solution completely worked out, he had begun to understand what he had to do.

The words of Kevin echoed in his mind . . . *It was time to choose!*

57

The next morning Franklin saddled two horses and he and Darlene went for a sunrise ride. Argonne was asleep and under the watchful eye of her grandfather, who had risen early to visit Shania's grave and talk about what he had in mind. After detailing as much of his plan as he had devised, he went back inside, checked on the baby, then went into his office.

He spent nearly two hours on the telephone, most of the calls to Washington, one to Saigon. When finished, he sat back in his leather chair and clasped his big hands behind his neck. For the first time in a long while he felt good about himself. He had done something positive for his family. He broke into a wide grin as he saw through the window Franklin and Darlene riding into the yard. He sat watching them; the two seemed to glow in each other's presence.

When he heard them come through the door, he met them in the living room and told Franklin, "I spoke with the Red Cross a few minutes ago. They've extended your leave for three more days."

"Thanks, Pop. I had planned to go back tomorrow."

"Son, you won't be going back. At least, not to Vietnam."

Franklin was stunned.

"Nor will I. At least, not for very long."

"I don't understand," Franklin said.

Samuel went on. "I've contacted the Pentagon and spoken with the vice chief of staff of the air force. He's an old friend of mine. We flew together in Korea. I've informed him it's my intention to retire from military service."

"Retire?" Franklin and Darlene both chorused.

"Yes. I've been through three wars for my country. I think that's enough. I explained the death of your mother, and your brother's injury. The vice chief understands. However, he did ask that I return and get things in order for my replacement. That shouldn't take more than a couple of weeks. Then, it's back home."

"What will you do?" Franklin said. "I mean, all you've known for nearly twenty-five years is being a lifer—"

Darlene laughed. Franklin covered his mouth like a child who had said something bad. "Sorry, Pop. You know what I mean."

"No need to apologize. I know what you mean. There're plenty of things to do. Just because an old warhorse goes to pasture doesn't mean there's nothing to do."

"What about Franklin?" Darlene said.

Franklin was wondering the same thing and saw Samuel looking at him with a glow in his eyes he'd never known from his father.

"What did you mean, when you said I wasn't going back?"

His father shrugged. "Do you want to go back?"

Franklin looked at Darlene. "No, I don't. Not that I'm a coward—"

Samuel cut him off. "You're no coward. I'm a general and that gives me certain privileges. Not many, mind you, but some. You volunteered for the draft nearly a year ago. That's a two-year hitch, which is nearly half-completed. I spoke with one of the powers in the Pentagon and pointed out to him that you are a combat medic with a lot of experience and expertise in what is now a new and different type of ground war. I also said that your experience could be used more effectively at the combat medic school at Fort Sam Houston, Texas, rather than in Vietnam; that you had been there, in combat, and that you are one of the few medics currently stateside who has seen the situation up close and can better serve your country in an instructor capacity for at least another year. He agreed; as a matter of fact, he thought it was a superb idea. Therefore, you are going to be reassigned to the combat medic school, where you can serve out your enlistment."

Franklin released a long, deep breath. "Pop, I thought you were opposed to any form of nepotism."

"I am. This is not nepotism. What you learned in Vietnam is more valuable here than going back and getting your ass shot off. You can talk with these young medics. Tell them the way the situation really is. I'm sure you learned something in the bush that is not being taught at Fort Sam Houston."

"Yes, sir. Quite a bit. The real thing is nothing at all like what we were taught, especially in the area of medevac and personal hygiene in the bush."

Samuel was already way ahead of him. "That's what I conveyed to the under secretary of defense."

Franklin was impressed. "You know the under secretary of defense?"

"Yes. Six months ago I was assigned to take him all over Vietnam on a fact-finding tour. He's a good man and understands my personal situation as well as the military benefit of this assignment."

"Is that all?" Franklin asked.

"That, and how embarrassing it could be for the government if I retired and wrote a book on why I believe the war is being botched, that more young men are going to die in what is becoming a war we can't possibly win."

There it was, thought Franklin. There's no way the government would want a bronco tromping through their carrot patch, especially when the price of his silence would be to exercise good judgment. Franklin knew he could contribute more as an instructor at the CMS, where his experience could be used to save more men than he could ever hope to save on the battle-field.

Darlene took Franklin's hand and pulled him toward his fa-ther. She took Samuel's hand and drew him from his chair and guided both men together.

As she walked out of the room, she turned to see the two embrace.

For the Sharps family, the Vietnam War was over.

EPILOGUE

1991

At Sabre Ranch, Dr. Franklin LeBaron Sharps sat at his ormulu desk, disinterested in his daily mail, with the exception of one letter that had arrived that morning from Argonne. At forty-seven, he was still sapling lean, his physique strong and durable, like that of a long-distance runner. He continued to wear a paratrooper haircut, his scalp shaved two inches above the ears and close-cropped on top. He allowed himself a narrow mustache, highlighting full lips, and wore a light blue jumpsuit.

When he finished reading the letter, a sudden movement from outside the house caught his eyes. He rose and walked to the French doors and watched a herd of antelope walk lazily through the front yard, ignoring his sudden appearance as he studied them through the glass.

He watched for several minutes, then returned to the letter and read it again. He then glanced to the wall and slowly swiveled his leather chair as he panoramically studied a multitude of family photographs, awards, and decorations. All of which swelled him with great pride. But it was his medical degree that gave him the most satisfaction. After being discharged from the army, he went to college, earned his bachelor's degree, then attended medical school at the University of Texas.

Life had been good to him and Darlene, whom he married in the fall of 1967. They had a child of their own, Jacob Le-Baron Sharps, now a first-year medical student at the University of Southern California. Franklin, an orthopedic surgeon, had his practice in Phoenix, where he commuted daily in his private airplane.

Slowly, his eyes scanned the wall carefully, ultimately pausing on one particular frame that gave him a great sense of pride, followed by heartache. As he always felt, when remembering one of the saddest days of his life.

Captured in the frame was a single sheet of paper the size of a dollar bill, bearing the name ADRIAN AUGUSTUS SHARPS II. The paper reminded him of a lightning storm at night, what with the brilliance of the name at the center, then the surrounding dark lead shading from the pencil he used to transcribe his older brother's name from the Wall at the Vietnam War Memorial. There had been other names on the Wall he had recognized on that first—and only—visit in 1983. But his brother's was the only one he had framed. The more than dozen others he had brought back lay within the cover of a book in the bookcase. The book was titled *About Face: The Odyssey of an American Warrior*. The author was Colonel David H. Hackworth, his former commander in the 101st Airborne.

He had visited the memorial with his father, Darlene, their son, Jacob, his younger brother Kevin, now an attorney working for the N.A.A.C.P. in Atlanta, and his stepdaughter, Lieutenant Argonne Sharps, now a graduate of West Point.

Instinctively, his eyes drifted to another photograph on the wall, this one taken four years ago at Argonne's graduation from West Point. She stood at attention, wearing the uniform of a cadet, saluting with her drawn sabre. Beside her photograph was a picture of his dead brother, wearing an identical uniform, the same sabre salute.

"Tradition." Franklin whispered softly, almost reverently.

Then he heard the front door open and Darlene's voice calling, sounding frightened. He hurried toward the living room, where he found her standing in front of the large front window. She turned, and he could see the worry on her face. He put his arms around her and felt her trembling body weaken against his. "What is it, sweetheart? Aren't you feeling well?"

"You haven't heard?" she asked, her voice nearly frantic. "It's just been announced on the news."

"Heard what? Darlene, you're not making any sense."

She went to the television set and pressed a button on the remote. She quickly switched the channel until she found CNN.

From Baghdad, Bernard Shaw's voice rang with excitement as the greenish picture, filmed with night vision cameras, showed the night sky of the Iraqi capital aglow with the tracer etchings of antiaircraft fire pouring upward from the ground.

He sat heavily on the couch, and the words seemed to be released like a desperate breath. "The air campaign has begun."

"Argonne! My God, Franklin. Her unit is in Saudia Arabia!" Darlene's words shrilled with fear.

Within seconds he was on the telephone to his father, who now lived in Falls Church, Virginia. He was given several numbers by Samuel of influential military men at the Pentagon, called them all, but could reach none of them.

For the next few hours, like most Americans, the two sat in front of their television set, knowing their daughter, along with other sons and daughters, was now journeying into harm's way.

In the desert of eastern Saudia Arabia, First Lieutenant Argonne Sharps sat at the pilot controls in the cockpit of a H-60 Blackhawk helicopter, the tarmac as dark as the night. The four massive blades were churning smoothly toward liftoff revolutions as she flipped down night-vision goggles on her helmet visor and glanced to the rear of the chopper.

Twelve army Special Forces soldiers dressed in desert camouflage sat strapped into the web seats, their faces coated with camouflage beneath their night-vision goggles, their bodies laden with huge packs, ammunition, and explosives. Their hands gripped automatic weapons and heavy machine guns.

Before she increased the throttle and pulled back on the collective, she reached down and touched a metal scabbard lying between her chair and the copilot's seat. The sword had been presented to her by her father when the order came down for her unit to deploy to the Gulf. Now, the sabre's presence gave her a feeling of reassurance, as though five generations of Sharpses were sitting beside her. Guiding and advising her of her duty and responsibility.

Then she heard her copilot's voice break in over the radio and jokingly say, "Pretty tight quarters in here, Argonne. I hope you don't get the cavalry urge and draw that blade. You might slice my head off."

"Not me, Rob. I was raised swinging that old sabre. I can split hairs with it." She could see copilot Lieutenant Robert Shelton's mouth turn upward into a grin. Then, she switched the radio to internal commo mode and said to the Green Beret team, "Hold on, gentlemen. We're on our way to Iraq!"

The sleek, black helicopter lifted off smoothly, creating a tornado of swirling dust and sand on the tarmac, then banked sharply and raced toward the east. In a matter of seconds, the chopper was gone from sight of the ground crews, knifing through the darkness with its cargo of American commandos.

Lieutenant Argonne Sharps was now a seasoned helicopter pilot with her father's former outfit, the 101st Airborne Division. Shortly after the Iraqis invaded Kuwait, the Screaming Eagles were dispatched to the Persian Gulf as part of Operation Desert Shield.

Like her great-great-grandfather, the old 10th Cavalry Buffalo Soldier, she was charging toward battle on a modern-day stallion made of steel and speed, carrying a gleaming, razor-sharp sabre!

Afterword

* * *

The following citation for the Medal of Honor was awarded posthumously to the author's platoon leader, First Lieutenant James A. Gardner, U.S. Army, Headquarters and Headquarters Company, 1st Battalion (ABN), 327th Infantry, 1st Brigade, 101st Airborne Division, for action near My Canh, Vietnam, 7 February 1966. For conspicuous gallantry and intrepidity at the risk of his own life above and beyond the call of duty. 1Lt. Gardner's platoon was advancing to relieve "A" Company of the 1st Battalion that had been pinned down for several hours by a numerically superior enemy force in the village of My Canh, Vietnam. The enemy occupied a series of fortified bunker positions which were mutually supporting and expertly concealed. Approaches to the position were well covered by an integrated pattern of fire including automatic weapons, machine guns, and mortars. Air strikes and artillery placed on the fortifications had little effect. 1Lt. Gardner's platoon was to relieve the friendly company by encircling and destroying the enemy force. Even as it moved to begin the attack, the platoon was under heavy enemy fire. During the attack, the enemy fire intensified. Leading the assault and disregarding his own safety,

1Lt. Gardner charged through a withering hail of fire across an open rice paddy. On reaching the first bunker, he destroyed it with a grenade and without hesitation dashed to the second bunker and eliminated it by tossing a grenade inside. Then, crawling swiftly along the dike of a rice paddy, he reached the third bunker. Before he could arm a grenade, the enemy gunner leaped forth, firing at him. 1Lt. Gardner instantly returned fire and killed the enemy gunner at a distance of six feet. Following the seizure of the main enemy position, he reorganized the platoon to continue the attack. Advancing to the new assault position, the platoon was pinned down by an enemy machine gun emplaced in a fortified bunker. 1Lt. Gardner immediately collected several grenades and charged the enemy position, firing his rifle as he advanced to neutralize the defenders. He dropped a grenade into the bunker and vaulted beyond. As the bunker blew up he came under enemy fire again. Rolling into a ditch to gain cover, he moved toward the new source of fire. Nearing the position he leaped from the ditch and advanced with a grenade in one hand while firing his rifle with the other. He was gravely wounded just before he reached the bunker, but with a last valiant effort, he staggered forward and destroyed the bunker and its defenders with a grenade. Although he fell dead on the rim of the bunker, his extraordinary action so inspired the men of his platoon that they resumed the attack and completely routed the enemy. 1Lt. Gardner's conspicuous gallantry was in the highest traditions of the U.S. Army.

> Entered Service: Memphis, Tennessee
> Place of Birth: Dyersburg, Tennessee
> Date of Birth: 7 February 1943
> Killed In Action: 7 February 1966
> Place of Burial: Murfreesboro, Tennessee

The White Rose Ball

*   *   *

In the writing of these chronicles of a family's dedication in military service to its nation, I have tried to maintain a distance from the events and characters as history has unfolded around them.

However, this book is different. This book represents a part of my life that I chose to share, hoping to shed light onto the shadowed faces of the gallant Vietnam veterans of our nation.

For more than three decades, I have been asked "When are you going to write a book about Vietnam?" I always replied, "It's a personal thing."

I quit high school at sixteen, joined the army two days after I turned seventeen, went into the paratroopers, and when my outfit, 1st Brigade, 101st Airborne Division, received orders in early 1965, I went to war. I was fortunate. Unlike many soldiers who would follow, I was led into battle by the finest officers and noncommissioned officers our service had.

John L. "Dynamite" Hughes is not a fictional character. He is a real and wonderful man who has once again come into my life as a friend and advisor on the writing of this book. It is his photograph that is used on the jacket of this novel. There were many to chose from, such as Hughes riding an elephant, clenching a rattlesnake between his teeth, or posed in his gun jeep, the one that struck a land mine, and blew John into the branches of a tree (he survived, thank God) . . . but our comrades Sheffield and Vincent were not so fortunate.

Colonel David H. Hackworth, America's most decorated living combat soldier, is a friend and advisor. I was one of his "kids," as he proudly recalls his troopers of "Tiger Force." He retired from the Army to reflect and write the critically acclaimed book *About Face*, became an editor and correspondent for *Newsweek* magazine, and serves as a constant vocal and literary warning to an American government policy that he—through experience—considered fraught with folly and certain death to American soldiers.

Colonel Hackworth is to this day, in my life, the flare drifting down from the flareship—giving light in darkness, the voice telling us, "Fight back!"

Leo B. Smith died in 1997. He was my "First Shirt," and would become the director and curator of the National Medal of Honor Museum. A great friend to all who knew and loved him, to his last breath.

Charlie Musselwhite and his wife Jackie remain true friends. They not only survived three tours of Vietnam, but the terror of the overthrow of Iran when America was forced from that country by the Ayatollah Khomeini. They left Tehran with nothing but their children and the clothes on their back.

Phillip Chassion was killed in Vietnam fighting to save his men, as he always had, tough as ever to the last moment. It's reported there were twenty-six dead enemy soldiers stretched out in front of his position when his body was discovered. It's reported he had twelve bullets in his body. He was one tough son-of-a-bitch who loved his young troops, kicked their asses to make them better, and was always willing to fight and die for them.

Phil Chassion was also a good man, of a wonderful heart. I know. I willingly gave him my beer ration. I don't like beer. I didn't even like Chassion. But I loved him. He kicked my ass one night to get me to the religion of battle. He said: "You might not like where you're at . . . but you asked to be here. Do the job. Die well . . . if you die. But do well while you live. You're a United States paratrooper. Don't piss on the silk!"

When his body was returned to the United States for burial, John Hughes saw to the burial requirements, along with others from the army burial detail detachment. But it was friends who served with him who made certain he was put into the ground with grace and honor. There are a lot of young soldiers who won't know, until now, that he died. In more ways that can be counted, we owe our lives to him.

Lieutenant James Alton Gardner, awarded the Medal of Honor, was killed on his twenty-third birthday, the day before he was to be promoted to the rank of captain. He was a great leader. Died too young. But . . . he died well. I don't know if that could possibly make up for the void he left, but he gave it all in a single, unselfish moment, so that others could have hours, days, weeks, months, years, decades . . . of life.

James Gardner gave it all with valor. Never thinking of himself.

The sergeant depicted in the battle of An Ninh was Herb Dexter, who had served four tours in Vietnam. I never knew the man personally. I only knew of his legendary courage, leadership, and character. What I could not portray in the story can be said now; he was a soldier's soldier. No one can imagine what it is like to be in a situation where there is no hope, and suddenly, you look up to see a sword shining against the enemy fire. To raise the courage of those frightened, to become lions, is a flight among the heavens of the valorous.

Herb Dexter was that sergeant.

And I never shared a beer with the man.

But he was a hero of the day, and that has to mean something. If nothing else, his name won't be forgotten where he died so others would live.

A great soldier.

There is one I wish to remember. Earl Wilson, Memphis, Tennessee. If there was ever a recon soldier, it was Will. I believe he is the essence of the combat soldier. The members of Recon Platoon, 1st Brigade, HHC, 1/327, knew who the best grunt was. It was Earl "Recon" Wilson. The only thing he was afraid of was snakes, and he ate them for breakfast to remind him of his fear.

Everything else was an appetizer . . . or the main course.

History can often be fickle, viewed in one perspective by one generation, considered entirely different by another. Regardless of how the Vietnam veteran may be viewed by history, one critical point will never change: The Vietnam veteran showed up for the roll call!

In 1969, my college fraternity held its annual White Rose Ball. It's a formal affair, and on my white tuxedo coat I wore the miniature medals of my decorations received for valor. It was the only time I've ever done so. I took a break from the festivities and went to the bar and ordered a drink. The bartender eyed the medals, delivered the drink, then snickered, and asked, "Where did you get those medals, kid? In the Boy Scouts?"

I pitched my drink in his face, and replied, "That's goddamned right . . . Above the Rest!"

As Chassion said, "Don't piss on the silk!"

—Tom Willard
July 1999